WHISKEY BARGAIN

A Foster House Novel

WALKER ROSE

LE Publishing

I thought I'd be miserable planning my ex's wedding, but a rugged cowboy turned distiller knows just how to relieve the pressure.

Coming home to Huckleberry Springs, Montana, is hard enough. Begging my family for a job because I'm blacklisted up and down the West Coast? That's tough. Patching up a broken heart after my cheating ex made me a spectacle? Stinks so bad. Drunkenly puking on Durban Hennessy, the hottest cowboy to ever work my daddy's ranch? That's just classic Campbell Hawthorne.

But even Durban doesn't blame me much for that last one, because my first job as Daddy's event coordinator? Planning my cousin's wedding to my cheating ex at the family guest ranch. Because if I don't, my uncle won't sign over his share of the business.

The only bright spot? Durban is now part owner in the local distillery, and while he doesn't do drama, distractions, or hot messes that just threw up on his boots, he's not averse to saving damsels in distress. Once a ranch hand and now a distiller with a superiority complex, he'll provide wet bar service throughout the wedding festivities—and some steamy, no-strings stress relief between events.

In return, I'll help him patch up his own ego after getting dumped by his long-distance girlfriend. But when impromptu hookups turn into sleepovers that include intimate pillow talk, I know I'm in trouble. Because our whiskey bargain is set to end when the bride says *I do*.

CHAPTER ONE

Durban

This night went to hell long before a tornado with sun-kissed skin walked into Bootleg Tavern. But babysitting the woman with chestnut hair so long a guy could wrap it around his fist isn't cheering me up.

Behind where I'm sitting at the bar counter, Campbell Hawthorne whoops with some women who must be tourists. "Rack 'em up!"

Her sultry rasp goes straight to my dick.

Dammit, I came to drown my sorrows, dump a little alcohol on my pride, before I get back to business as usual. Not listen to vocal cords formed straight from every man's wet dreams.

She's not mine, she's not for me, and I don't want her to be, but as inconvenient as it is, she's a beautiful woman with a voice meant for sin. That's probably how she sounds when she recites her grocery list.

Before, I could ignore it. I was taken. I had a girlfriend, and it didn't matter that she was two thousand miles away. But now, my brand-new single-guy status makes me aware of it—and irritated. I pinch the bridge of my nose as snippets of my recent phone conversation run through my head.

"I don't think it's a good idea to talk to each other anymore. I think we need to break up."

"I'm sorry. The jokes are cute, but they're distracting, and I can't have that."

"I know you don't get what it's like. College. Graduate school. Research. This program is the most important thing I'm doing, and I've got so much invested."

"I knew you'd understand. You have that laid-back lifestyle. Easy breezy."

Easy fucking breezy. And my jokes could not have been that bad of a distraction. I'd waited for Natalie for almost four years. She'd assured me she was ready for a long-distance relationship and we'd figure out the rest when it was closer to her graduation.

With her graduation imminent, I'd been asking about where she planned to find a job, if she'd like me at her graduation, and I'd reassured her that I'd give her transition time. Assuming her vague answers were from the stress of planning her thesis defense, I'd quit asking questions and started sending her jokes. Simple science ones to lighten her day.

Too simple. Too easy breezy.

Her words have been on constant replay since I hung up. Mostly, I can't shake the sound of a guy laughing in the background. She might've been around friends. Is that better or worse? To get dumped in private like it was a long, agonizing decision? Or to get dropped while out for a good time?

Is he her study partner?

Why do I care?

Because I waited like an optimistic, proud-as-hell dumbass for four years so she could pursue her second PhD. I was just happy to be in her orbit. Now I'm not.

"Silas, another round," Campbell calls.

I ignore the heat the sound of her voice sends curling through my veins. It's frustration and heartbreak. Nothing more.

Campbell laughs and shimmies, the skirt of her loose dress swinging around her hips and tickling the tops of her cowboy boots. That woman does not need another shot. She's had four since she arrived. I might want to go home and let her fuck around and find out, but my ass stays planted on my stool. Someone has to be responsible, and as soon as I saw her tonight, I knew it wasn't going to be her.

Silas steps in front of me to line up three shot glasses with scratched images of a cowboy boot on them. His weathered expression is impassive as he selects the tequila bottle Campbell's group has been drinking from all night.

"You should water them down," I say. "At least hers." One of the women Campbell linked up with only sipped her last shot, then gave it to Campbell to down the rest.

Silas doesn't have to ask who I mean. "She can hold her liquor."

Another whoop in her dulcet tones rings out. I cock a brow at Silas, and he shrugs. As long as the cops aren't called, he doesn't care. He also isn't worried about cutting customers off or taking keys from them. He wouldn't twitch unless they drove drunk right into the bar.

Silas slides the little glasses toward the open spot next to me. "Got yer order, Campbell."

I hunch over my whiskey on the rocks. The half-melted ice gives it the mellow flavor I prefer, bringing out the vanilla and smoothing over the bite, but I don't take a drink. A cloud of tequila and the sweet floral scent of huckleberry blossoms surround me.

"Thanks, Silas." Campbell tries to gather them all at once and fumbles, almost tipping one.

"Jesus," I mutter.

She thumps against the counter, draping a little too far across it. "Got a problem, Durban?"

"I'm trying not to have one."

Usually, she rolls her eyes when I call out her antics. Ever since I've known the youngest Hawthorne sister, she's been carefree, flitting through life on her daddy's money and her sexy looks. A smile and a giggle, and she got her way. My oldest brother married her oldest sister five years ago, and they're the reason I'm here. Iverson and Jamison don't need Campbell breezing into town and getting herself into trouble when Jamison is having some health concerns with her second pregnancy.

But there's no eye roll. She'd probably get too dizzy. Defensiveness puffs her lips out. Is she trying to look tough? Or like a trout asking me to put it back in the water? "What's that supposed to mean?"

"It means that maybe you should skip this round."

"Durban knows best," she mocks.

"Do I have to keep proving it over and over?" I should stop. This is only going to get her riled up, but I can't help myself. I hold a finger up. "The day trip on the river after the wedding?" She was late, and our party of six lost their booking.

Guilt flashes in her eyes. "I told Jamison to go without me."

I tick up another finger. "At the opening of the distillery, I told you to take a small sip, and you gulped it." We practiced our tasting presentations on friends and family. She spewed a mouthful all over me and my youngest brother, Haven.

"I did take a small sip. It was, like, a hundred and forty proof!"

It was a cask-strength whiskey, but it was one of the last lines we served for tasting. The strongest was saved for the end when her palate should've been conditioned, had she listened. I add a third finger. "And then there's Kacey's dog."

She glares at my offending digits. "I was told Coal would be a midsized dog."

The rescue mutt puppy grew bigger than our niece by the time he was six months old. Coal ended up being a Labrador-and-Pyrenees mix. She's a gorgeous, well-tempered dog, and also huge. "I'd hate to see what you think is large."

"And I hate to be blamed when others lie to me." Her glassy eyes flare, and she hiccups. She puts the back of her wrist against her mouth.

"Maybe skip that shot."

She narrows her eyes and brings the little glass to her lips. She doesn't throw it back. Instead, she slowly tips her head. Those lush lips of hers open, and the golden liquid flows into her mouth. She swallows without wincing, but the fight of her life is happening in her eyes.

"How's that burn?" I ask smugly.

She inhales sharply, but it's to cover a gasp.

"Smooth," she rasps. "Now, if you'll excuse me, I'd like to have a good time, and you're a bit of a downer."

I've heard I'm a distraction. "Sure."

I riled her up, and I shouldn't have. She's going to retaliate and drink more. She's like that. Jamison tells her to slow down on horseback, and Campbell gallops faster. Her daddy tells her to find a stable job, and she goes into event planning. I tell her to sit down, and she dances around me—after she picks a song she thinks I won't like.

She did that at her parents' anniversary party a couple of years ago and asked the band to play "Barbie Girl." Too bad for her, I know all the words. I have a good memory, and the guys would play it during poker nights when I lived in the bunkhouse on Hawthorne Ranch, back in the days when I was nothing but a hired cowboy.

Now I'm a businessman and a distiller.

I take a sip of my whiskey, rolling the rich Foster House Gold over my tongue. This is one of my batches. I used locally grown corn and wheat, and we sell it as a special barrel line. One of the first made in Foster House's new location, right here in Huckleberry Springs, Montana.

I understand a whole lot, Natalie. And I didn't need school to do it. I didn't have a chance to get one degree, much less the third or whatever she was on.

An hour ticks by. I scroll through my phone, making notes for new recipes and shoring up details for a meeting we have at Hawthorne Ranch tomorrow. Campbell doesn't return to the counter. Silas leaves me alone to nurse my whiskey. People come and go. The ones I know toss me a wave and a few come over to chat—

about the weather, the distillery, and my brother's soon-to-be new arrival. People I don't recognize come and go. Tourist season is gearing up now that spring has officially hit Montana.

A few guys enter. I tense as they look for a seat and eye Campbell's group. Seasonal workers. They could be in town to work at the Hawthorne Ranch, in which case, Campbell is very off-limits. Iverson learned that the hard way when he hooked up with Jamison, not knowing she was our boss's daughter.

Campbell can do what she wants as far as I'm concerned, but she's drunk. So those guys cannot do what their overly interested gazes say they want to do.

The cloud of huckleberry blossoms returns. "Silas," she says in a singsong voice and kicks a hip out.

All I have to do is lean back, just a few inches, and I can see the way her ass pushes against her dress material. She's got a purse strung across her body, and the strap only clamps the dress closer to her lush, round butt cheeks. Heat punches low, and my long-neglected dick wakes up.

Down, boy. I'm not interested. I'm just deprived.

I look at my phone. The screen is a snapshot of my palomino, Duke. No new messages. There won't be, unless it's from my brothers. I set it on the counter so I can monitor the Campbell situation.

Silas hobbles to her. The guy glowers at everyone else, but she gets an indulgent smile. She's a Hawthorne, so she probably tips him more than anyone in town.

"What can I get you?" he asks.

"A nice cold beer." She sings that too—off-key.

"Aw hell, you're mixing drinks?" I can't mind my own business. I'm here to mind hers.

Silas ignores me and taps on the counter to get her to quit glaring at me. "Any preference?"

"Shurprise me."

Fuck me. "Campbell, you can't mix drinks."

"It's nooo problem." She turns to face me and has to adjust her stance. Her eyes are even glassier, and her cheeks are a rosy red. Even the tip of her nose is red.

"You're going to make yourself sick," I insist. "A mug of beer is more than one serving, and since you've already been drinking—a lot—you're going to consume more beer than you think."

She lets out a frustrated snort. "Ever get tired of trying to be smarter than everyone?"

"Ever get tired of going through so many jobs?" That's a low blow, but I wanted a quiet night at home, to have a whiskey on the deck and read while the birds chirped, and it got too dark to see the words.

The view from Bootleg Tavern is not as nice as my deck, and it's not every day a guy gets dumped from across the country.

She lets out an indignant gasp and sways backward before catching herself. "Ack-tually, no. I get tired of horrible managers." She smacks her lips. "And I'm home for a job."

"Your dad hired you?" Jamison said Campbell was in town, but she didn't know why or for how long. Campbell, oddly, wasn't talking, and neither were her parents. As long as I'm not dragged into the drama. I like the calm life I have now. I'd just like to spend it with someone.

A flash of anguish passes over her features so quickly, I might've imagined it. She cocks that damn hip again.

"Yes, and I have a client." She swallows hard and looks away.

There, I'm not seeing things. Something's bothering her. Is that why she's on a one-woman mission to drain the bar dry?

"Campbell!" one of the women calls. "Gonna shoot some more balls?"

"There are a few balls I'd like to shoot," she growls, and the corner of my mouth twitches. She's drunk, but if she can still insult me, she's not that far gone.

Silas slides a frosty mug that probably should've been run through the dishwasher one more time in front of Campbell.

"Well, Durban." She purrs my name, and goddamn, there's no need to like it that much. "It's been fun as always. That stick up your ass is really holding firm." Just then, my phone screen flares bright, and her gaze dips down. Her eyes light up when she sees the name. "Natalie? That's your girlfriend, right? The schuper smart girl you're seeing?"

I'm a grown man, but I'm going to lie to save my pride. It's too soon to come clean, and it won't be in front of a sexy, drunk woman. "She lives across the country. Getting her second PhD. I send her science jokes " I tack on like I want to be awarded for my efforts.

"That's cute."

Right? It's a goddamn good boyfriend move. But I keep my mouth shut.

"Does she have a full . . . juicy . . . IQ?"

I nearly groan at the way she says it, all tease and temptation. I take a bigger gulp of my whiskey and swallow wrong. I cough and sputter.

She pats me on the back. "Sorry, smartypants. Didn't

realize you were new to drinking." She picks up her beer, making the head slosh over the side, and saunters away.

I glower at my traitorous whiskey. Silas appears back in front of me. "Told ya she could hold her own."

The alcohol is starting to hold her. "Check again after that beer."

He harrumphs and goes to fill another order.

Natalie's name flashes again, and I snatch up the phone.

Natalie: I really am sorry.

So am I. I met Natalie when she'd just finished her first PhD in Bozeman. She came to Huckleberry Springs with friends for a rafting vacation. We dated for a few months, and I tried to lock it down, but she decided early on to do a second PhD in bioethics on the East Coast. Just far enough away to make regular visits difficult. I haven't been out there for a year, and she hasn't been here since that summer vacation four years ago.

I don't feel like talking to her, but I have to hand it to her. She didn't make me fly out there to break it off. Guess the answer to my earlier question is that I *do* appreciate getting dumped with some unknown dude in the background.

Durban: Me too.

I down the rest of my glass.

Silas turns from where he's handwashing a few glasses in the bar sink. I've quit questioning how often he changes the water, or if he ever does. No one comes to Bootleg if they're worried about health code violations.

" 'Nother?" he asks.

Since it doesn't look like Campbell's quitting early . . . "Yup."

For another hour, I sip my second whiskey and read through distilling blogs and articles to keep me from being a sad sack at the bar. When I get done, my ass is starting to hurt, so I help Silas take and fill orders. I replace the cold dishwater with fresh stuff, adding more soap than Silas ever does, and keep an eye on Campbell.

She's on her second mug of beer, and now the three guys who are probably seasonal help have joined her group for pool.

Any other night, I wouldn't care how many guys are hitting on her, but she's drunk. Her laughter's gotten louder, and her balance is shit. How has she not fallen on her ass?

I shake my head and clamp my teeth together. I can't go over there and haul her to my pickup, drive her home, dump her in bed, and tell her to sleep it off.

Why can't I?

Right. She wouldn't cooperate.

I like the thought of throwing her over my shoulder too much. Finally, her impromptu friends start putting away pool cues and giving her hugs.

Good. I can get home and stroke one off to the memory of Natalie and— Nope. I'm single now. That routine is over, and I won't torture myself with it.

Campbell's bell chime of a laugh rings through the bar. The three guys are eyeing her like wolves would a newborn calf on slippery ground. Their ringleader is touching her—a hand on her hip, leaning in close, even feathering his fingers over her hair.

Not on my watch.

The ringleader drags her to their table, and he scoots his half-full beer toward her.

I round the bar and I'm at her side in seconds. "Hey, Campbell. Do you have a ride?"

She sways when she spins around and grabs on to the string of her cross-body bag. Her green eyes are glassier than they were before. "I've got it taken care of."

That's Campbell code for no. "I'll drive you home."

She gives me a saccharine-sweet smile. "Don't worry that pretty little head of yoursh."

The ringleader puts a proprietary hand on her lower back. "We'll make sure she gets home."

Anger dings at my temples. I'm a bronc that's just thrown its rider—pissed as hell, and I just want to leave.

A flash of worry crosses her face, but she smothers it. She doesn't want to be at that guy's mercy. Why in the hell can't she just make this easy?

"Give me your keys," I tell her.

She pouts. "You're not in charge of me, Durban." She teeters and tries to punch a finger into my shoulder.

The men surround me. I didn't grow up with two brothers in the foothills of the Beartooth Mountains to let them intimidate me.

"The lady said—"

I spin, getting in the ringleader's face. I tower over him—over all of them—by a few inches, and years of wrestling cattle have made me fearless. "The lady has a goddamn name, and if you don't know it, butt the hell out."

"Take it outside, Hennessy," Silas calls from the bar. He doesn't care about the fighting. In fact, he'd be the first one out the door to watch, but he hates broken glass and busted tables. The high-top we're standing around has a splint around one leg because Silas refuses to replace it.

"God, Durban," Campbell moans. "Schtay out of it."

I didn't waste the last three hours to let her push me away. If Iverson or Sunny found out I left her here, I'd get the shit beat out of me worse than these guys could ever do, and Jamison might spike her blood pressure.

"One last warning," I tell her.

She frowns and makes a move for the beer.

Oh, hell no. I bend and put my shoulder into her gut, wrap my arm around her curvy, muscular legs, and lift. Her purse digs into my shoulder, but I barely notice when I have an armful of lush woman.

"Durban!" She kicks her feet, and that only makes her body jiggle against me.

"Whoa, whoa, whoa," one of the guys says, but I ignore them. I propel her out the door and make sure she doesn't get slammed in the head with it. She's an inch taller than her sister, but much shorter than me. She flails her legs until I hear a groan. Cool spring mountain air surrounds us.

She bats at my back and my butt. "Durban." Her moan almost gives me pause.

The door whacks open behind us.

"Listen, asshole," one of the guys says. "You can't go around abducting women."

I'd admire their sense of protection if I thought they actually wanted to look out for her. My brothers and I have had too many experiences in Bootleg rescuing women from the seasonal staff that comes to town. Some of them are decent. A lot are college kids. Some of them roam from job to job to stay under law enforcement or child support's radar.

I continue to my pickup.

"Durban." Her croak doesn't sound good.

"Should've given me your goddamn keys," I growl.

"Hey, fucker! We're talking to you."

They are also catching up to my longer strides. My pickup's parked at the edge of the lot, backed in so I can drive out without watching for drunks stumbling around.

A hand grabs my shoulder just as she clenches my ass, and a loud retch rips from her. I set her on her feet, but she falls to her knees and vomits. I drop with her and gather her long, silky strands away from her face.

The ringleader, who had it bad for Campbell, jumps back, disgust twisting his face. "Fucking gross."

His buddies look equally horrified. They ditch us and rush back into the bar.

Well, that's one way to take care of them.

The pool of puke grows behind my pickup. Campbell's narrow shoulders shake as she heaves, rocking forward to throw up, then back to catch her breath.

A sob wrenches out of her, and she drags a shaky wrist across her mouth. The smell rises around us like a noxious cloud.

"Are you done?" I ask.

She spits, but nods. "I think so," she wheezes.

"I think I have some napkins in the truck."

"Okay." She sounds so small my normal irritation tamps down, but not far. All of this was preventable, but she won't fucking listen.

I help her up and hang on to her shoulders as she stumbles to the passenger door. She doesn't get in.

"I think . . ." She swallows. "I think I got puke on my dress."

It's in her hair too. "It's fine. I'll clean up everything in the morning. Let me get you home."

She still doesn't move. "I don't want to go home." She sniffles.

"Where else are you going to go?" I snap.

Her shiny eyes fill with tears, and there's a weird twist in my chest. "I can't go home like this."

"What were you planning to do when you were pounding shots?"

She sniffs, but a couple of tears roll down her cheeks. Maybe they're just from the effort of heaving her night of fun onto the pavement. "I would've figured it out. I can take care of myself, Durban."

"It looks like it."

She huffs out a breath. "I've made it this far without you."

"And without me, you'd have made it under one or all three of those guys. Does that sound better?"

More tears gather, and she looks away. The tip of her nose matches the flush of her cheeks. "Maybe I should just sleep it off in my car."

"Where those assholes can find you?"

She scrunches her nose. "I'll sleep in the back. They won't be able to see me." She smacks her lips and pulls a face. "I need mouthwash and a shower." Her expression turns stricken. "I guess I should go home."

I can understand her earlier trepidation. If her dad saw her like this, he'd lose his shit. He's uptight on a normal day, but something about the meetings at the ranch this weekend has him wound tighter than a bowline knot.

I can't bother Iverson and Jamison. As impetuous as Campbell is, she'd never forgive herself if Jamison stressed herself over this. Avery, the middle Hawthorne sister, lives outside of Salt Lake City.

"Get in," I say.

Her expression crumples, but she recovers as much pride as a puke-stained drunk woman can summon. She holds her skirt and climbs into the pickup. She nearly slips out, and I move to catch her, but she plants herself in the seat before I can help her.

I close the door and round the pickup. I stop to toe some dirt over the vomit splatter, not worrying about covering it entirely. It joins one of many soaking into Bootleg's parking lot, and Campbell's pukefest may not be the last of the night.

I hop into the driver's seat and start the engine. The soft weight of her gaze rests on me as I pull out of the parking lot.

When I turn in the opposite direction from Hawthorne Ranch, she peers out the window. "Where are we going?"

"You can stay at my place, use my shower, and I'm sure I've got a spare toothbrush somewhere." From all those times Natalie couldn't come visit.

"I can't. You've already . . ." She erratically waves a hand.

"You got a better option?"

She hunches her shoulders. I know I'm being hard on her, but come on. We don't say anything until I pull up in front of my house. I built this place a few years ago, after the major renovations on Foster House's second facility, Foster House Gold, were done.

A foolish part of me wishes she could see it in the daylight. Would she admire the size? Be impressed that a simple distiller like me could afford a place like this? I was the hired help for part of her life when I worked for her dad on the working side of his ranch. He had the guest ranch that was for show, and then the real cow-calf operation to supplement his income.

She's probably seen my place before. Iverson and Sunny have probably given her the grand tour of our family land, the legacy my father left behind. But my headlights only light up the sprawling two-story log cabin. I made sure it had a deck that faces west so I can watch the sunset over the mountains.

I hit the button for the garage door and pull inside. My space is neat and orderly. I'm working at the distillery much of the day, but I have a few chickens and some cattle my brothers and I run grazing the forty acres between us in town.

"Nice place," she says quietly.

"Thanks." I climb out of my pickup, and her feet are hitting the ground before I'm on the other side.

My chest damn near puffs up with pride when I lead her from the garage into the house. The entry space doubles as both mudroom and laundry room, and I gave it more square footage than necessary. After years of living in a bunkhouse with a bunch of cowboys, I like being able to spread my shit out without anyone else's ratty underwear hanging in my face.

She's toeing out of her cowboy boots, hanging on to the doorframe for dear life, when I remember I have a dryer full of clean clothes.

"I've got a sweater or something here for you." Rummaging around in my clean clothes, I find an old Dee's Sweets sweatshirt I bought when the bakery in town first opened. I grab that and a bath towel.

She blinks, trying to focus on the logo when I hold it out to her. "You bought merch from Elodie?"

Elodie's the quiet baker who owns Dee's Sweets. "I'll

buy all of her merch if it keeps her open. No offense, but your dad didn't let the guys have the good desserts unless we paid for them. Elodie gives regulars ten percent off."

A giggle bubbles out of Campbell. "Daddy can be such a cheap bastard. And everyone thinks Elodie's so sweet, but she upcharges so she can make it seem like locals get a discount."

Disbelief swells in my chest. I scoff. "Not Elodie. She's too timid to tell Pete Creighton to leave when he smells like he's slept in piss for a month and stares at her tits."

"But she'll tell her cousin, Deputy Palmer, and he'll come and remove Pete." She smirks. My astonishment must be scrawled across my face. "She's devious, churlish, and she can be underhanded if it means a few extra bucks."

"You don't like her?"

Campbell recoils and nearly loses her balance. Confusion lines her brows. "She's one of my favorite people."

I bark out a laugh. Campbell's always full of surprises, and usually, I don't like it. But right now, this is the most honest I've seen her. She's not acting out for show, being the center of attention. She's got crusted vomit on her, and she needs to sleep it off.

I gesture to the washing machine. "Just toss your stuff in. There's a bathroom on the main level. Go through the hallway by the office and take a left. It's right there. There's a guest room next door, so go on in when you're ready." I scratch the back of my neck. I haven't had a woman in my home, other than my sister-in-law, and it wasn't supposed to be *Campbell* naked in my shower, or sleeping between my sheets.

She's my guest, and I have a guest room. That's all.

Her nod's shaky. She twines her fingers together and scrunches her toes into the rug. She looks so fucking young and vulnerable. What would've happened if I hadn't stopped in tonight? How has she survived this long without getting hurt or taken advantage of?

She fiddles with the ends of her hair, grimaces when she touches some dried strands, and drops them. "Thank you."

"I have chores in the morning, and I gotta run to the distillery." Then I have a meeting at Hawthorne with Iverson in the afternoon. A nice, busy day after the shit night I've had. "I'm going to get a later start since I had to watch out for you."

"I didn't ask you to." The flare of irritation infuses color into her cheeks. Good.

"But you needed me to." I hold her defiant stare until she drops it. "So you can give me a call to give you a ride to your car, but I can't promise I can get here right away."

"I'll figure it out."

"Fuck's sake, Campbell. You can't do anything on your own, so quit trying."

Hurt swims in her eyes.

I'm a bastard. I really meant to tell her it's okay to ask for help. That's not how it came out. I can't quit pointing out all the many ways she crawls under my skin.

"Call me when you need a ride to your car, and I'll get back when I can. Night." I rush from the mudroom and into the kitchen. I gather water and some over-the-counter pain meds to put in the guest room while she's in the shower as a way to forget how luminous her big gray eyes are. How they draw a man in.

Nothing will wipe how she felt tipped over my shoulder and how silky her hair is. I'm not attracted to Campbell Hawthorne. Obviously, she's gorgeous. Full lips and fuller hips. Powerful legs that make a guy think about having his head between them.

Good thing I'm not a guy driven by base desires. Or it'd be fucking torture to think about how she's started the washing machine, and that means she's buck-ass naked in the next room.

CHAPTER TWO

Campbell

Fuzz fills my mouth and my head when I wake. I groan before cracking an eyelid open. What room am I—

The mortification of the night comes rushing back, and I pull a pillow over my head. The comforting smell of fabric softener dulls the faint alcohol smell still clinging to me.

Why did I drink too much?

Stanford fucking Baldwin. The love of my life, who fucked my cousin and is now marrying her. And they want it to be a happy family adventure!

Assholes.

I peel a dry eyelid open. A bottle of water and a vial of ibuprofen greet me, along with some crackers. Who did that?

I sit up. The drumbeat behind my temples thrums impossibly harder. I close my eyes as I chug the water and down a couple of pills. Chasing them with the crackers, I study the room for a momentary reprieve from recalling how Durban watched me heave all over Bootleg's parking lot. And myself.

"Wow," I croak, both at my humiliation and my cozy surroundings.

Finished logs line the outer wall, and the others are adorned with nothing but a few simple pictures. One has a bear running full speed toward the camera. Another has three moose grazing in a valley. The frames are as rustic as the furniture. Nothing says mountain cabin like this room.

I like it. Daddy could do with more of this at the big house on the guest ranch, but the sprawling lodge was built to be majestic. To be inviting while at the same time astonishing that something so grand could be in a tiny Montana town. The aesthetic helps sell guest ranch packages worth thousands of dollars.

A little room like this makes me want to hide in it for the day. For the week. For the six weeks until the wedding is done and the bride and groom are on the Tahitian honeymoon I'd once talked about with Stanford.

I rub my eyes and wince at the pain. I need to check my phone and figure out how to get to my car without calling my knight in cozy flannel. Durban's mustache-scruff combo should only work on actors and country music stars. The girls I hung out with last night kept asking if he was single. I took more than a little glee in dashing their hopes. That know-it-all downer is taken by some other woman I'm sure is super dull and responsible.

My purse is lying on the floor. It's dry after my wobbly scrubbing last night. I was sober enough to do a decent job. If I hadn't thrown up the last two beers I'd had, I'd have been a mess. *More* of a mess.

I dig my phone out and a groan slips free.

Jamison: Elodie said your car is still at Bootleg. Where are you?

Jamison: Hey, call me.

Jamison: Mom's asking where you are.

Jamison: Call. Me.

Jamison: Now Daddy's on my ass.

Avery: Why are Mom and Dad asking where you are?

Jamison: Campbell, where the hell are you did you go home with some guy are you dead in a field have you been dumped on the side of the road???

Jamison: No, seriously. If you're not okay, I'm going to kill you. And then I'm going to cut off Can't Stanford's nuts and dangle them on your tombstone like a pair of steel hitch balls.

Avery: We could take turns displaying them.

I snort and prod at my aching temples. Jamison can't stand Stanford, and she said it so often after the breakup—*I can't stand Stanford*—the words slurred together and he became Can't Stanford. When I blink, my vision goes fuzzy. A hot tear rolls down my cheek. If it wasn't for my sisters, I'd have bought a travel van and found some remote camping spot to hide in for a few years.

I'd also probably have a broken-down vehicle, be lost in the forest somewhere, or dumped in a ditch. That's how it goes for me.

Time to face my reckoning.

I text Avery first.

Campbell: I'm fine. I'm just not sitting at

breakfast and smiling pretty for Stanford and January.

Avery: Nor should you be.

I take a deep breath and call my oldest sister.

"You'd better be okay," she says instead of hello.

"Is that offer to chop off his balls still good? I'll hang them from my fender since I don't have a tombstone."

"Don't tempt me. So—spill it."

I pick at the hem of Durban's soft, warm sweater. I eyed this one when Elodie first opened Dee's Sweets, but Stanford hated the blue. I thought it looked like the Stillwater River in June after most of the spring runoff flowed downstream. He claimed it washed me out.

"I, um, went to Bootleg last night."

"Uh-oh," she drawled. "No good decision starts with that sentence."

"It worked for you." She met Iverson in the bar, and he hadn't known she was his boss's forbidden daughter. Daddy had made me and my sisters off-limits to the cowboys working for him, and Iverson had had no idea "Sunny" was Jamison Hawthorne. Which she had known full well was the case. That's why she introduced herself as Sunny.

"Once," she says. "Once in the history of that dive has it worked. Are you telling me that's what happened?"

That's the last thing that'll happen. "I went home with a Hennessy, but I can assure you it didn't work out the same."

Durban Hennessy always looks at me with that slightly perplexed frown of his, the one that says he can't believe I'm not lost in the woods somewhere, batting my eyes at the big, bad wolf. Joke's on him. I can't read a map, and I wander off trails, so I don't hike without someone who's more adept than me.

"You went home with a Hennessy? Not Haven. Oh my God. You did not—"

"No, not Haven."

Iverson made the comment once that I remind him of his youngest brother, who's still older than me. Reckless. Impulsive. It's only celebrated in good-looking guys like Haven and less desirable in a young woman.

Besides, I'm not reckless. Impulsive, yes. Forgetful? Too often. "Um, it was Durban."

"What?" Rustling comes over the line like she's switching ears. "You went home with *Durban*?"

"More like he hauled me out of the bar because he thought I couldn't take care of myself." I sound inane to my own ears. I wasn't able to walk straight last night. I knew it at the time, and I figured I'd dive into my back seat and sleep it off. Silas wouldn't care, and I'd probably be left alone.

Probably.

My gut gurgles at the odds. The likelihood that I wouldn't be bothered had been better before my new acquaintances left, and the three guys set their sights on me. Yeah, I was irresponsible.

"You were that drunk?" she asks, shocked and concerned.

"I mixed drinks. My bad." I also didn't eat a decent dinner.

"Campbell."

"I said my bad. I just wanted to forget."

A sigh gusts over the line. "You should've stayed at the lodge. Then Mom and Dad wouldn't worry about you."

"I can't take up a room in the garage." Our childhood home isn't the same as the lodge where guests stay. Doesn't mean it's a good hiding spot. "Mom keeps asking if I'm okay. Daddy won't quit about the wedding."

She makes a disgusted sound. "Can't he see— Anyway. I guess that's what the meeting's for. How are you doing now? I thought Iverson was with Durban at the distillery."

"I just woke up." Something pricks at my brain. Didn't he say something about being gone in the morning? To call him to figure out my car situation? Right. My car's at Bootleg. "Hey, um, is there any chance you can give me a ride? Only if you're feeling up to it," I rush to add.

"Not you too."

"What about me?"

"Treating me like I'm fragile. I swear, Iverson is afraid I'll break into a million pieces. Durban won't even let me open a door on my own. And now you? If I wasn't pregnant, you'd have told me to quit prying and come pick you up already."

The corner of my mouth tips up. "Fine. Quit prying and come pick me up already."

I hang up, grateful she's able and willing to rescue me from a really nice, cozy house. Iverson does fret, and he'd glare at me for using that word. Durban seems to think women are breakable creatures who need a guy like him to protect us.

I'm not doing a good job of proving him wrong, since my clothes are in his washing machine, and I'm in his sweater and in his bed. Add in that I woke up and immediately partook of the pain meds and water, and I do appear as if I need to be taken care of.

I roll out of bed and wait for any lightheadedness to make me dizzy, but it doesn't happen, probably thanks to heaving out my last couple of drinks. I tiptoe out of the room and into the quiet house.

I blink. "Damn."

The rest of Durban's home is simple yet rustic and welcoming. Wooden beams bisect the arched ceilings with a rock wall acting as a mantel for the fireplace. His seating is all deep browns and mostly leather, and the bookshelves that match the wood tones are lined with impressive tomes.

There are stairs by the office, but I won't snoop He built this place for a family. With his PhD girlfriend?

I creep through the hallway and peek into the modest kitchen. The house isn't large, but it's still roomy and cozy. In the laundry room, my clothing is folded neatly on top of the dryer beside a stack of Durban's clothing. He either stayed up late or got up early to dry my stuff. I didn't think that far ahead last night.

I take the pile to the bathroom, which I barely recall from when I showered. My towel is hung up. Didn't I towel dry my hair and leave it on the counter? Using the same toothbrush I found in the cabinet last night, I brush my teeth and clean up. He has a spare comb too, but I finger comb my tresses, the tangles tugging at my scalp. I have the dried, drowned-rat look going on, but at least I'm puke-free. My skin is sallow—and it's not from the sweater, Stanford!

After I'm dressed, I go to the kitchen. Ooh, a banana. Surely he won't mind. With all those muscles, Durban probably huffs protein shakes and throws back steaks like they're potato chips.

I munch on the banana. Where's the garbage?

I set the peel on the counter. I'm opening cabinet doors when there's a knock. My food lurches into my throat, but I swallow and rush to the front door. Sunny's SUV is parked by the driveway.

"Hey," I say when I open the door to a pregnant sister in a violet flower-covered dress, tenting over her belly, and her feet stuffed in flip-flops. She's put her brown hair in the standard ponytail she's been wearing since her first trimester, when she had morning sickness. "I've gotta grab my purse. Be right back."

I find my boots in the mudroom and return to Jamison.

She frowns. "Where's your purse?"

Shit. "I'm a little scatterbrained today." I run and retrieve my bag, toss the strap over my head so I don't forget it again, and leave with her.

Once I'm buckled in, I steal a pair of her sunglasses to ward off the bright spring sun.

I thunk my head on the back of the headrest. "Why did it have to be Durban?"

"You're lucky it was Durban."

She's right. "Did you text Mom and Dad?"

"I told them you went to Billings with a friend and were doing some shopping this morning."

By the time I get my car and return to the ranch, it'll be just after lunch. Almost plausible if someone bought that I was a morning person and was at the store as soon as the doors opened. "Thank you."

Her excuse sounds a whole lot less pathetic. I owe her.

"They were worried, though." She gives me a side-long look, the light streaking across her sunglasses. "You can back out. No one will blame you."

"And give Stanford and January a reason to blame me for any snafus during their happiest day? No, thanks."

Sunny grunts, disgust twisting her mouth. "January's gotten her way too often."

"She's the apple of Uncle Rayburn's eye, and Sydney's the worm."

We exchange a smile. My mom said that once about our cousins, and my sisters and I have taken it and run. Sydney's a sweetheart, but her efforts always fall short in her parents' eyes, where those of her sister are celebrated, no matter how many people they hurt. It's weird that I wasn't best friends with her instead of January, but January and I are the same age.

She casts a worried look in my direction. "You can tell them to fuck off. I will back you. Iverson too."

If I had a job and a place to live, I could leave. But I don't. Daddy hired me as Hawthorne's Guest Ranch event coordinator. I have to actually prove I can take care of myself. "Can I buy you lunch?"

"No, but I'll eat with you."

I close my eyes. She won't let me buy because she thinks I don't have money. I got a nice severance package at my last job. I had a lot to negotiate with when I got "laid off."

She pulls into the big lot in front of Springs Cafe. Hunger rumbles through my belly. Solid, greasy food is about to hit home, and I can't wait. We sit in the cracked leather booths. Thankfully, my dress has long sleeves, so my skin doesn't stick to the tabletop.

Greta stops by, hands tucked in the pockets of her waitress apron. The owner has worked as a server for as long as I can remember. "Couple of Hawthornes. How ya doin'?"

Jamison smiles at her. "Good. How's the family?"

She beams and gives us a ten-minute spiel about her three kids and five grandkids. My mind buzzes in and out of the conversation as new faces come and go. I love when it's tourist season in town, and I'm granted some level of anonymity. I don't see the guys from last night. That's how it works. You either cross paths a million times or once.

". . . they're my dears." The finality of Greta's tone draws me back in. Dang, I missed all the updates. "What can I get you girls?" She winks. "The same?"

"With an extra pancake?" I ask, admiring how Greta can twist her black hair into a bun without a million flyaways.

"That kind of morning, eh?" Another wink.

"Same for me," Jamison adds. Neither of us looked at a menu. It hasn't changed for as long as I can remember.

When she leaves, I study the street on the other side of the window. The bar is around the corner on the edge of town. It's why it can have such a big dirt lot. The tree-covered Beartooth Mountains line the horizon. I can't see the rolling foothills from here, but Huckleberry Springs lies at the base. Daddy keeps the guest portion of his ranch facing the mountains, but the working ranch is along the sprawling valley, where there's space for cattle to graze and lush grasses.

Main Street is lined with tourist shops, small retail stores, offices, and a grocery store. Outdoor recreation businesses surround the edge of town, closer to either the mountains or the river. Whether it's hiking, skiing, fishing, or kayaking, there's a place that offers it.

I have the urge to talk to Jamison about whether I should contact Sy's Water Adventures before or after the wedding. Do I need to capitalize on my sudden free time, or should I prove myself first? But I don't want to witness her hesitancy again. Her trepidation that I'm going to mess this up too.

"How are you feeling?" I ask.

"Good. I can't do much. I'm a breath away from being under *activity restriction,* and that'll drive me nuts. I'm already in a desk-heavy job."

"Accountants aren't known to go wild at work?"

"They get thrown in jail when they do."

"And that'll raise your blood pressure."

She laughs. "Exactly. But since I'm so close to my due date, and I can work from home, she just wants me to take it easy—at home. No chores, keep my stress down and my feet up." She takes a drink of water. "Did Avery get ahold of you?"

"Yes. I told her to go back to bed and give Thea a sloppy kiss from me."

Her expression turns droll. "You know they both probably ran a marathon before dawn."

"And then personally stocked a local food bank." I cup my hands around my glass of ice water. "Sometimes, I wonder if Mom and Daddy pretend Thea's the third daughter they wished they had."

"Only because Thea can actually catch a fish."

"Fishing's *boring.*"

Her smile fades. "Life isn't always exciting, and we have to deal with it anyway."

Acid churns in my gut. "Thanks, Mom."

"Oh God. I sounded just like her, didn't I?" She rests a hand on her belly. "I'm sorry. I know you're not just chasing a thrill. I told Iverson to say no at the meeting."

I don't want to think about this afternoon when

there's still a dull thud at my temples. "Durban might tell Stanford he made a good decision," I say wryly, masking the burn behind my sternum.

"I don't know what man January is a good decision for." Jamison rolls her eyes. "I mean, seriously. That girl couldn't form an independent thought if she was being dangled off a cliff."

"It's why she took what wasn't hers." I hate to think of the overlap. The comparisons when they have sex. Does he make more of an effort for her?

January might be vapid, but she exudes intelligence. I'd rather ask a statue for advice, but somehow she garners respect and I don't. She's also an unrestrained people pleaser and too conflict-avoidant for her own good. Until now. Because she and Stanford have decided to have their wedding at Hawthorne Guest Ranch and make me plan it.

<hr>

CHAPTER THREE

Durban

Iverson's driving and we're on our way to Hawthorne Ranch for our mysterious meeting. It's about Foster House and an event at the ranch. William Hawthorne has long mentioned combining our services with his, but until now he's been content to order Foster House products and serve them in the bar in the lodge.

I haven't told Iverson about the breakup yet. He's been critical of Natalie since I met her, asking subtle, probing questions to point out that there's too much distance between us, literally and figuratively. Neither of my brothers ever really connected with her, probably because I was the only thing they had in common. I don't want to let them know they were right.

"So, uh." Iverson clears his throat. "Jamison told me what this is about."

Makes sense she'd know, as the Hawthorne Ranch's accountant. "What'd she say?"

He blows out a breath, and my interest perks up. Aren't we just meeting about providing bar services for a special event?

"You remember Campbell's ex?" he asks.

"That dick who thought we were all too hick to understand his job?" He's an insurance broker. I might not have gone to college, but I can do research. "The one who left her for her cousin?"

I don't like the cousin either. I met her at Iverson and Jamison's wedding, but I can't put my finger on why she's like a splinter you want gone ASAP.

"They're getting married."

Figures. That has to be hard for Campbell to hear— Wait. "Is that why Campbell was getting wasted last night?"

He slides his gaze to me, then back to the road, unsurprised. If Campbell got a ride from Jamison, the news of her staying at my place would've made it to Iverson. "Probably. And probably because they want to have the wedding at the guest ranch."

"You're fucking kidding me." Anger explodes from me so fast I nearly spit my words.

"That's not all. They want Campbell to plan it."

I'm dumbfounded. No one can be that callous. "And she told them to shove it so far up their—"

"William thinks it's a good idea, but he's leaving it up to Campbell."

My fury mingles with my astonishment. Then compassion seeps between the cracks in my resentment toward Campbell. She was drowning some emotions last night, and for once, I can't blame her. No wonder she didn't want to go home wasted.

"So, anyway," he says gruffly, "thanks for taking care

of her last night. Hate for Hawthorne Ranch to lose its newest event coordinator," he finishes bitterly.

"No problem." The event coordinator was gone from my house before I went home for lunch. I didn't tell Iverson how bad she was, only that she didn't want to go home. Must be why he thought to share the news about the meeting.

A meeting Campbell apparently has today too. Good thing she cleared out early.

I didn't think to tell her not to bother her sister, but she must have called Jamison anyway. She probably would've forgotten my warning before she woke with the world's worst hangover anyway.

She wasn't in my house long, but her presence was stamped on everything she touched. She left my shower smelling like strawberries and sunshine. The whirlwind that went through the bathroom didn't take me long to clean this morning, but when I stopped home for lunch, I had to tidy the guest room too and throw away her banana peel. Why not take a few extra moments to look for the garbage?

She's not my problem anymore.

"What's Natalie going to think about your overnight guest?" Iverson asks, his hand draped over the steering wheel.

Now would be the perfect time to tell him Natalie has no reason to care. "She probably won't be worked up about it. I don't take advantage of drunk women, and she knows I have issues with Campbell's level of responsibility."

He gives me a sidelong look before turning down the winding road that'll take us to the front of the lodge.

"Did Natalie ever tell you what she's doing after school? Getting a third PhD?"

I snort. If she had, would I have waited through another three or four years? "She's been getting offers here and there."

"Are the 'here and there' offers anywhere near Montana?" he asks.

"There's a faculty position in Bozeman she's waiting to hear on." My stomach ties into a knot as if I'm lying, but I'm not, technically. She did apply, only it no longer matters.

"Yeah? In what?"

"Molecular biosciences."

He coughs out a laugh. "Shit."

Yep, she's a smart girl. And I was the laid-back guy she wanted for a while.

"Is that what you two talk about all the time? Molecular shit and ethics?" He's asked questions like this before.

"Yes, and I talk about distilling."

He snorts. "Does she listen?" I shoot him a perplexed look, but he shrugs and keeps his attention on the road. "Just saying, she likes to talk about herself a lot."

"She has a lot going on in that brain."

Iverson's observations burrow into my mind like a persistent worm. She listened. Didn't she? She'd turn the conversation back to her, but of course, she knew the important stuff, like my niece's name. Didn't she? I try to recall her saying it, or even asking about Kacey.

Again, that's all water under the bridge. Despite how easy-breezy Natalie thinks my life is, I do have responsibilities. I tug on my sleeve. I don't look like I'm a part owner in a business. Much like the old gold mine that the distillery is in, I'm just a piece of Montana that's been dressed up a little.

I'm wearing my nicest flannel and jeans that don't have holes. Iverson's wearing a yellow-and-black Foster House polo with a flannel over it, jeans, and boots. That's the most effort we're putting in. We could use this gig and the exposure it'll bring, but if I'd known what William was going to talk to us about, I'd have kept the clothes on that I did chores in.

Disgust prickles the back of my neck. Who the hell would cheat on his girlfriend and then marry their affair partner in his ex's backyard? Either Stanford never cared about Campbell, or he's obsessed with her, and I don't like enabling the fucker.

"I can't believe we're doing this," I mutter.

"No kidding." Iverson grunts. "Jamison said Campbell's avoiding the topic. Instead of telling William no outright, I figured we might as well make an appearance and stand behind Campbell when she faces her dad."

My normal censure when it comes to her isn't there. She should be able to handle her own battles—and her own dad—but I know about a parent bulldozing over what's best for their kids. Yeah, we'll stand behind Campbell.

It's a good view at least.

I stare out the window, searching for something to take my mind off Campbell's ass swaying in her dress last night.

In the distance, a guide on horseback leads a group of five riders through the pastures. Guests on a tour. I never led those. We weren't classy enough. William Hawthorne needed performers to lead tours and work with the guests, to be really showy about branding with an old-fashioned branding iron and wrangling calves by hand. He didn't want us talking about electric branding irons or squeeze chutes that make our job quicker, easier, and usually safer. He told me once, after a long discussion about the different cuttings of hay and what they offer, that I would bore an entire tour to tears.

Resentment clouds behind my eyes. I liked working for him, but until I started at the distillery, a company I'm part owner in, I didn't realize how unfulfilled I was.

Iverson rounds a curve, and the big house comes into view. The guest lodge makes my home look tiny. Down a small hill, there are three smaller cabins that some of the staff and seasonal workers stay in. Not far from those is a sweeping red barn and stable, then a sprawling shop. Even farther away is the bunkhouse where I used to live with Iverson, Haven, and the other guys. Another barn and shop are close to the bunkhouse.

"Do you ever miss it?" Iverson asks. We haven't been out here together much.

"No," I say without hesitation.

I wasn't unhappy as a cowboy for hire. It's honest work that leaves a guy ready to hit the hay at the end of the day. The cattle I wrangle now bear a brand I'm part owner of, and the distillery carries my name as an investor. I take pride in both things, but also comfort that there's something for me even if I'm too beat up to get into a saddle.

"Yup," Iverson agrees. "Can't beat cowboying for a living, but I also like having a retirement plan."

"Yup." I like having something to offer someone besides my tired ass at the end of the day.

I glower at the lodge as Iverson pulls into a spot on

the far side of the parking area where the employees park. A thought hits me, and I stiffen. "That dickhead isn't going to be here, is he?"

"Can't Stanford?"

I nod, long familiar with Jamison's name for her sister's ex.

Iverson thinks for a moment before dread fills his expression. "Fuck, I hope he's not here."

After seeing the state Campbell was in last night, I hope not too. We get out and start for the main entrance. The employee entrance is off to the side by the kitchen, but those days are over for us.

A few guests who likely skipped the trail rides mingle along the walking paths that lead to the barn and a sitting area. There's a sizable pavilion and a firepit behind the lodge. Staff wearing name tags roam the grounds, working on the flower beds and cleaning the dust and grit off windows and exterior doors.

Jamison and Campbell's mom, Christine, greets us with a tight smile, her blond hair pulled back and her blue eyes bright. Her jeans don't have a speck of dust on them, and her boots have blue and purple stitching. The bluebell-colored blouse complements her eyes and I can see each of her three daughters in her.

She nods at me and gives Iverson a quick hug. "I'm glad you left Jamison at home."

"I'm not stopping her from doing anything," he says lightly. "She doesn't trust her hormones in a situation like this."

"Good, she told you." A nervous laugh leaves her. "It's certainly unprecedented, but William has his reasons."

His reasons usually have dollar signs, and I've never

been more upset with the man. Why would he make his daughter do this? As for Campbell, she's an adult. Why would she go along with it?

My comments about her jobless state from last night drift through my mind. Does she feel like she doesn't have a choice? Moreover, can she plan an event without being late or missing one of the hundred small details that go into it?

Christine leads us through the sitting area where social hour often takes place, past the entrance to the small bar, and to a concealed door behind a bookshelf. The meeting room.

Inside, William's waiting at the head of the table. His bushy white mustache is the first thing anyone notices about him. He's usually boisterous, greeting guests and making them laugh and smile. Today, he's grim. His mustache practically droops.

He glances from me to Iverson. "I take it you know what we're meeting about?"

"I do." Iverson doesn't take a seat, and neither do I.

"You can't let this happen," I add.

"I'd like to wait for Campbell to get here before you guys level me with your righteous opinions." He checks his watch and huffs out a breath.

We're early, but Campbell isn't.

Christine sits, waving for us to take a chair. I finally pull a seat out, and she gives me a grateful smile. I'm not here to create drama, and Christine was always nice to the ranch employees. She accepted Iverson into the family with no hesitation. She even hugs him like our mom never did. So, yeah. I can sit my ass down when she asks me to.

Iverson relents too. We're not turning our back on

our convictions. But we are willing to hear the rest of the story.

"How's the herd?" William asks us, tapping his fingers on the tabletop. Campbell continues to be a no-show as we chat about calving season. Haven's taking over for us, watching for any new calves or mamas having birthing trouble.

Lane and Cruz Foster are working the tours and tasting room at the distillery. They're the other partial owners. Myles Foster controls the most shares. He's the founder and CEO, but his brothers are taking more responsibility with the whole company and not just the Huckleberry Springs' site.

Five minutes after the scheduled time tick by, we're still chatting, but Christine is discreetly tapping into her phone.

Another five minutes later, Campbell breezes into the room on a cloud of huckleberry blossoms and sunshine. Her chestnut hair is gathered in a clip at the back of her head, but lighter strands fan out around her face. Her cheeks have a fresh blush, but the tip of her nose isn't red.

The dress from last night is gone. She's in jeans—these most definitely have dust on them—and a hoodie with the Hawthorne brand across the front, an *H* over a squiggle. William claims that's to represent the Stillwater River, but the inside joke is that it's really a dollar sign.

"Sorry," she says, out of breath. "I didn't mean to keep you waiting."

William pointedly looks at his watch again.

She sits across from us and avoids my gaze, but she doesn't offer any excuses. I have to respect that. Unless she was rescuing puppies or solving the answer to world peace, it'd sound irresponsible.

"I'll just come right out with it," William says. "Stanford and January want their wedding at the ranch, and since Campbell's our new event planner, she'll be planning the wedding."

Campbell's gaze is on the wood grains swirling through the tabletop.

When she doesn't say anything, William continues. "I know everyone thinks we shouldn't allow it."

"No shit." I clamp my teeth together. I didn't mean to have an outburst like that, but what dad would put his daughter through planning her ex's wedding to the cousin he cheated on her with?

William shoots me a scowl. "I'm not happy with my brother for pushing it either. Stanford, the dumbass, should have more sense, and well, we all know January doesn't."

Campbell puffs out a small laugh, her attention remaining on the wall.

"I think it's important in this case to be the bigger person." His shoulders are stiff as he continues. "To be infallible when it comes to how we conduct ourselves."

I shift in my seat, but Campbell's gaze flicks up and she grimaces, as if my movement projects all my judgment onto the tabletop. Rich girl gets a job from her daddy when she can't hold her own.

She's wrong.

Well, that's *absolutely* what happened in her case. But I don't judge her for it. I didn't grow up rich, but I have the job and my land because of what my dad left behind for me and my brothers. For a long time, the only family assets we had were detriments. Her dad loves her, and he wants to help. She accepted that help. In that, we're no different. It's how we use advantages that makes the difference, and she's been thrown into the fire.

He scrubs a hand down his face, and for once, he looks old. Bags hang under his eyes, and strain shows in the frown lines pulling down at the corners of his mouth. "Rayburn also owns half the ranch."

"What?" Iverson and I say at the same time.

"The guest ranch is mine. The money it makes or loses is mine, but we were both left the land the working ranch is on." He blows out a hard breath. "If we do this wedding, he's agreed to sell it to me. Then I can leave it free and clear to my daughters. All but a portion he wants to keep for Sydney. January wants the wedding, and she doesn't want anything else to do with the ranch."

A sarcastic snort leaves Campbell. "She probably hasn't told Stanford, or he'd be counting the money he could squeeze out of you, Daddy."

Christine's derisive sniff lands between us. "That girl just wants to show you up more than she wants a part of her family's legacy. She always was a jealous kid."

My mind's whirling. The situation is shitty for everyone involved, but it's all Hawthorne drama. The only other family involved is Stanford's. "What's our role in this?"

William lifts his gaze to Campbell.

She crosses one leg over the other. If she were wearing the dress from last night, it might've slid down her knee to reveal some skin.

And why would I care?

She has nice legs. I'm not interested, but I still notice things.

"They would like the local distillery with deep roots in Huckleberry Springs history to provide the spirits and bar services." She says it like she's trying to recruit our business, and the way she's selling it would've worked if I hadn't just heard the story about why.

"We can provide the spirits," Iverson says. He taps his fingertips together. "Is there a reason why the staff here can't do their normal duties with the bar? Or why they can't provide a wet bar?"

"Stanford thinks you're an asshole and he wants you to wait on him," Campbell says simply.

I cough out a laugh. "Way to get to the point."

I mean it as a compliment, but her shoulders droop farther. "It's a guess. I shouldn't have said it, but this isn't really a standard pitch for your services." She bites into her lower lip, and I'm fixated on the spot where her white teeth are sinking into red flesh. "At the wedding, Stanford thought both of you were presumptive asses and dismissed him. Haven too. He doesn't take kindly to that, ironically, because he thinks he's better than anyone. So when he was presented with a chance to have a wedding at the ranch and make you three dance for his money, he couldn't resist."

"Fucker," I growl.

Christine leans over to put her cool fingers on my forearm. I tense for her censure.

"I'm so glad we're of the same mind when it comes to this craziness." She pats me in the most maternal gesture I've ever experienced before pulling away. "I say we should tell them to take a hike."

The venom in her tone tells me she's used harsher words to describe what Stanford, January, and William's brother can do.

"We can," William said cautiously.

"We don't need their business to succeed," Iverson says. "Foster House is doing just fine, and the Foster House Gold products are growing a niche whiskey, vodka, and gin audience, just like we planned. It doesn't need some dickwad's wedding."

"But it would help," Campbell says in a soft voice. "It would help you and your growing family for Foster House to have more stability and faster growth." She runs her gaze over me, a resolute glint in her eyes. "You're supporting a lot of people in this small community. Iverson, you're married, but the other owners are mostly single guys who may also be settling down soon and growing families."

Is she shouldering the responsibility of how our company is going to support all of its employees? My admiration for her grows. Just a little.

"I can tell them no," William assures her, but the stress and fatigue weighing him down are almost palpable.

"I have no problem telling them to fuck off," Iverson adds.

"He'll have the full Foster House fuck-off behind him," I say.

Christine's nodding, but Campbell's studying me, as if she can't believe that I'm on board to keep her from getting bossed around by two people who hurt her. She's annoying, but I don't wish that for her. I'm a better man than her ex.

We all watch her. She licks her pink tongue out, wetting her bottom lip, and once again, I'm riveted. Damn, it's been a long time since I've had sex.

That determination from earlier hardens. "I think we

should do it. I'm going to plan their wedding, and I'm going to do it well. Because I'm good at what I do. No matter what anyone thinks." She casts a glance in my direction. Point taken. "I think Foster House should participate. You can serve the wedding and get your products on more palates, but you'll also be factored into the biggest talk of the town since one of Daddy's cowboys ran off with his daughter."

William and Christine chuckle. Iverson looks pleased with himself.

"I'm going to plan the hell out of this wedding," Campbell says, "and I'm going to do it with a smile. I'm going to look blissfully happy that Stanford is no longer my problem, and I can't think of anyone better to be saddled with him than my backstabbing cousin."

William dips his head. "Amen to that."

Neither Iverson nor I jump in. It doesn't feel right. Everyone involved in hurting Campbell can stay in Portland or Seattle, or wherever Campbell was living before she moved home.

"When you put it like that . . ." Christine sighs and rolls her neck. "Then I'm in. Whatever you need, even if it's just moral support when Stanford's pompous parents show up."

The relief and gratitude pouring through Campbell's smile at her mom tugs at my heart. Damn, she's pretty when she's not irritating me. She's not just doing the wedding to spite her ex. She wants to help her dad—and us. I thought she was self-absorbed, but her selflessness didn't just appear overnight.

Iverson and I exchange a glance. I know from his hard stare what he's thinking. He wants to back Campbell. He doesn't want to incur his wife's wrath for agreeing to the wedding, but he wants to help Campbell. So do I. But neither of us is going to be Stanford's dancing puppet. Fuck that guy.

"We'll agree," I say carefully. "But the bride and groom are going to realize quickly that we'll provide services at our discretion, when it works for us, and we can jump off this train wreck whenever we want. They can go buy a few six-packs if they piss us off."

Her eyes widen with each declaration, but then a radiant smile breaks through. "I can't wait to tell them."

Iverson glances at me. "Jamison's due right around when the wedding is. Mind taking point on all this?"

"No problem." Just because Campbell Hawthorne is the event coordinator doesn't mean I can't be professional.

CHAPTER FOUR

Campbell

A week after the meeting that determined my future for the next six weeks, I coast through the trees at the entrance of Foster House. The distillery looms at the edge of the parking lot, a polished gem that once housed the loud, heavy equipment that crushed pieces of the surrounding mountains freed by miners to liberate any gold inside.

The equipment is long gone, hauled out by the mining company when they declared the hills empty of gold, platinum, and palladium. The inside sat empty for decades, and the elements took a toll on the metal sheeting blanketing the outside and the logs making up the headquarters. You'd never know now. Silver metal gleams along the sides, rising to peaks of three different levels, and some of the timber has been replaced. The newer pieces are lighter than the restored older wood, giving the whole building a rugged, industrial aesthetic.

I got a tour once, shortly after they opened. Jamison dragged me and Avery through. The higher levels are now offices, one each for the Hennessy brothers and Lane and Cruz Foster. The main level is where the tanks and stills are housed, and there's a small area in the back for the production line. A large garage door faces the far end of the lot where a long rickhouse has been built. It's a new structure, but it matches the metal, log, and timber look of the tasting room and merch store.

The whole property is a complete one-eighty from how I knew it most of my life. I grew up being told never to roam the dangerous area full of abandoned mine shafts, but it's private land anyway. Hennessy land. As a kid, I had no idea the only remaining Hennessys worked for Daddy, but for a lot of my life, the boys didn't live in Huckleberry Springs.

There are stories about them. Tales that tear my heart. The three boys were left alone after their dad died on a hike. They told no one that they had no guardian. Eventually, though, they were taken into foster care and then shuttled to their mom. All the time they worked for Hawthorne Ranch, no one connected the dots that they were *those* Hennessys, or if anyone did, they kept it to themselves.

I park and enter through the main door.

Inside, Elodie's little sister, Clementine Palmer, arranges a display of vodka bottles, all with the familiar yellow house on the labels. Her long dark hair is pulled back into two Dutch braids.

She brightens. "Hiya, Campbell."

"Clem, how's it going?"

She dusts her hands off on her jeans. She's wearing a simple yellow shirt with a Foster House logo. Same house that's on the product labels, only in black. "Good. Are you stopping in for wedding stuff?"

I don't have to tell anyone about what I've been working on for the last three weeks. News spread around town faster than when Jamison announced she was marrying one of *those* Hennessys. "Yeah. Is Durban around?"

"He sure is. All the guys are in a meeting. The big boss is in town, but Durban told me to let him know when you arrive."

She picks up a phone, and my traitorous belly does a little swoop. Normally, I can acknowledge what a good-looking guy Durban is. He's tall, with thick dark hair that makes a girl want to run her hands through it. The way he styles it is always a little unkempt, like he meticulously combs it, then runs his hands over his scalp regardless. The guy's so uptight, he's probably constantly frustrated and tugging on those rich, almost black strands.

All the brothers are undeniably attractive with similar good looks, but I've never noticed the others quite as much as Durban. Iverson is my sister's husband, so he's been off-limits since I met him. Even then, I only thought he was hot in that general, *my sister bagged herself a hot cowboy* kind of way. Haven's more casual demeanor instantly put me at ease, and while he's a genuine panty incinerator, mine have no singe marks.

But Durban's always had that slightly disapproving frown that makes me more . . . aware. I can't miss the way his whiskers fail to hide the cleft in his chin. Or how a deep dimple flashes when he smiles, but he's never aiming that ovary annihilator at me. I never cared. I was with Stanford.

Now I'm not, and his frown a week ago was deeper than I've ever seen it. Yet he took me home without even knowing the whole story.

After he abducted me from the bar for my own good, I figure I'll feel humiliated around him for the rest of my life. Now's my chance not to flub and show him I'm a competent adult. Maybe I'll figure out why it's important to me to redeem myself. It's not because I'm interested in him. He has a girlfriend. A smart one.

"He said you can go on up," Clem says. "They're almost done, and you two can use the meeting room."

"Thanks."

I wind through the merch store and up the wooden staircase with metal handrails that reflect the rest of the distillery's style. An elevator was added during renovations, and it's often used by tourists. The second level looks over the trees and into the mountains behind the building. Guests receive some gold mining lore as part of the tour.

Three guys, none of them Hennessys, but all still shockingly handsome, exit the meeting room. Like the Hennessy brothers, the Foster brothers resemble each other. I met Lane and Cruz at Jamison's wedding, and I see them running errands around town and chatting with business owners. Both are tall, with black hair and blue eyes. Lane's short hairstyle does nothing to hide his shrewd gaze, while Cruz's stylishly long hair just highlights his devil-may-care grin. They're both tall, but stockier than their oldest brother, Myles. Jamison told me once that Myles is Lane and Cruz's older half brother.

"Bring Wynter and the kids next time," Lane tells Myles. "And if you're not bringing Mae herself, I'm not letting you in without her chocolate chip cookies next time."

Who's Mae?

Myles smirks. "I dropped them off at your house. Along with the eggs." He glances at Cruz. "Yours too."

Cruz grins. "I knew I gave you my code for a good reason." Cruz waves me over. "Heya, Campbell. Durban said you were coming by today. You ever meet my brother? Myles, this is Jamison's sister, Campbell."

I tuck the box under my arm and stretch out a hand.

"Nice to finally meet you." He gives my hand a firm shake. I've never felt shorter than I do now around the Foster brothers, except for when I'm standing around the Hennessys. "Thank you for helping Foster House Gold break into the local events scene."

"Seems to be our common goal," I say, and again, there's no flutter. Myles and his brothers are hot. No reaction. But the thought of Durban being through that door with his glower has my nerves tingling on high alert. What's going on with me? "Nice to meet the oldest Foster."

"And now we've shown her that it doesn't get any better than me and Cruz," Lane jokes.

"Now she knows you're full of shit," Myles says smoothly. "And I'm not buying lunch."

"Haven can get it." Cruz folds his arms, and his biceps bulge. "He lost the last bet anyway."

"What can I get?" Haven's the next to leave the meeting room, Iverson on his heels. They both nod their greetings to me.

"Lunch," Cruz answers.

I brandish my box of pistachio-crème-filled cruffins. They're my favorite of Elodie's creations. I already ate mine, or I'd be wearing half of the sugar coating. I can eat gallons of her custard. I open the lid and all the guys peer inside, interest lighting up their faces. "There'll be dessert waiting for you when you get back."

Myles snaps his fingers. "Thanks for reminding me. Wynter wants me to bring home a dozen of something."

"Sure," Lane says. "It's Wynter and the kids asking for the goodies."

Myles mock scowls at him. "Elsa likes to bake, but she changes the recipes without understanding the science behind them. Her last three batches of cupcakes have been . . . interesting." Pride shines in his eyes regardless of how the cupcakes must've been. "She's going to work as Bourbon Canyon's baker, but she likes to sample other goods."

A dad who's proud of his daughter despite her mishaps. Who'd have thought?

The Fosters filter out. Iverson gives me a light slap on the shoulder as he passes. "Ready to kill them with kindness?"

The "them" in question is Stanford and January. "And competence."

"You'll do fine."

He heads down the stairs after the others. I can't tell from his tone if he's really convinced I'm going to do okay. I *am* good at my job. I love planning and coordinating events. Meetings, gatherings—it doesn't matter. It's just too bad I had to come home in order to do it.

When I turn around, Durban is in the doorway, an unreadable expression on his face.

I startle, and the lid of the box falls closed. "Jeepers. Scare a girl lately?"

He cocks an arrogant brow. "Just the jumpy ones."

Fright is not what's swirling in my belly and sinking lower. Fear isn't making me appreciate his wide shoulders and the natural power in his stance. This guy doesn't have to boast and intimidate to get respect or authority. He possesses it to the point where I might beg him to use it.

Oh God. Get off the subject of his body and what he can do with it. He's so not my type. If I keep saying it, maybe it'll become true. "Aren't you going to lunch?"

"I have an important meeting." He checks his watch. "And you're early."

"You can thank my three timers for that."

Bewilderment flickers in his eyes, but he stands back and ushers me into the meeting room, a minimal but stylish area like the rest of the building. Two walls of windows overlook the line of pipes running from the stills. There's only a simple stained wood table, a nook with a coffee station in the corner, and office chairs that look like I could sit in them for hours.

"Have a seat," he says as he takes a seat.

"Cruffin?" I slide the box across the table and pick a spot across from him.

His gaze dips to the pink bow printed on the container. "No, thanks. The sugar sticks to my mustache."

"Lick it off."

He pauses, shuffling papers that look like they have the wedding schedule I designed on them. "I assure you, there's nothing I like more than licking sweetness off my whiskers, but there's a time and a place for it."

Heat hits me like a tidal wave. Surely, he doesn't mean . . . In my mind, a picture forms: my legs splayed open with him in between, his lips and chin glistening with—

"What exactly is this ex-prick of yours expecting from Foster House?" he asks like he didn't just say *that*.

But mention of my ex and his wedding snaps me out of my lustful daydream. For a few blissful moments, this ordeal wasn't the center of all my thoughts. I'm so desperate for a distraction, I'm lusting after Durban. "I only ask you don't refer to him as Ex-prick on Hawthorne grounds. He might overhear. Or the happy bride could."

"Is he here?"

I let out a heavy sigh. "He's going to be soon. I've been corresponding with them." I had to unblock his phone number for this shit. "His family is going to arrive about three weeks early. They want to make a vacation out of the wedding, with the ceremony as the cap to it all."

He does a quizzical shake of his head. "You don't have to plan his family's vacation too, do you?"

"More events, more money."

He narrows his eyes, but I don't feel any heat of disapproval. "That's fucked up."

"It's a job. I've done plenty of events where I don't like the people involved. This is no different." Is that a glint of respect in his eyes? "My main role is to make sure the bride and groom are happy with what they've booked."

"Do they really deserve to be happy?"

"I really don't care. Like I said, it's my job, and once it's done, I don't have to have anything to do with them anymore."

Sympathy darkens his rich-brown eyes. "Were you and January close?"

We've veered off topic, and normally, I'd charge away from this subject. But the unexpected compassion in his voice encourages me. "I considered her my best friend outside of my sisters, though she seemed to want more of a mentor out of me—how to dress, how to flirt, what's the best mascara. Probably because of her mother. Her birth mom wasn't interested in being a mother to her or Sydney, and her stepmom is hyperaware of looks and status." I shrug. "In the end, January wanted to be me, and she made my bed. Now she can lie in it."

"A lumpy mattress?"

A smile traces my lips. "Poorer quality than I thought at the time." I don't have a paper schedule, but I pull up the information on my phone. "So Ex-Prick has said he wants guests to be able to order any whiskey- or vodka-based drink possible." He opens his mouth, but I hold up a finger. I'm laying all of Stanford's cards on the table, and now I'll inform Durban of which ones I've flicked off. "I told him that the best plan would be to have Foster House offer a menu for them to order from. Three to five of each if you're going with whiskey, vodka, and gin." I wave my hand in the air. "Makes it feel more exclusive, especially if you offer at least one different cocktail for each spirit just for each night."

His brows draw together. Crap. Does he think it's too much? Too simple? Did I somehow insult his whole personality?

"You seem to get into their heads," he says. "How much psychology goes into this job?"

Startled he's asked such a serious question, I consider

my answer. "Um, a little." I think about clients I've talked out of a panic over the years. "A lot. Besides, I've been placating Stanford for years. That's like second nature."

Both his brows lift. "You shouldn't have had to do that."

Shame heats the back of my neck. I didn't know I was doing it at the time. "I emailed you the times. So far, the couple would like a Foster House bar at the dinner for Stanford's family when they all arrive. Then there'll be the bridal luncheon the Thursday before the wedding, a groom's dinner Friday night, and the wedding ceremony and reception Saturday evening. The wedding is at seven. If you could arrive forty-five minutes to an hour before each gathering, that'll give us a buffer if there are any hiccups."

He leans back in his chair and crosses his arms. "Like what?"

He's unusually agreeable. Is this distillery a different dimension, or is the situation extra pathetic? I don't want to know the answer. "Broken bottles, missing equipment—speaking of that. Do you want to use what the ranch has in its bar?"

"Yes, and I'll haul all the spirits I'll be using, but I can store them there until the wedding's done." His phone buzzes where it's sitting by the laptop. He glances at it, and the corner of his mouth quirks up as fondness crosses his face.

Jealousy pokes dead center in my chest. "Would you like me to arrange with Chef to provide you with garnishes and syrups?"

"I can do that."

His phone buzzes again, and that little smile is back.

"Do you need to take that?" I'm being nosy and I

don't care. A guy doesn't get that look on his face for a text from his brother, and they're all probably still driving to town.

"No." He taps in a quick message.

It must be her. The spot on my sternum flares hotter. His girlfriend is across the country, and she gets that look? Jesus. "Natalie?"

His expression darkens for a quick second. "No. She's getting ready to defend her thesis so she can graduate. This is Kacey. She's bored and making your sister send me and Haven photos of her drawings."

My heart softens, but it doesn't negate the intimidation. I hated college, and his girlfriend is on her second PhD. I was late to class all the time, and I'm shit at taking tests. "PhD in what?"

I don't know what would make me feel better, but it isn't his answer of "Bioethics."

"Oh, wow." I summon a foggy memory. "What's one of the jokes you sent her?"

"You remember that?"

I give him a *duh* look, but I'm surprised myself.

He hesitates for a second. "I was going to tell you a joke about sodium, but nah."

"Why not?" Doesn't he think I'll get it?

His gaze flickers, and he sits forward. "That's, uh, the joke. The element symbol for sodium is N-A, Latin for natrium."

"Right." I let out a nervous laugh. I barely get it I didn't like the sciences. They made me feel stupid, and I had enough of that growing up.

He clears his throat, and yep, this moment is as mortifying as it feels. "What can we really expect with this first dinner where it's just his family? None of yours will be there?"

"January will." My laugh is hollow, and he doesn't crack a smile. Tough crowd. "His parents and maybe an aunt or uncle and some cousins will be at the family dinner. They are all too much like Stanford. You'll instantly see why he is the way he is. As for the Hawthorne side, you met them all at Iverson and Jamison's wedding, so no surprises there." The small, intimate gathering at the ranch was where I earned my first scowl from Durban. "Which also happens to be where Stanford first met January."

"Did they have a nice chat when you were tearing up the dance floor?"

I tense. Is that censure in his voice? "Probably, but you have to admit. I tore it up good."

"And loud."

"Line dances shouldn't be quiet." I exhale a gusty sigh. One of my goals today is to prove myself, not defend myself. "Don't worry. There's no rowdy country music allowed at the reception, but I'm the event planner, so I'm not allowed to dance anyway."

His mouth forms a troubled line. "You're still family."

"Not to her anymore." One of my alarms goes off. "Oh, sorry. I don't mean to cut this short, but I have to meet with the band's manager."

He quirks a brow. "A live band?"

"Of course. Locals out of Billings. I don't think they want to do some small wedding gig in a place like Huckleberry Springs. Fingers crossed meeting them in person will change their mind."

"I used to foster with June Bee."

"Shut up!" Hers was one of the songs I cut up the dance floor to during Jamison's reception. "Jamison told me you guys fostered with the Copper Summit family when you were young. I hope that's okay she said something."

He nods, his expression revealing nothing. "It's not a secret. In fact, I'm surprised it's not talked about more."

"Jamison would only tell me and Avery, and neither of us will say anything. As Hawthornes, we learned to keep it in the family." We're too prominent, and that makes it too easy to feed the gossip mill. "So, June Bee, huh? She talks a lot about her adoption story. Did you know she was going to be a star when you were fosters?"

"Junie and her three sisters were already adopted when we were there, and my brothers and I only stayed for a few months."

"Then what?" I'm aware it's none of my business, but I want to know more about the serious Hennessy brother. Is he just the strong, silent type around me?

"We went to live with our mom."

His features don't change, but his tone tells me a lot. "It was like that, huh?"

"It was the complete opposite of how you grew up."

"Is that why you don't like me?"

He cocks his head. "Is that what you think? That I'm jealous?"

"No. I think you think I'm a mess and I take people for granted."

"You were a day late for your sister's wedding." He says it like he's stating a fact, which, fair.

"Yeah. I was."

Stanford didn't want me to go without him, and he'd scheduled a Very Important Meeting the morning I told my family I'd be there. I didn't miss the wedding, but I lost out on a lot of family time.

My second alarm goes off. "Apologies, but I really do have to be off. Stanford and January would like to arrange a tasting, so if you could give me a time that could work, I'll wait to schedule the rest of their family events until I hear back. I anticipate the rest of the crew will like a tour and tasting too. I have to entertain them for almost three weeks until the official wedding activities begin. Let me know if you want to meet at the ranch sometime in the next few weeks, and we'll go over where you'll set up for the various events."

"Why were you late to Iverson and Jamison's wedding?" he asks as if I didn't just rattle off a bunch of details he should be writing down. Does he have a photographic memory, or is he just brushing me off because all of this is frivolous to him?

I'll worry about that later. I push out of my chair. If I don't stand, I might keep talking. I planned some buffer time for construction. "Does it matter? I was late. Everyone was irritated."

He rubs the scruff on his jaw. The faint scrape makes it hard to suppress the thought from earlier about Durban and spread thighs. "The why matters."

"No, it doesn't. People hate it when you take their time for granted. I never felt like I was doing that, but now it's my job to figure out how to be on time, and I'm doing it."

He stays sitting. "What other tools do you use?"

I scoot around the opposite side of the table toward the door. "Alarms mostly. Apps to block notifications on my phone and laptop. Automated reminders to keep me on task."

I stop at the threshold, my gaze on the stairs and the network of copper and steel pipes behind them. My parents taught me to take responsibility for myself, and I have. But planning this wedding, what would've been *my* wedding, and watching hearts-in-her-eyes January hang on a man I used to love . . . I'm so tired of taking other people's responsibility. I covered for Stanford while we were together, and I'm still doing it.

"The main tool, the one that has had the most significant impact, is getting dumped by a small cheating man who tried to manipulate my time."

I leave the room with my chin held high, despite knowing I've just shown Durban one more time how pathetic I am over a man who didn't deserve me.

CHAPTER FIVE

Durban

She bends over me, hair sweeping across my chest as she makes her way down my body. When she reaches the erection bobbing in front of her face, she looks up at me, rewarding me with a sultry grin. Eagerness lights her gray eyes—

I come awake with a start. My heartbeat throbs in my dick, pounding at a steady rate, demanding I finish what my dream started.

Fuck. Is my brain getting revenge on Natalie by replacing her with Campbell? I have to think of something else.

Definitely not how wet her lips would be—

No. Not that. What do I need to do today?

My daily to-do list trickles into my head. I have to meet Campbell at the lodge. Must be why she's on my mind. The revelations from my meeting with her last week have stuck with me.

Stanford made her late for her sister's wedding. Why wouldn't she throw him in front of everyone's judgment?

And three alarms? At least she knows she struggles with time and tries to adjust for it. Though it doesn't always work.

My phone vibrates. As if I've summoned her straight off her knees in my dream, she texts me.

Campbell: Stanford and January are here FYI

Not the best news, but everything's beginning. I set the phone down. My erection is still determined to stick around.

I sit up, wincing at the way my boxer briefs throttle my cock. Rubbing at my eyes, I slide out of bed and trudge to the shower, bringing my phone with me.

Time for a stern talk with myself. Dreams aren't real. They don't reveal hidden obsessions. I've been fielding texts and reminders to download some planning app from Campbell. That's why she appeared in my dream—with those ripe, full lips and that long, satiny hair.

I turn on my country playlist and start the shower. My erection's barely flagging, and I need that damn thing gone before I meet Campbell to go over the layout. She offered to tell me over the phone or email a diagram, but my dumb ass said I'd meet with her instead.

I wash myself, ignoring my insistent erection until I'm clean. Then I sigh and grip the base, squeezing just how I like it.

Pleasure courses through me, and images flash through my head. Tits. A round ass. Chestnut hair with blond highlights that is so damn soft . . .

Hell no. I can't think about Campbell. She's my brother's annoying sister-in-law. She's too young for me.

She's no longer the "barely out of college" girl I first met.

By now, blood's hammering in my dick, and I'm pumping faster, re-creating the weight of Campbell's body in my arms, how her ass wiggles right in my face, and the graze of her breasts against my shoulders. Arousal pumps hot through my veins, and I forget that I should get some soap or lotion to stroke myself with. The shower-fresh smell of her on my sweatshirt rises nice and crystal fucking clear in my head.

I come on a long moan, hot spurts hitting the wall and the floor of the shower. I catch my breath and sag against the shower wall. What the hell? I never get myself off that fast.

Dammit, now I have a mess to clean up and images I have to forever push out of my head when I'm around Campbell Hawthorne.

There's no way that sexy-as-hell image is leaving. It's burned into every neuron in my brain, and it's from my *imagination*. Shit.

After I dry off and get dressed, I heat a breakfast sandwich and eat it on the drive to the Hawthorne Ranch. When I pull into the parking lot, guests mill around the grounds and chill on the front porch. How many are Baldwins?

I don't like them on principle.

Inside the lodge, I spot the happy couple cuddling on the couch. Stanford's running his hands through January's hair—hair that's even closer to Campbell's shade of highlighted brown than before.

Why does January look like the queen of the rodeo ring with her studded blue jeans, pristine cowboy boots, and a plain tee tight enough to be a second skin? It's like the easy country style Campbell wore for the meeting last week—minus the easy. Stanford has black slacks and a light-pink dress shirt on. They look like a poster for opposites attract.

They don't deem me worth a glance as I stride past them toward the meeting room, and after the morning I've had, that's just fine.

I enter to find Campbell with her face buried in her hands. All this has got to be affecting her sleep. Clearing my throat, I take a seat.

She jerks back. "Oh. Sorry. I should've known you'd be early."

"If you're on time, you're late." It's a cliché, but one that Darin Bailey drilled into us during our time fostering with him.

"I never understood that." She sits back, her complexion wan, and picks at the sleeves of her loose blouse. "I mean, if I'm on time, I'm on time. Before that, it's my time, and I don't need to give that up for someone."

Good point. "So argues the youth."

She blinks at me. Blinks again. "How old and wizened are you?"

"Forty."

She licks her tongue across her bottom lip. "I'm twenty-eight."

"See? Youth."

She reclines in her seat and lets her gaze travel over me. If she keeps it up, she's going to find a very prominent bulge behind my fly. I'm not immune to a beautiful woman's attention, and Campbell is another level of sexy altogether. "Well, you look good for your age. I would've guessed thirty-nine and a half at the most."

The chuckle that leaves me is startling. "It's the complete lack of sunscreen use. Keeps a guy young."

Her laughter tinkles right over me. "It's the fresh mountain air that ages a guy."

We share a grin, and my heart does a hard clench, as if it's been orbiting in one direction and suddenly shifted. I rub my sternum and take a seat. Back to business. "Do you want to show me where you want everything? I'll need to access the location with a delivery truck."

She frowns, and I don't like that one bit. "Are they still making out on the couch out there?"

Seeing that must've been hard. She could be over him six ways to Sunday, but the sting would remain. "Couples that have to prove to the world they're solid are often the most fractured."

"Except you know how the youths are." She shoots me a knowing look. "Are you saying you wouldn't be out there sucking face with Natalie?"

Definitely not, and I should say so. I don't. "I'd take her aside in an empty room or a closet, and then I'd make damn sure she had time to gather herself after so people wouldn't look at her and know exactly what we'd done. Because that's for us. No one else."

The person I'm with in that dark closet has highlighted chestnut hair. My shower experiences aren't staying in the shower, dammit.

Her lips puff open, and there's yearning in her eyes. Stanford never made her feel that special? "Isn't spontaneity romantic?"

"I never said it wouldn't be spontaneous."

The apples of her cheeks flush pink, almost like they

were in my dream. "Maybe you should give Stanford some notes on romance."

I'm the last guy to talk to about romance. "He's not getting a damn thing from me other than an amazing drink, and only because my pride can't serve him a weak one. But once this event is done, the one we're doing as a favor for *you*, then he's not allowed to step foot on Hennessy property. I'm sure the rest of the guys will agree to ban him from Foster House too."

Her eyes glisten. "You'd do that for me?"

"It's the principle."

"And you're a man of principle."

I nod.

She looks at the door, then back at me. "Can I ask you something personal?"

"Shoot."

"The whole long-distance thing. You've never wanted to . . . You've been loyal?"

"Have I ever cheated?"

She nods.

"No." I bypass the explanation of how I'm a single man. My brothers already think my loyalty is misplaced.

"Hmph. Then you really do need to give him notes. I practically lived with the man, and he still found time to step out." She straightens her spine and pushes back. "We'd better get to work."

"You got any alarms set?"

"Just the one to meet with Chef tonight to go over the final menus, but that's not until after he's done with the evening meal."

The kitchen provides food for all the guests and the workers for both sides of the ranch. "Let's go then."

She marches out of the meeting room, and I follow

her. She doesn't glance at the couple on one of the plush couches. January's cupping Stanford's face in her hands, practically straddling him. Groans and whimpers can be heard, but Campbell doesn't react.

I hate both of them even more.

We go out the front door, and she takes the stone path that curves around the house and leads all the way to the pavilion in the back. She's not wearing a dress today, but the air has a spring chill to it that'll be gone by this afternoon. Instead, she's got on rust-colored leggings and a spring-green sweater that falls past her ass. Her cowboy boots are the same as the ones she wore at Bootleg Tavern.

The breeze ruffles her hair, and once again, the memory of the silky strands haunts my fingers. Noticing the way her hips sway doesn't help. I refrain from adjusting myself. I'm not going to get an erection just because I'm walking behind a woman.

Perhaps it makes a difference when the woman is Campbell Hawthorne.

The pavilion is safe to look at. Comprised mostly of beams, the long rectangular structure has the same rustic Western style of the guest lodge behind us. If the winter is mild, William has the staff set up firepits or domed tents with their own heaters so guests can relax and take meals in the great Montana outdoors. This whole idea is a new development since I left.

Campbell steps off the path before the pavilion and points down to the barn. "He wants to ride a horse into the sunset with his bride. After the, uh, vows." Tension lines her face. "He wants to swoop her up and ride away." She blinks and wipes at her eye. "Sorry. The wind must've blown dirt into my eye."

"You're kidding me, right?"

She sniffs. "About what?"

"If the extra work of readying horses and hoping like hell Stanford can keep his seat and not dump his bride doesn't give the couple pause, the pure corniness has to."

She scowls. "It's not corny."

"It's corny. Cheesy. Lame. Whatever the kids say these days. Moreover, it's a hazard. The horses the guests ride are used to people. They're used to the trails and cattle. They're not used to galloping away with two riders."

"I reiterated all that to the bride and groom, and it's not lame. It's romantic."

I scoff. "A groom riding in on horseback?"

"Maybe not that part, but riding off into the sunset. With the mountains in the background?"

"Superfluous at best."

She lets out a frustrated huff. "It is not. There's nothing more Hawthorne Ranch than a wedding with horses." She stomps toward the pavilion.

Why is she championing some over-the-top nonsense the bride and groom—

Shit. I charge after her. "It's what you wanted."

She stops, her body ramrod straight.

Aw hell. The birds around us chirp away, unaware that I just insulted Campbell's dream wedding that she has to plan for her cheating ex and her cousin. "You wanted to ride off into the sunset with the love of your life, and now you have to plan that for January."

She stuffs a boot into the grass. "Like you said, it's corny anyway."

"No." Yes. I shove a hand through my hair and grip the back of my neck. "It's over the top, yes, but if you can't be over the top on your wedding day, then when can you?"

"Good cover, but you think it's silly. You made it clear." She pins me with her sad gray eyes. "Just don't make your opinions known to them, please."

The *please* on the end cuts right through me and lets the guilt pour out. "I won't."

"The ceremony will take place on that end." She pretends like the moment never happened and points to the far side of the pavilion before swinging her arm to the middle. "The chairs will be moved and tables set up for the meal, and the wet bar will be in the back. Dance floor and band where the altar was. We can roll the partitions down for any sun, wind, or rain that interferes with the day, and we have the screens for when it's getting dark and the bugs are out. The family meal will be in the bar in the lodge, but the bridal luncheon and groom's dinner will be out here."

Her tight-lipped smile does nothing to make me feel better.

I meet her gaze with an assessing one of my own.

"Are you sure you don't want someone else to bartend?" she asks, catching me off guard.

"Why?"

"Can you serve drinks without looking at someone like they're the most inane person you've ever met?"

"I do it every week."

She cocks her head. "Do you though?"

I cross my arms. "Care to explain what that's supposed to mean?"

Waving her hand in front of her face, she gives me a *you know?* look. "You say a lot without saying a word."

I've never heard that before. "I do not."

"Do too."

I almost keep going with the childish argument. "No. I don't."

She cocks a hip and adopts an *I'm sick of your shit* expression, followed by a *You're a dumbass* flat look. Then she juts her other hip out and gives me an *I don't want to be here* eye roll that could also say *I don't want* you *to be here*. Finally, she does a long blink while staring right at me, her mouth in a neutral line, but her eyes say everything. *Do you have any idea what you're doing?*

Flummoxed, I prop my hands on my hips. "I don't look like that."

She plucks at invisible lint on her sleeve. "You look at me like that all the time."

"How do you know that's what I'm thinking?"

"Because you don't look at your brothers that way. You don't look at Jamison or Avery like that. Or my parents." She tips her head back and forth. "Mostly. You give Daddy this look."

Her face screams *I can't believe you.*

She's right. All of it. I can *feel* those expressions on myself, and yes, from when I've been around her. "You can think what you want. Doesn't mean you're right."

"People write me off as scatterbrained and clueless. Doesn't mean they're right." She pivots and takes off across the lawn. "That's all I need, other than to let Chef know you'll be giving him the list of supplies for each bar setup. Now, if you'll excuse me, I have to talk to Grady, the guest ranch manager, and verify which horses will work the best for the superfluous sunset ride. If anything comes up, you know how to reach me."

I was that guy who wrote her off. Despite what Natalie thinks, I'm a smart man. I won't make that mistake again.

CHAPTER SIX

Durban

I walk into the distillery. It's closed to the public on Mondays, but the guys and I still work. So do Clem and Edna. It's only been a couple of days since Campbell asked for a time to host a tasting for the bride and groom, but I'd rather get it over with.

Doing the tasting sooner also means that I'll see Campbell sooner.

Clem's at the front desk. Her lips are moving, but no sound is coming out. She must be practicing her tour speeches. The guys and I used to take turns with them, but Lane and Cruz are continuing to shuttle between here and the main site in Denver, Iverson has a growing family, and I'm not sure what Haven's issue is. My tour assignments must've been cut due to my not-so-resting dick face.

How did she read me that easily?

My morning jack-off sessions should've stopped while

working with Campbell. Instead, need rides me hard. My sessions have been lightning quick, and I quit fighting the images rising in my mind of gray eyes and full hips. Fantasies don't mean a thing, and they do the job. Smart women have always been a thing for me.

I need to get a hold of myself. I'm the logical one. Campbell and I have to work together for the next month, and I have to have some blood in my brain when I'm on duty.

Clem glances up as I pass. She has her dark hair in what Jamison calls space buns. "Hey, Durban. Iverson's looking for you."

"Did he say what he wants?"

She shrinks back. "No. Sorry?"

What the hell? I take out my phone and turn the camera on, flipping it around so I can see myself. My mustache makes my mouth look like it's a flat line, and my dark eyes glitter in the lights pouring through the windows over the entrance. I look pissed. "I'm not upset."

"Okay?"

Goddammit. "I've heard I can look . . . insulting."

She ticks a brow up, and for the first time, I get a glimpse of the real Clem, the one I see joking around with Edna, our bookkeeper. "Do you need a shirt that says, 'I'm sorry for what my expression says'?"

I bark out a laugh. Apparently, there's something to what Campbell said. I say a lot that I'm not aware of. "Get me one in a few different colors."

Her grin is the widest I've ever seen. "Will do, boss."

Shaking my head, I enter the distilling area. The smell of warm grains surrounds me. Open tanks of mash bubble away. Overall, it's smaller than the main headquarters outside of Denver, but we make smaller batches too, and multiple spirits. We don't have the distribution needs either, so fewer trucks have to navigate the winding highway here.

Iverson is at the tanks, Kasey sitting on a stool next to him, swinging her legs and holding a clipboard. She's scribbling on it like she's logging important data.

"Hiya, Uncle Durban."

I muss her hair. "Keeping him in line, little one?"

She nods. "I'm doing what Mama told me."

Iverson turns from where he's monitoring the water fill for a new mash. "Durban, I know you have the wedding bull—uh, business, but can you cover chores for me if Jamison delivers early? Haven said he can help too. We're trying to get everything figured out, since this wedding is going to take up any grandparent help we usually get."

"Of course. Everything okay?"

He brushes a hand across the back of his forehead. His scruff is shaggier than usual, like he's rushed out of the house after getting Kacey ready, but not himself. "It's fine as long as her blood pressure is. She's working from home a lot so she can have her legs up."

I can see the circles under his eyes. Excitement simmers in his dark irises, but he's also worried. And stressed. "Christine doesn't care if she'll miss the wedding," he continues. "She wants to support Campbell, but you know how it is. Campbell might get blamed if her parents aren't at the wedding party's beck and call."

"Auntie Campbell's fun." Kasey kicks her feet against the stool.

Auntie Campbell won't be having a lot of fun these

next four weeks. "I have the tasting in an hour, then I can do whatever needs to be done here so you can cut out early."

Iverson scratches the side of his cheek and looks around. "Do you mind getting Kacey a snack?"

"Sure. Oh—I have a couple mash bills I can send you too." Formulas for new recipes we can try. "And I found some other companies that do small-barrel aging successfully."

"Yeah, sure. We're planned out for the year, but go ahead. Send me what you've got."

I clamp down on my tongue. This place has a lot of cooks in the kitchen. Lane and Cruz could each run the distilling side, not just the business end, but Iverson has taken to distilling like it'd been his calling his entire life and not wrangling cattle. I don't want to ruin that for him, and I definitely don't want him to feel like his role at Foster House is slipping because he's growing a family. Iverson and Lane function more like supervisors—Lane on the company end, and Iverson on the distilling side. But that all leaves me feeling like I'm asking for permission, not collaborating.

"Come on, kiddo." I hold out my hand to Kacey. I'm not putting pressure on Iverson when he's already under stress. "I'll make you a Shirley Temple while I'm getting the tasting room ready."

She climbs down from the stool, and I bring that with me too, setting it by the standing desk and computers we use to log our times and temperatures.

I unlock the tasting room and usher her inside. We're greeted by clean finishes that match the timber-and-steel look on the outside. Large windows face the parking lot and the rickhouse adjacent to the main building.

She scurries toward the bar and yanks a barstool out. Clambering onto it, she slaps her clipboard onto the top of the counter. There are drawings of . . . cats? A dog? A tick? It's round and has four legs sticking out from various points around its body.

"Want a cherry?" I ask, getting a special plastic cup we store for her.

"Three," she says with a toothy smile.

I fill her cup with Sprite and grenadine and plop in five cherries. She giggles.

"That's why I'm your favorite uncle," I tease. It's not true. Haven's the fun uncle. He swings her around while I avoid nursemaid elbow. He gives her endless refills of Shirley Temples while I cut her off at two. She could murder someone, and he'd make it a game to hide the body. I'm more likely to teach her about different soil types and how long body decomposition takes.

She draws more . . . creatures . . . while I dig out bottles of our gin, vodka, and whiskey. While she's occupied, I'll work on the menu for each bar we're providing at the wedding.

I take out the notepad where I like to scribble mixology notes. So far, I've stuck to common cocktails for each spirit. For whiskey, we'll offer a Manhattan and an old-fashioned, then our spin on some classics, like a mint julep with cherry liqueur and our own whiskey-infused cherries. Definitely not the ones I gave Kacey.

I drop three more regular maraschino cherries into her glass.

She digs them out. "Can I have more?" she asks around a mouthful.

"Let me get you some crackers instead." I dig into the cupboard where we keep a stash for her. "Want a beef stick with cheese?"

She nods, and I prepare a preschooler charcuterie board for her, complete with two more cherries.

The door opens, and Campbell breezes in on a gust of huckleberry and sunshine air. Her hair is pulled off her face in a loose braid, and when she grins at Kacey, my heart rams into my ribs.

"Kacey!" Campbell barks out like she's at a football game.

Kacey launches herself off the stool and sprints for her aunt. "Auntie Campbell!"

Campbell swings her around.

"Careful, or you'll be wearing her Shirley Temple," I caution.

Campbell's smile dips. "I'm not going to get her dizzy."

She thinks I'm chastising her again. "I've been doling out cherries like parade candy. Just giving you a warning."

"Lots," Kacey happily replies.

"Just know how you don't like vomit on your clothing and hair." I can't help myself.

Campbell's sharp inhale resonates between us. Her eyes flash daggers, and I don't bother to hold back my grin. She narrows her gaze. "I'm going to swing her around a few times and hand her off to her uncle."

"Haven's not here yet."

Finally, she cracks a smile. "He'd probably finish off the jar with her."

"Can we?" Kacey asks.

"Definitely not," I say. "Want a Shirley Temple, Campbell? Or the real thing?"

"Just what would that be?" She's led to the bar by Kacey.

"Dirty Shirley." I grab another glass. She won't go for any alcohol. I might've assumed that before, but I'm getting to know her better. I want to know more.

"A regular Shirley is fine." She slides onto a stool and helps Kacey onto hers.

"Can I have a Dirty Shirley?" Kacey asks.

"Not for many more years." I add a splash of Sprite to her cup and fill up Campbell's.

"I'll have what she's having." Campbell inspects her niece's little plate of cut-up beef and cheese sticks. "Is that Hennessy beef? Or Foster? Do you all ranch together too?"

"My brothers and I are separate from the Fosters." I slide her drink in front of her. She got three cherries too. "The three of us built on Hennessy land, so we just fenced it off and split the duties between the three of us." We surround the mine on three sides. Lane and Cruz bought land on the other side of the highway that passes our land.

"I bet that helps at times like this when babies are due." She plucks a cherry and puts the whole thing in her mouth, stem and all. Is she going to eat it?

"Yep." I continue collecting bottles from the shelves behind the bar for the cocktail sampling.

I squat to grab the cranberry juice out of the fridge. When I rise, Campbell's setting a perfectly tied cherry stem on the napkin by her glass.

Lust steals all the air from my lungs. I'm supposed to be above base sexual gimmicks, but the dream's flashing through my head like a strobe light. Campbell bent over me, her hair brushing along my abdomen. Her full lips hovering over my aching erection. Arousal pumps hard through my veins, because I am certain that she can tie my dick up just like that stem.

I clear my throat. The shower is one thing. Having those images in my head when I'm at work and she's right in front of me is not allowed.

"You know what name I want?" Kacey asks me.

My niece spins my mind around the way she changes subjects. Today, I welcome it. "Name for what?"

She looks at me like I have two heads. "My new brother or sister."

"Try to keep up, Uncle Durban," Campbell says sweetly.

She's teasing, and it goes straight to my dick. Everything she says does. "Cole if it's a boy?"

Campbell's laugh rings out. "Like their dog?"

"Spelled different, obviously," I say.

"Obvs." She continues to snicker, but Kacey seems to be mulling it over.

"Rachel." Kacey ticks one finger up, then she does the same with her pointer finger on her other hand. "Or . . . Blue."

"Blue or Rachel." No doubt from some shows she watches. "Have you told your parents your suggestions?"

She nods, pride ringing across her face.

Movement outside catches my attention, and my good mood falters. "They're here."

A car's pulling away. Stanford's sauntering toward the door and January's tucked under his arm. He looks like he's scowling, but January's giving him doe eyes. They got a ride from someone at the ranch, and the driver parks at the far end of the lot to sit and wait.

Stanford's brows draw closer when he enters and sees Campbell at the bar with Kacey.

"Oh," Kacey says in a flat tone. "It's him."

Campbell coughs, and it sounds suspiciously like she's covering a laugh. She slides off her stool.

"Isn't she a little young to be taste-testing cocktails?" Stanford's trying for casual, but there's a censuring edge to his tone.

"Hey, Kacey." January's purr doesn't seem fake. She might genuinely like her cousin's kid.

Kacey ignores her and leans over to Campbell. "Mommy said she hurt your feelings, and I don't like people who hurt your feelings." Her whisper's as loud as a church bell. "And I'm not invited to the wedding."

January's eyes mist over, and she glances away.

"And that's why we're having a kid-free wedding," Stanford says. "I thought I wouldn't have to specify that all the events are child-free too."

Anger thumps a beat at my temples. "The tasting is a courtesy set up by your wedding planner. If the circum-stances don't appeal to you, we can go ahead and cancel. We're normally closed Mondays anyway."

He holds my gaze like I'm bluffing. I don't fucking care. I'm not the one in the wrong, and Foster House doesn't need this cocksucker's business.

Campbell stares at me, and I'm hit with that damn guilt. I don't want to make her life harder, and having to find another vendor will do that. It wouldn't be her fault, but she'd take the heat.

"Oh no, it's fine." A tremor runs through January's

voice. "Kacey's family, and I would like to see as many as I can while I'm in town."

Stanford stiffens and nearly shoots her a glare before catching himself. This guy is a piece of work. "Of course, baby. I just want this wedding to be perfect for you. I know it's your dream, and I'm going to make your dreams happen."

Campbell's knuckles are white on the purse strap across her body. She's paler than usual, and I miss her natural blush.

Iverson enters, and his features harden when he sees the couple at the counter. "I'm all done, Kacey. Time to go."

"I want to stay with Auntie Campbell."

Campbell rubs Kacey's back and swoops her up. "I know you do. We'll have to make a girls' date in a few weeks."

Kacey wraps her arms around her aunt's neck. "Can we paint our nails?"

"Nails, hair, it's all getting done. How 'bout I walk you out?"

"Ooh, I love cherries." January sits primly on a stool. "Can you add extra to mine?"

Stanford's gaze drops to the neatly tied stem on the napkin in front of where Campbell was sitting. His shoulders sag just a little, but he catches me watching him. I snag the napkin and toss it, but I keep the stem and tuck it into my shirt pocket. Envy glints in Stanford's eyes.

That's right, asshole. Campbell's too good for even his dreams.

Campbell

My throat's thick as I polish off my Shirley Temple. Stanford and January have amped up how much they hang all over each other. Her hand is either on his back or his thigh. Twice, she's brushed it higher to stroke over his groin. Their loud kisses turn my stomach. It's not the first time I wish I had the filthiest of Dirty Shirleys in front of me.

I don't want Stanford back. I want the self-respect he robbed me of over the years, but that's not happening until the wedding's over.

"So what's this again?" January's smashed into Stanford's side. "Strawberry?"

"Raspberry," Durban says for the second time. "Vodka raspberry lemonade. We'll have raspberries the day of to use for decoration."

I got a mocktail version without the vodka. Bits of bright raspberry swirl inside, and a vibrant red tints the glass. "I've seen a recipe that uses raspberry vodka instead of muddled berries with simple syrup."

January frowns at me like I shouldn't be talking.

"We're going to start infusions later this year," Durban answers, moving over to stand in front of me. "Using fresh berries and syrup does double duty, so we can make a nonalcoholic version for guests."

"It'll change the flavor." I hold the glass up to the light, admiring summertime in a drink. "And the look of it." Infused vodka might have the color, but it won't have the rustic invitations of the crushed berries.

Interest lightens his eyes. "It won't be as sweet, but that's not what people come to the distillery for."

Stanford tosses a smirk at me. "It's not always about how pretty something looks."

The old urge to shrink in on myself and think about how right he is because he's the one who has his shit together hits me. I inhale, fighting off that inferior feeling. Stanford's still the successful insurance broker with his own corner office, but I'm not that struggling event planner who barely got through college anymore. Yet I *am* the girl whose daddy had to create a job for her.

A muscle jumps in Durban's jaw. "The cocktails have to look good no matter what's inside."

Durban and Stanford are going to get into a fistfight if they glare at each other any more. This whole event could slip through my fingers, and it would be even more humiliating than my last foray in the professional event planning world. Then there's the way Durban seems to be defending me and the funny things it's doing to my insides.

My heart rate climbs, and my lungs are tight. I need some space. "I have to take this." I wave my silent phone. No one's calling me. No one's texting. "Excuse me."

I put distance between me and my insufferable ex and his future bride, and the man who's tying up my emotions. I can't leave behind how it should be me sitting on that stool—albeit with a different groom— tasting cocktails, laughing and giggling, while I bury myself in the love of my life.

I duck into the storeroom across from the bathrooms beside the bar counter. I've been in the bathroom before, and there are two stalls. I don't need January popping in, but she won't snoop in the storeroom.

I flip on the light, fold my arms, and lean my back against the wall. This is supposed to be my wedding. I'm supposed to say "I do" on my family's land, with the mountains as my witness. I should be the one telling my planner all the things I've ever dreamed of.

I've dreamed of my wedding my whole life. I'm that girl. The one who knew before she was in high school what dress she wanted, who'd stand up there with her, and exactly how it'd look. It was like I manifested Daddy building that pavilion.

Now, if I do ever get the wedding of my fantasies, it'll be a recycled version of Stanford and January's. I'll stand in the pavilion, gaze at my groom, and remember what it was like when two people betrayed me in that very spot.

I push off the wall. Fuck the mocktails. There's gotta be something in here I can drink. The whole room is full of bottles of whiskey, vodka, and gin, all from Foster House. A wall is dedicated to different glasses, but they're all in boxes. Only a row of curved glasses that remind me of tulips isn't contained. Next to them are a few open bottles. Perhaps just a sip.

"Whiskey," I mutter. "Figures."

"What do you have against whiskey?" Durban asks from behind me.

I bite back a yelp and spin around. He's in the doorway, leaning against it. "What are you doing here?"

"Checking on you."

I scowl at him. "You can quit doing that." I wave

toward where the bar would be. "Don't the happy couple need you to walk them through the tasting?"

"I served them a Tom Collins. We got a few minutes."

"A Tom Collins?"

"Gin, maple syrup, lemon juice, and club soda. I made his extra tart, and he's pretending not to notice." He prowls across the room and upends a curved glass. "What's your thing against whiskey?"

"It overpowers whatever it's in."

A disappointed rumble leaves his chest, and he rifles through the already opened bottles of whiskey. "You haven't been having the right cocktails."

"I've had plenty."

"Have you had Foster House?" He selects a bottle with *barrel proof* written on the label and pours a splash into one glass. The other gets a pour that just reads *single barrel* on the label.

"Yes, of course. It tastes like any other whiskey. Did you like the stuff before you started making it?"

"I liked it just fine, but now I know the art and the science of it. Not just the entertainment." He hands me a glass of the single barrel. "This isn't barrel strength, so we'll start with that."

"What does that mean?" I accept the glass. I should be worried about looking stupid in front of Durban, but something about him makes me unashamed of being curious. Perhaps because he admitted to having had to learn it all too.

"It's not watered down. The bottling proof isn't more than two degrees lower than when we dump the barrel."

"Why do you dump it?" When did we get only a couple of feet apart?

The corner of his mouth ticks up. "That's what we say when we empty a barrel for bottling. It has to get strained first." He tips his head toward the glass in my hand. "Swirl it, smell it, sip it."

"Only if you tell me why."

"Swirling releases the aromas. The tapered neck of the glass captures them while the flared opening lets the alcohol dissipate so you don't suck it in."

I gently swirl, then lift it to my nose.

"Open your mouth," he says in a quiet growl that sends shivers coursing over my skin. "And inhale."

Flutters erupt in my stomach as I smell, taking in pleasing notes of vanilla, caramel, and spice. I blink and smell again, concentrating. He's giving me a tasting, not coming on to me. "Cherries?"

"Yes. Now sip and let it coat your palate. This is an eight-year-old ninety-two proof."

"The distillery isn't that old."

"Lane and Cruz made some single barrels in Denver to get us going while our product ages."

"So none of this stuff is from Huckleberry Springs?"

"Some of it. We can use it for tasting, but we can't sell bottles in-house if it's not all made in-house. Drink, Campbell."

I would guzzle it if he spoke to me like that again.

Ugh. This is *Durban*. I'm not supposed to find it so appealing. I can appreciate his mountain-man good looks, but finding his judgmental ass irresistibly sexy? No. I'm not the lonely girl looking to poach someone's man—and if he can be seduced away, I don't want him.

I take a sip.

"The flared base—"

I cough and sputter.

Laughter dances in his eyes. "—of the *glass* allows the liquid to coat more of your tongue. So let it coat your palate."

Do regular tastings here always sound so sexy? I keep my breathing calm. Every time he talks in that deep voice of his, my chest constricts. I take another sip, and spice fills my tongue. Vanilla, oak, and caramel. Those cherries I smelled. "Mm."

Satisfaction etches his features. "If we were doing this for real, I'd add a couple of drops of water."

"What does that do?"

"Opens up the flavors. Softens some. That's part of the fun. Finding out."

"Durban Hennessy, I didn't know you were a wild man."

He smiles at my gentle teasing and switches glasses. My fingers brush against his warm skin. More butterflies careen through my stomach. I rein them in. This man is not mine, and I won't accept attention from any guy just to stave off the loneliness.

"Your girlfriend probably appreciates it." There. I put it out there. A reminder for me—and for him.

His brow furrows, and a shadow passes over his face. "I think she's enjoying someone else's wild side."

My fingers tighten around my glass. "What?" Who would do that to Durban? I have a special hate for cheaters.

"At least it's probably not with my cousin, so there's that." His smile is tight. "She broke up with me."

"Oh." He's single? Those butterflies aren't forbidden? This moment between us doesn't make me on par with Stanford? More importantly, it doesn't make Durban similar to my ex. "Were the jokes that bad?"

His chuckle is soft. "I don't think they helped." He tips his head toward the whiskey in my hand. "Go through the process again. This is stronger and older. More hints of oak will come through."

Message received. He's done talking about Natalie. Even if he's telling the truth, I'm not on the dating market. I have a job to do, a career to reignite, and family land to get back.

I swirl, gently inhale with my mouth open, and sip. The liquid tingles along my tongue, and I roll it around. I look into his deep-brown eyes, losing myself in their fathomless depths. "I taste cinnamon."

"Good girl. That's the American oak."

Praise from him should put me on the defensive, not make me want to strip down, but knowing he's single only makes it worse. Laughter from the tasting room reaches us, and I shoot the drink back before I can think twice. I'm also single, and it's for a damn good reason.

"They're getting to you." It's not a question.

"Yes," I hiss. "It's going to be a long four weeks."

"All this to look like the bigger person?" His gaze strokes over my face. I'm open and raw, but his proximity is soothing.

"They'd do it anyway. In the end, my only revenge is to look unbothered, and that's hard to do on the sidelines." I set the empty glass down and shoot the other one. Warm whiskey coats my insides, and I close my eyes. "Besides, each time I'm in the same room as them, January has to be wondering if he still loves me. She has to wonder if he's checking me out when she's not looking. When I walk by, she has to question how well he remembers me naked and sucking his dick."

I open my eyes. Tension is scribbled across his face, and his pupils are wide. He's focused on my lips.

"That's gotta be a mindfuck," I say, my voice husky. The stiffness in my limbs is melting away as the small amount of alcohol I drank soaks into my veins. "And I hope it's a special hell for her. I hope that no matter how much she tells herself that he chose her, the thought of me still taints her wedding."

Several moments tick by. Did I go too far? Does he think I'm demented and that I'm not at all the bigger person? I'm a childish, selfish girl when it comes down to it. I'm scorned, and I want some retribution.

"Good girl," he says again and drags his gaze up my face to meet my eyes. "And I can assure you, Campbell, that he very much remembers you sucking his dick."

CHAPTER SEVEN

Durban

I drive down the road to the lodge. The tasting with Stanford and January was only a few days ago, and instead of dreading the family dinner, I'm struggling to stay under the speed limit.

Images flash through my head as quickly as the countryside. Her pink lips on the glass. The sounds she made when she tasted the whiskey. Her questions. She was curious, and fuck. I liked sharing my knowledge, and when the attractive recipient is equally interested, well . . . it's hot.

I just got out of a relationship. It can't be a coincidence that now I'm undeniably single, my lust has attached to Campbell like the most powerful Velcro in the world. I'm not ready to dive into something with anyone, and I might be learning more about Campbell, but she's not my type.

I'm not hers. If she goes for the Stanfords of the

world, then I'm not the guy she's looking for, and she's likely not looking for anyone at all right now. The upcoming weeks will be her reason to stay single, and after that, she's still got a career to build.

We don't belong together. Knowing that, I can control myself.

I'm coasting down the long drive to the guest lodge. A woman is swaying on a black Morgan, Hailstorm. He's one of the most requested horses the guests use. Impressive looking when he's freshly brushed, and a giant teddy bear with a penchant for treats, he's a perfect guest horse.

The woman's hair is tucked under her cowboy hat, but I recognize the flare of her hips. Campbell's in jeans, and the strong muscles of her legs are evident, gripping the sides of Hailstorm. I've never been envious of a horse before.

Time to flex that control. No ogling Campbell. But I can wonder what the hell she's doing. Tonight, we're deep in the wedding bullshit. What's she doing out for a pleasure ride?

I slow even more and roll my window down. Hailstorm's tail swishes.

"Enjoying yourself?" I ask.

"As much as I can." She cocks her head so she can see me from under her Stetson. Her hips roll with each step, and her back is straight, making her breasts jut out. Fuck, she looks good on a horse.

"Cutting it close, aren't you?" The dinner is supposed to start in an hour and a half.

She purses her lips. "Stanford wants to use Hailstorm to ride away with the bride, and I have to start working with him and January. Stanford needs lessons, and he has to learn how to lift January into the saddle." She rolls her eyes toward me. "It has to be photogenic, you know."

"Hailstorm will be. Not sure about them."

"It's my job to make sure they all are," she says woodenly. She continues riding, and I keep my speed even with her.

Her job is planning. She can't possibly mean she's doing the rest. "You aren't training them, are you?" William has staff who can do it.

She smacks her lips. "Personally requested."

"You're fucking kidding me."

"You're not the joking type." She smiles when she says it, and fiddles with a silver chain around her neck.

"I repel girlfriends when I tell jokes, remember? It's like oil and water."

"Is that a science joke?"

"Seems I *am* the joking type."

Laughing, she reaches over the saddle and rubs a hand over Hailstorm's gleaming withers. "It's a bad one, but I almost pulled a muscle laughing so hard, so it wasn't the jokes. Had to be her."

I was only kidding, but she's sticking up for me. My appreciation for her grows, and it has nothing to do with the flare of her hips from the way she's astride Hailstorm, or how the sun makes her eyes dance.

She juts her chin toward the other side of the pickup. "I'm cutting in front of you so I can get to the barn. Stanford and January want to meet Hailstorm. Then I have to run home and get cleaned up. Then I'll meet everyone in the bar."

I brake so she can pass in front of me. "See you in a few."

"I'm gonna need more than a few," she grumbles as she rides past.

I watch her retreat, looking like a natural. I never paid attention to talk about the Hawthorne girls when I was an employee of the ranch, but didn't she use to do rodeo? Barrel racing? Or was that Jamison? Maybe it was roping? I could see her doing breakaway with that lithe, powerful body.

She's going to look back and find me staring. I hit the gas harder than intended and spin out some gravel. Hailstorm doesn't break his stride. He's chill as can be, his tail swishing. He's a good choice to ride into the sunset with, but Stanford shouldn't be making Campbell train him.

I park and make sure my mind's in the right place. Admiring Campbell's thighs isn't making me presentable in the groin department. Neither is the memory of her laughing at my joke. I can't believe she remembered to ask in the first place.

If I sit here any longer, I'm going to keep thinking about Campbell. She's already consuming an inappropriate amount of my thoughts.

I walk into the back entrance of the guest lodge to avoid the guests roaming in the front and sitting on the porch. I'll be seeing them soon enough. This whole situation is unbelievable. At least it was until Campbell told me why she's really doing it. She might be wanting to strike back at her cousin because of the hurt, but she probably doesn't realize how much she's tormenting Stanford.

I have a hard enough time fighting off wet dreams about blow jobs and wide-eyed questions about whiskey.

Then somehow whiskey became part of the blow job, and I've been awake since three in the morning.

Stopping in the kitchen before turning into the bar, I marvel over my change in circumstance. Five years ago, I would've had to justify my presence in the guest lodge. Now, I gave Campbell a list of what I need for tonight, and she took care of it with Chef.

Chef Cecil has worked at Hawthorne since before I did, and his meals are next level. They're one of the things I've missed since living on my own. He glances up from the beef Wellington he's preparing for tonight. His usual jovial expression is replaced with grim determination. "Durban. What can I do for you?"

"Other than cancel this wedding?"

He barks out a laugh. "I would if I could. That poor girl should not be enduring this. Have you heard the latest?"

"About the horse training, or is there more?" I hover by the entry. Anyone who's been in Chef's kitchen knows we can only go so far. Two more steps and I'd have a hair net slapped over my head, a beard net clamped across my ears for my mustache, and an apron tied around my neck. And then Chef would scowl at my cowboy boots, as if I'd walked through a cured manure pile right before I entered.

Chef sucks his lips against his teeth. "That's it, but there'll be more." He shoots me a knowing look. "That boy's just getting started."

A rolling cart full of lemon and lime wedges, maraschino cherries, fresh simple syrup, and other cocktail supplies is waiting for me. "Thanks for this."

"Anything to make this easier for one of my girls."

I appreciate that everyone around here is rallying around Campbell. It says a lot about her.

I push my goods to the bar. Tables are butted together and surrounded by chairs. Campbell talked them into serving the family meal in the bar so the drinks can flow. The bar's ambiance has a more classic Western vibe than the dining room, and I'd rather work behind a counter than a little cart.

I spend the time putting my supplies away and lining up the bottles I'm going to use, making sure the labels are visible. Eventually, people start filtering in.

A young woman flops onto a stool. Her shoulder-length blond hair flares out at the ends. "Is it too early to order?"

"Sydney." An older woman with a severe bob, wearing black slacks and a loose cardigan, glares at her. "We are sitting at the table, not the *bar*. There's no need to be drinking yet."

Sydney's shoulders go rigid. "There isn't going to be enough liquor for tonight." She pushes away from the counter and drags her feet to the table.

"Is there a seating arrangement?" another woman asks, smoothing her hands over her black cocktail dress. The pearls at her neck catch the light.

Mother of the groom? She has the same pointy chin, and the hair in her chignon is only two shades lighter than his. A man strides in, a hand in his slacks pocket and his charcoal sport coat hanging open. He stops beside the elegant woman and scowls at the setup.

Stanford sweeps in, January hot on his loafers. The back of her hair is mussed, and her face is red. Stanford's fly is half open.

He stops, frowning. "Where's the planner?"

"You mean your ex?" Sydney mutters.

I almost fail at holding back my smile.

"Late like always." Stanford stomps to the bar. "Vodka raspberry lemonade."

January stands on the same side of Stanford that Sydney's on. "I'll have one too."

Sydney leans over. "Wanna tell your beau that the barn door's open?"

"Jesus, Syd," January snaps. "What?"

Sydney recoils and looks around. Everyone's attention is on them, their disapproving stares on Sydney. "His fly's open." She says it loudly and wiggles her index finger by her head. "And you might wanna fix your hair. What were you both doing out in that barn anyway?"

My stomach sinks. The barn. Did Campbell have to witness what they were doing, or had she finished with Hailstorm by then?

I crush the raspberries, grateful that she isn't here to witness the casual bickering. She'd probably get blamed for it.

"Where do I sit?" January's mom says louder than before.

When the attention switches to her, Stanford jerks his zipper up. I finish making his drink.

"She's late again." Stanford rubbernecks toward the door.

"As always," January says in a snide tone.

I slide the bride's cocktail over and toss two raspberries in. They plop, creating a tiny splash. Her dainty frown is no match for the lack of shits I have to give.

Stanford gulps half of his, but his gaze is plastered on the doorway.

Finally, Campbell arrives. Her hair is pulled back in a

high ponytail, and she paired her lilac summer dress with a loose-knit cream sweater. Instead of cowboy boots, she has on suede ankle boots. A long necklace makes her ensemble fit the classy Western vibe of the bar. No one would know she was dusty and smelling like horse sweat a little over an hour ago.

Her cheeks are still flushed, like she ran here from her parents' house, but with the tension around her eyes and the tautness of her movements, it's not from her afternoon ride.

"Campbell," Stanford says smoothly. "Nice of you to join us." Her cheeks pinken even more, but she doesn't respond. Stanford lifts his cocktail. "Help yourself to drinks, everyone, while we get this seating arrangement figured out."

Campbell's forced smile falters. "It's a family dinner. There are no seating assignments."

"It's a formal dinner," Stanford's mom complains. "There are always seating assignments at formal dinners."

Campbell barely misses a beat. "Of course. The couple will sit at the head of the table, naturally."

I really need Campbell to be able to tell them off.

Stanford's dad ignores the seating assignments and bellies up to the bar. "Macallan. Neat."

"We only serve Foster House," I say in a bored tone. I'm not kissing this guy's ass.

"Why would I want Foster House?"

His snide tone roughs up my eardrums and my pride. I hold his gaze. I'm not playing games either.

Our face-off is interrupted by a cloud of huckleberries. "Is there something I can get you, Mr. Baldwin?"

"Damn good whiskey," he replies.

"You are invited to sample what Foster House offers. Your son and future daughter-in-law's wishes are to feature local spirits, and Foster House is the pride of Huckleberry Springs." She aims that fake-as-astroturf smile at me. "Durban, do you have that barrel proof available, or one like it? I believe that's right up a whiskey connoisseur's alley."

The man's frown deepens like he can't tell if he should keep complaining or take the flattery. "Fine. I'll take the best you've got."

Admiration sneaks in as I pour the drink, but so does worry. Campbell appears to effortlessly defuse the situation, but it's costing her. She has a little over three weeks of festivities. I'm not involved again until the bride's lunch, but she's got to entertain the douche crew for weeks.

While everyone's either taking their seats or giving me their order, I catch Sydney giving Campbell's hand a squeeze. They exchange tight smiles. At least she's got an ally in the group, but Sydney seems like she's in the same rickety boat as Campbell.

I serve drinks until only one more person stands in front of me. Stanford's mother. She huffs. "I can't believe we have to go *to* the bar to get our refreshments. That's not how dinners work."

"What can I get you?" I ask mildly.

"Decent service, but I can't imagine you know what I'm talking about."

Does my expression say that I'm sick of people's shit? "What can I get you?"

She rolls her eyes like my lack of engagement spoils the fun. "Gin and tonic."

I make it quick and slide it in front of her. Sooner she's gone, the better.

"Campbell, dear." This comes from the woman with the bob. She must be January's mom. "We're missing a seat. Aren't you joining us?"

January puts her hand on Stanford's chest, her gaze distraught. He shakes his head.

"I'm on the clock," Campbell says smoothly. "I want to make sure this night is perfect for all of you."

Fuck, I could choke on all this pretend kindness. Since everyone's seated and they all have a cocktail or a drink, I duck into the long storeroom-slash-break room behind the bar the staff uses.

Is Natalie like Stanford's mom? Was I that wrong about her? About us? Shame leaves a bad taste in my mouth.

I'm surrounded by the inventory of the Hawthorne bar. All I need is a swig to take the edge off my irritation. I open a new bottle of Foster House whiskey and take a long pull from it. I'll buy it later.

Spice and heat fill my mouth. I swallow and it spreads down my chest, warming my gut.

"Fuck me sideways until Sunday," Campbell says from behind me.

I turn to find Campbell slumped against the wall by the light switch. "They're that bad."

She jumps and slaps a hand over her mouth. She drops it. "You can't keep scaring me like that," she whispers loudly. "What are you doing in here with the lights off?"

"Taking a breather." Letting my pride pick apart scabs. But it's not Natalie I hear in my memories. It's Mom's rough voice.

I have more important things to do.

You couldn't possibly understand.

Why do you suck the fun out of everything?

Campbell prods her forehead. A small shudder racks her body.

I move closer, setting the bottle on a shelf next to her. "Is it that bad already?"

"They were in the barn. Stanford and January." She lets out a quiet but scornful laugh. "Caught them with their pants down in the tack room after they petted Hailstorm a few times. I turned him out and was going to put the halter and lead rope away."

"Aw, hell, Campbell. I'm sorry."

Her eyes shine in the weak light. "They were so loud." Her lower lip trembles. "I don't even want him, but it's not fair, you know. He wasted years of my life. She's stealing the wedding plans I told her about when we were kids. It's not fair that she gets to swan around out there in her post-orgasmic glow and be the center of attention. It's not fair that he gets to be satisfied right before he's allowed to be a controlling bastard to me—again. It's not fair. None of it. And I was late again because I have to face them and be polite and professional when I'm so damn angry. They should be wound up as tight as me for having to suffer through them."

Her chest is rising and falling. She's hurting, and what I felt minutes ago pales against what she's going through. The disrespect continues. Stanford and January probably intended to be heard and possibly seen.

Those assholes. Something should be done. At the very least, there should be a way to relax her. A way to get the couple back without anyone knowing.

When I walk by, she has to question how well he remembers me naked and sucking his dick.

I told Campbell that Stanford absolutely does remember. He probably obsesses, and that's why he's so hard on her. He detests the hold she has on him, and that's why he plays her.

So what if he suspects she is also getting satisfied? What if he goes out of his mind, wondering if the pretty blush staining her cheeks is from an orgasm? At the very least, a climax will decrease some of her tension.

"Then make it fair," I say, my voice gruff. Am I actually going to suggest this?

"How? I'm not interested in stealing him back."

I should shut my damn mouth, but my logic got scrambled as soon as she entered this room. I've been burned by these people, but she's been scorched. "Be satisfied. Just like them."

She laughs, and her minty breath wafts across my chin. "You're kid—" Her breath hitches. "You're not serious?" she whispers.

More serious than those fucking science jokes. "Why not? A little—or big—*O* before you have to deal with them? Takes the pressure off. Makes tonight a fuckton better."

Only her breaths are audible in the room. "Now?"

"Would you rather go out there and face that crowd like this?"

Her gaze strays to the door. I wish the light was on only so I could watch the sexy flush creep up her neck. "How? It's not like I can just grab the nearest guy."

The nearest guy to her very much wants to be grabbed, but I can't comprehend those complications. "You're an independent woman. Do it yourself."

She doesn't laugh off my suggestion. Instead, she worries her lower lip between her teeth. "I could use a drink."

I stifle a groan. If she's going to do it, I could use a big fucking drink too. I'm already strung tighter than a newly repaired fence, my erection ready to form when I even think of her.

But I need to have a clear head if we're going to get away with this.

I grab the bottle I drank from earlier and lift it to her lips.

"Swirl, sniff, and sip?" she asks, her voice huskier than normal.

"Just drink." I tip the bottle, and she sucks some liquid into her mouth.

I shouldn't touch her. I shouldn't be doing any of this, but I grasp her wrist. My fingertips on her warm skin scatters any remaining logic. I bring her hand to her mouth.

"Wet your fingertips," I order.

Her lips part, and it's all I can do to keep from tracing them—with my finger or tongue.

Her eyes glitter from the ambient light, but she opens her mouth and sucks her index and middle fingers inside. My groan echoes loud between us. I give her another drink. She swallows and licks her fingertips.

I release her arm, set the bottle down, and crowd closer. "Now lift your skirt and touch yourself."

A moment passes, and I think she's going to refuse. Maybe she'll shove me away and face the Baldwins with her chin held high. A small part of me will die inside. She's been starring in too many of my fantasies for me to be deprived of a very real experience and not end up a changed man.

Instead of pushing me away, she gathers the fabric of her dress up. My erection roars to life, growing so hard I'm damn near lightheaded. Her breaths grow shaky. She moves, and in the dark, I can only picture her slim fingers burrowing under the hem of her underwear.

A small gasp leaves her, and fuuuck.

"Are your fingers on your clit, Belle?" The nickname slips out, but I don't take it back. My pulse hammers a beat behind my zipper. I'm hard to the point of pain, and no shower jack-off session is going to help. Only hearing her sweet release.

"Yes." Her whisper is faint.

"Are you wet?"

"Y-yes."

A moan rumbles in my chest, but I keep it quiet. "Is your pussy throbbing? Is it pulsing, waiting for that sweet release?"

"*Yes.*"

I place my hands on either side of her head. Looking down, I can only see where her hand disappears under the fabric of her skirt. She lets out the faintest of whimpers.

"Keep going," I coax, my voice gruff. If she stops, I'll shrivel up and die. This moment is all I'm living for.

"Durban." Her eyelids are hooded, and she's resting her head against the wall.

"You're getting wetter. Fuck, I bet you're tight too. Dip those long fingers inside of yourself." My forehead is tipped toward hers, but we're not touching. I cage her against the wall.

Her shadowed eyes fly up to mine, but she does it.

"Christ, Belle. How fucking wet are you?"

"So wet." One of her legs lolls to the side, and she's rocking her hips against herself.

"Rub that clit again. Tight little circles."

"Durban," she whispers. "I'm going—"

"Do it. Come as hard and as long as you need."

I'm millimeters away from her, my attention and focus on her. She arches her back, and her tits brush against me. The hard little points of her nipples graze my chest, and I have to clamp down on my control before I come in my pants. I can't tend bar with a wet spot.

Her mouth gapes open, and I hover, ready to catch any sound that slips out.

"Oh my God," she rasps quietly. "Oh my God. *Yesss.*"

I soak it all in, imagining just how hot and soaked she must be, how she'd squeeze around my fingers—or fuck, my dick—if I were inside her. With a final jerk, she sags against the wall. She lets her skirt drop and her arms hang. She might be spent, but I'm fighting for my life. My cock throbs, and I think of cow shit. Getting slammed into cattle panels. Stubbing my toe.

You don't know what it's like. College. Graduate school. Research.

That does it. Blood drains from my erection. I can concentrate on Campbell and her reaction. Her eyes are closed, but her breathing has evened out.

"You okay?" I ask softly.

"No. I can't believe I did that."

We did that, but I don't correct her. I'm keeping this glorious moment to myself.

She's about to slap her hands against her cheeks, but she gawks at the one she used to get herself off.

I take the bottle, turn her palm up, and pour a splash onto her skin. She rubs her hands together like it's sanitizer. Close enough.

I don't back away from her. "Now go back out there, smile, and know that I'll be seeing how you orgasm in my dreams tonight."

Shock flickers in her gaze a heartbeat before she looks stricken. She's stiff again as she ducks out from under me. "They can't know."

"They won't. You only need Stanford to suspect to make him suffer. If anyone asks why you're flushed, say you got too much sun out riding."

She takes a step, then stops. "This can't happen again."

If I never get to experience another one of her orgasms, I'm going to die a sad man. "Maybe you should wait and see how well it works first."

CHAPTER EIGHT

Campbell

I sit with Jamison at the house she and Iverson built. The big picture windows face the mountains. They're Durban's neighbors, but I can't see his place from here. I'm taking a much-needed break from Hawthorne Ranch and wedding planning. Nothing was planned for yesterday, but somehow, I've become the official vacation guide for the Baldwin family. After suggesting they go to Bozeman and try some of the amazing restaurants in town, they actually listened and left me alone for the day. Alone with my thoughts about the family dinner two nights ago.

I can't believe I did that.

I can't believe *we* did that.

Those two sentences have been on repeat since I got off in the storeroom with Durban. Somehow, I managed to avoid him the rest of dinner.

It worked, though. The way Stanford narrowed his

eyes when I breezed out of the storeroom lit me up with the most invigorating satisfaction. Even better—when January noticed her fiancé noticing me. The punch of insecurity in her gaze was watered-down payback for all the times I worried about whether Stanford was actually working late.

And when Stanford's parents got snide about the quality of food in the middle of nowhere, Montana, their insulting tone rolled off my freshly orgasmed skin.

Only one thing overshadowed the entire experience. Once the bride and groom and their family cleared out, I ditched the place too. I went to my parents' house, hid in my childhood bedroom, and tried to answer the question of how I wasn't messing up my redemption story. If someone had walked in on us? I'd have looked like a floozy who couldn't control herself through one dinner—and it would have been true.

I would've climbed Durban like a mountain if he'd asked me to.

He didn't ask, but he told me to do a lot of other things.

"I would ask what's wrong, but I know better," Jamison says, her hands wrapped over her belly. She's officially on maternity leave now, but she's climbing the walls. Her husband called me in to make sure she at least keeps off her feet instead of cleaning an already clean house while he takes Kacey to the playground in town.

"The usual," I lie.

I've been replaying the storeroom climax over and over and over. Between reruns, a litany of questions streams through my head. Is he really single? I can't ask anyone without them wondering why. What would I say?

Well, you see, he talked me through masturbation during the family dinner, and I don't want guilt on top of that.

If he is single, when did he and Natalie break up? He told me at the tasting, but guys say a lot of things to get what they want. Every interaction we've had since I've returned to town is studied in a new light, but I have no new answers. And the loop starts again. His gruff voice in the dark. The way he loomed over me, cloaking me in his body heat and caramel-whiskey scent. I stroked one out, right in front of him, on the other side of the wall from a bunch of people who I had thought would one day be family. Some *are* my family!

I was on the clock. At my job. With my sister's brother-in-law.

I'm a hussy and I need to be ashamed.

But I can't deny that it worked. The release took a lot of stress with it. I have a naughty secret, and Stanford can suck it.

Male voices sound from outside.

Jamison sits up, keeping her swollen legs on the footrest. "Haven and Durban are here."

I bolt upright, and all the confusion from the last two days knots in my stomach. "I should get going." Shit. I can't. Iverson's not home yet. I'm on sister duty. "Never mind."

She frowns at me. Her lips are fuller, her nose too, and she's radiant like she was when she was pregnant with Kacey. "You can go if you need to. I promise not to run a marathon while you're gone."

I'm not shirking my responsibility, and I'm definitely not doing it in front of Durban. "I'm fine. I need the reprieve. Stanford and January's riding lessons start tomorrow."

"We both know Stanford should not be swinging brides into the saddle or riding off. He doesn't have the experience. He's going to hurt himself, her, or Hailstorm."

"Daddy made him sign all kinds of releases."

She lets out a disapproving grunt. "Still a dumb move."

"It keeps me from spiraling. I get to have a nice ride and they think I'm working."

"So true. I miss it."

"Soon," I reassure her.

"Iverson's looking for a pony for Kacey to start with."

My heart twists. I'm so happy for Jamison. I'm going to be a proud aunt when Kacey becomes an accomplished rider. It doesn't change that I thought I'd be at the same point as Jamison by now, or at least close. I'm starting single life all over again, and I haven't even nailed down a career yet. It's like Adulting 101, but I'm almost thirty.

"Do you think Bryce is around?" He's the owner of the rafting and kayaking tour company in town. "I want to ask if he could use my services now that the tourism season is opening."

"He's often at his office downtown, and if he's not, I'm sure he's at the river location." She frowns. "But he's still cranky that you didn't go to prom with him, and then you turned him down after college."

My shoulders hunch. I already had a prom date, and then I was strung out after the stress of finishing school. Dating had to take the back burner. I'm home now, but dating is the last thing I want to do. I'm also not interested in Bryce. The drawbacks of trying to make a living in your hometown. Grudges. "I thought he was dating Winnie."

"She moved to Idaho with a guy she met on a kayaking run."

"Ouch."

The guys' voices get close to the door. I want to run. I can't face Durban and act normal. Already, my nipples are hard peaks, and my body's flushed with heat. For a girl who isn't a fan of whiskey, I'm craving it in the dark with his voice in my ear.

"Iverson said he could use you at the distillery, though," she says.

"Me?" My initial inclination is to brush off the help. I need to prove myself, but after this wedding, I might need an easy win.

"Yes. Nothing full-time, but they're getting asked about office parties for the holidays already. Last year, he said that planning took up more time than expected."

"But there's a lot of them." Three Hennessy brothers and two of the Foster brothers.

"They're dudes. You think they want to figure out what to do with Edna's crochet club?"

"Some guys would."

"Some would enjoy it. *They* do not, and Iverson will be tied up more with two kids. His brothers are already pitching in a ton. Lane and Cruz were even out here to help with calving this last week."

"You married into a whole family of dudes who've got each other's back." I rub my hands together and peer out the window while ignoring the twinge of longing.

I was so excited to meet Stanford's family. I grew up close to my sisters, and while my parents are overbearing and constantly point out where I fall short, I've missed them too. After meeting Stanford's parents, I appreciate mine more. At least they cared when they asked me about the jobs I left or was fired from. Stanford's mom and dad always acted like I'm too country, working a pointless job and worthless for conversation because I don't follow the stock market.

Last night brought all those memories back. All the eye rolls Priscilla didn't think I saw. Or the way Chester stared at my tits but wrote off my intelligence. Stanford had to get it from somewhere.

Yet they approve of January. My cousin, who sells jewelry and works the same job she got out of college. Perfect, demure January who does what she's told.

The door opens, and Haven and Durban spill inside. The urge to sprint out the back door surges inside me.

"We brought food!" Haven shouts. "But don't move. We've been ordered to give you lunch in bed."

"I'm on the couch," Jamison calls.

"Lunch on the couch, then," he says, carrying grocery bags through the house to us. The smell of roasted chicken fills the air. Jamison's main pregnancy craving.

Jamison scoots up. "Rotisserie chicken?"

"We were told we'd better not show up without it." Durban's behind Haven with his arms full of paper towels and disposable plates. "We were also told that we'd better not touch the thighs or you'll gut us."

His deep voice ripples over my skin in a way Haven's doesn't. I need to go, or I'm going to be a mixed-up, turned-on mess, while Durban is as handsomely casual as can be.

"I'll fight a bitch for those thighs." Jamison pats the spot next to her. "Wanna sit by me, Campbell? The guys can join us and have the chairs."

The warm brush of Durban's gaze strokes over me. My belly somersaults. If I have one bite of the food, I'll heave it all over the coffee table. I don't need that on top of the wedding stress. "Uh, no. Thanks. I should get going."

"You're missing out. Living room picnics are the best." Haven digs out grapes, sliced melon, and fresh bread that makes my hunger knock on my stomach walls. It's from Elodie's bakery. Maybe I'll run there right now, buy a dozen of everything, and hide from the way Durban's studying me, as if he wasn't just leaning over me less than forty-eight hours ago, telling me what to do as if he knows my body better than me.

"You're leaving?" Jamison puts her legs down, but I wave her off.

"They want to be proper guests on the ranch tomorrow," I say, "so I have to check in with the staff and make sure we're good to go."

There'll be branding, and that's always a huge draw. Daddy makes it a production with roping and wrangling and hot-from-the-fire iron brands, instead of chutes and panels and electric branding irons.

She rolls her eyes. "They aren't going to appreciate it."

They'll be horrified. I can't wait. "No, but maybe they'll get shit on them and I can celebrate that it's part of the experience."

"Don't forget to peek at the kittens." She rubs her belly and eyes the food. My stomach clenches at the delay. "Patches is keeping them in the barn, and they're ready for interaction."

"Sure." I told her I'd help get the kittens used to

humans before Kacey charges in a little too loud, a little too unpredictable for the mama cat.

I give the guys a tight smile without meeting their eyes and scurry out of the house, using the door off the kitchen.

The pressure doesn't ease off my chest as I cross the gravel loop to the barn on the other end. I find Patches curled up in an old rabbit hutch that Jamison found in a thrift store.

"Hey, Patches," I say softly and crouch by the fenced sides to let her get used to me. The little tortie that showed up last fall blinks and meows and pushes her face against the wires. I chuckle and scratch her cheeks before rising to coo at her and the four little kittens snoozing on her. "Look at you, Mama. Doing a good job."

A tiny orange kitten hisses at me before I carefully lift him. His little ears stick straight up. He closes his eyes and leans into me when I scratch him.

The three others start moving around, their little mews reaching me.

"Just wait your turn." I giggle at the wiggling body in my grip.

"I think Iverson's been out here spoiling them."

I whirl around at the deep voice. Tingles race down my spine and spread outward. Guilt immediately follows. "You've got to quit sneaking up on me."

Last time, I was the one who snuck into the room he was in.

He lifts his chin at the kitten I'm cradling. "I think they've been getting human attention for far longer than Jamison knows." His shadow only amplifies how wide his shoulders are. They blocked out the storeroom when he was in front of me.

Envy joins the other tangled emotions. My sister has the man, the house, the kids, a dog, and even kittens. I'm planning my ex's wedding while living with my parents.

I set the kitten down with the others and pick up another tortie with one white paw. "Are you accusing your own brother of spoiling barn cats?" I ask lightly. I want to run, to get away from his confusing presence, but not as much as I want to stay.

"Yes." He shoves his hands into his jeans pockets. The move pulls his dark-green T-shirt tighter. "That one's going to be my next barn cat."

I clutch her to me. She bumps her tiny nose against my chin. "Putting her to work so early?"

"She's got a month, and then she's moving."

And the mama cat is getting fixed. I knew the plans, but I didn't know which kittens were going where. "What are you naming her?"

He clicks his tongue against his teeth. "Bold of you to think Kacey doesn't have them named already. She's Bootsy."

I laugh and Bootsy mews. I trade her for another cream-colored kitten. One more and I can ditch the handsome cowboy standing in the doorway, making me wish I wore a dress today.

As if he's reading my thoughts, he rakes his gaze down my body. Appreciation fills his eyes. I'm only in jeans and an old Hawthorne Ranch shirt.

"What's wrong?" he asks.

His question takes me off guard. I swap for the last kitten, an all-black one. From the way they're not squirming to get away, they've been handled plenty already.

"Nothing, other than dealing with my cousin and her groom." Maybe referring to them like that will make it all sting less.

"Campbell."

A shiver whispers over my skin. He called me Belle in the dark.

"This is different," he says softly. "You've hardly looked at me since the other night."

The other night. When I practically came in his arms and he talked me through it. He helped me then, and he wants to do it again. I'm apparently a sucker for that. "Were you being honest? You don't have a girlfriend?"

"Ah. That." He drags in a deep breath, looks behind him, and saunters farther in. "We aren't together."

"I know we're not together. I want to make sure you and Natalie aren't either." I haven't eaten anything, but the center of my chest burns. I put the last kitten down. It was almost asleep, and I would've held it longer if it weren't for the potential cheater in front of me. Do I know how to pick them or what?

I didn't pick Durban. It just happened. I wouldn't have chosen another guy who thinks he's better than me.

"No, I mean, me and *Natalie* aren't together."

"You didn't do that thing where you broke up with her right after, so technically, you're not a bad guy, and I'm not a horrible homewrecker?" Nausea hits my stomach. "Because ugh. Technically, I still would be."

"That'd make me an asshole. I'm not your ex, and I don't string women along until they're not convenient anymore." The offense in his tone makes me feel both better and worse.

I'm insulting him, and now I have guilt wrapped up in the mix of feelings inside me. I wring my hands. "My dating history hasn't left me with the best worst-case scenarios."

The hardness in his jaw eases. "You should never be wrong for taking someone at their word. The night at the bar? I went there because she had just called and broken it off."

"Oh." The agitation in my stomach finds a different reason to continue. He didn't owe me an explanation, but I'm spinning out, so he gave me one. Now the guilt grows. I gave him shit about his girlfriend, and he played it off because he was sitting there, heartbroken, and wanted to save face. I just stomped salt into his wound. "Oh God, I'm sorry. No wonder you were so grouchy."

"Couldn't you read it in my expression?" he asks lightly before he turns serious again. "Four years of waiting, and it's over. Just like that." He takes his hands out and crosses his arms across his chest. Oh, that's worse. The flutters are back in my belly. "She said I was too distracting at such an important time for her."

"Ouch."

Four years is a long time to be cut out so quickly. I know how that feels. He said he didn't string women along until they were inconvenient, but that sounds like what his ex did.

"Why?" It's none of my business, but suddenly, I want to know everything about the Durban who's human and makes mistakes and gets dumped just like me. I grip the horseshoe charm on my necklace and run it back and forth along the chain. "If she's almost done with school, why now?"

"She's busy." The muscles on either side of his jaw pop. "I don't know what it's like, being in college and especially not at that level. It's a critical time for her."

"Harsh."

"But true."

"Fuck that." I snort. "Trust me. I know how much it sucks to have people think you can't possibly understand when it's them who have no idea what you're dealing with."

His gaze narrows on me, but he doesn't speak.

I don't know what else to say. Relief is starting to flood in, making the cool inside of the barn almost chilly. I could continue questioning Durban, but I believe him. What makes him more trustworthy? His focus is on me. Am I that needy? "It helped. Dealing with Stanford and his family after *that* was easier."

Satisfaction fills his eyes. "Yeah?"

"I found his parents and my aunt and uncle much more tolerable. I think Stanford suspected something, so good."

The same interest I saw in the storeroom flares in his eyes, and the corner of his mouth tips up. "When do you have to deal with them again?"

"He wants riding lessons. Given by me. January will be there though."

"She won't let him out of sight around you."

I shake my head. I'll take small ego strokes where I can.

"When?" he asks.

"When what?"

"Riding lessons."

"Tomorrow after dinner. They'll do dude ranch stuff all day, have an evening meal, then riding lessons." For acting like they're so much more sophisticated than rural Montana, the Baldwins sure want all the rural Montana experiences and adventures. Probably to laugh about them with their social circle when they return to Seattle. "The riding will be just the couple."

"Then I'll see you tomorrow." He spins on a boot heel.

"Wait—what?" I admire his ass while attempting to process what he means. Because I have to be wrong.

He doesn't turn back around; he just speaks over his shoulder, his profile strong. That mustache of his makes me wonder things. Same with the whiskers. How much would I feel them . . . down there? "You're going to make it through these next few weeks as stress-free as I can get you."

"But . . ." Does he mean what I think he means?

He does a half turn, brow cocked.

A full-body shiver racks me. I don't have it in me to say no. I don't want to. I want his growl back in my ear. I want his hulking frame over me. I want to be an unbothered hussy when I'm taking orders from Stanford and January.

It can't be a smart idea. I'm trying to get taken seriously, and if anyone finds out, I'll be humiliated. Satisfied, but embarrassed.

"No one can know," I finally say, succumbing to the siren song of how he can ease my pressure. "I don't want my reputation worse than it is." Even if I earn it this time. "And I'm not risking the land deal my uncle made with Daddy."

"Your sister would have my balls if she thought I was

fucking around with you. Both of them. Your parents too. I don't want to tarnish the relationship between the distillery and your family ranch."

"What about Natalie?"

"What about her?" Confusion ripples over his face, but hurt still shines strong from his eyes too. "There's nothing there."

There was a short window where I hurt so much after Stanford dumped me that I would've opened the door to him had he shown up full of remorse. I'm not proud of it, and I don't want to be in that window with Durban if it happens to him. "Not even when she gets her shiny degree and realizes she was too stressed and made a mistake?"

"Probably not."

Probably? Does that mean he still wants his brilliant scientist? That if she showed up at his door, he'd dive right in like he hadn't talked me through the best orgasm of my life?

"I'm a single guy," he continues. "That's that."

Even if he did ghost me for his ex, he's single right now, and I'm in the throes of wedding festivities. It's an offer I don't want to refuse. "And we're just going to . . . mess around? You don't like me."

"I never said I don't like you. Besides, you're not my biggest fan, but you still came for me."

My cheeks burn hot. "That's not— It's just—" Pressure smashes against my ankles. Patches. I pick her up, needing an obstacle between me and the guy who's offered to continue getting me off. "What about you? Aren't you going to want something in return?"

I'd tremble if it wasn't for Patches. I want to touch him. Put my hand on that bulge— Oh God. Is he hard right now? If he's not, then how big is he when he's erect?

Why do I want to know so bad?

He scratches the back of his neck and avoids my gaze. "If you think I got nothing out of hearing you climax, then you don't know what I like." He shifts to look at me. "We do whatever you're comfortable with."

"Whatever we won't get caught doing?"

He gives me one curt nod. "Just between us."

It's a tantalizing offer. Anonymity. The thrill of getting caught. The risk. Do I want to deal with that? I could tank my name in my own hometown, where I'm hoping to get a fresh start.

But I'm so tired of trying to prove myself—to my parents, to my ex, to his family.

I need a way to let off steam that's more powerful than cuddling kittens, and Durban's dangling it right in front of me. He didn't say no strings attached, but he means it. I'm not his type.

No strings. With a hot man who gets under my skin?

I lift my chin and hug the cat. "Deal."

I have my arms folded, pacing across the tack room in the barn. The vet was out earlier for an abscessed hoof, and all the horses are out grazing. I have Hailstorm, Mildred, and Clyde in the pen closest to the barn.

I'm set to take Stanford and January riding in an hour. Then we'll work on getting Hailstorm used to two riders before we progress to swooping brides up.

Durban said he'd see me today, but I never clarified how that'd happen. Is he just going to show up? Am I supposed to meet him somewhere? Did he come to his senses, unlike me, and realize what a bad decision this would be?

We're creating an uncomfortable destiny for ourselves, to be with each other for every family get-together Iverson and Jamison ever have. Awkward birthday parties and self-conscious barbecues. Do I want to see what kind of woman he'll bring when Iverson and Jamison host Christmas next?

I should call Avery and talk to her, but she'll ask me what the hell I'm thinking and tell me to keep my hands to myself and not fuck up the wedding because it'll all come crashing down on me. Avery's the coldly logical one.

I pace the room, pinging from the wall with the headstalls and lead ropes to the rows of saddles jutting out from their posts in the other wall. The smell of wood, dust, and faint horse sweat rises up around me. Comforting, but not soothing enough.

"The dress was much easier to work with."

I let out a cry and whip around. He looks as delicious as yesterday. "Is scaring me foreplay for you?"

Heat sparks in his eyes. "If that's all you think is in my foreplay game, I'm hurt."

I roll my eyes and hold back a smile. I notice him *a lot*. "I wasn't sure how this would work."

"The spontaneity will make it fun."

I keep pacing. "How are we going to explain why you're here?"

He enters all the way and leans against the table across from the halters. "I have business at the ranch until the wedding is over. We have Jamison to discuss and how we're going to help her and Iverson when it's baby time." He shrugs. "We'll think of something."

"That doesn't explain why you're out *here*."

"I miss the animals."

He says it so simply, I almost believe him.

Nerves zip up my body and back down. I hug myself.

He pats the counter next to him. "I'm not going to jump you. Come and have a seat. We'll talk."

I reluctantly do as he says. "This is weird." I lift myself to sit. I'm still not at eye level with him.

He turns and brackets me in, his hands planted on the surface on either side of me. "How's your day going?"

A nervous chuckle leaves me. "Not the best." It just got infinitely better as soon as his body heat radiated into me. The knots in my muscles start to relax. Our faces are close, but I like being able to see the dark striations in his irises.

"Why not?" His question is a caress, as if he's feathering his fingers down my cheeks.

"I called Bryce to arrange a time to meet up, see if there's anything I can do for his company, and he asked me out."

His nostrils flare. "You said no?"

"Of course I said no. I've been turning him down most of my life. He used to try to spy on us on the bleachers." I give him a deadpan look. "He used to try to look up our *shorts*."

He snorts. "You realize those three stooges from the bar work out there?"

No, I didn't think of that. Anxiety ripples through my stomach, but I pretend like it doesn't bother me. "Stooges? How old are you?"

"Older than you. My dad used to love them."

Surprise flickers through his gaze before there's a distance back in his eyes.

"Yeah?" I like this side of Durban. The one who acts like he wants me, and that he can't help himself from showing me the real him. "I bet he was nicer than Chester Baldwin."

A second ticks by. "He was. A lot nicer."

"Did our dads know each other?" My fingers tingle to run through the soft strands of his hair. I grip the edge of the counter.

"I don't know. Maybe. Dad would've been older than William. Dad met my mom when he was twenty. Had Iverson not long after."

"Then you and Haven?"

He swallows and looks down, which happens to be at my lap. "There's six years between Iverson and Haven. She left not long after Haven was born."

"Oh, Durban. I'm so sorry."

His gaze shoots up to me. "Don't be. We were better off without her."

"Did you live with her?"

"Yes. After Dad died, we had to. We would've been better off if they'd left us alone in the old house."

I can't resist touching him anymore. I cup his face. Whiskers tickle my palm. "Is that Haven's place?"

"Yes. Our mother hated that she couldn't take all this away from us. We haven't talked to her since we moved out." He clasps my wrist and turns into my touch, kissing my sensitive skin. Then he puts his mouth against the inside of my wrist.

Shivers trace through my body, and I widen my legs. He steps closer and places another kiss farther down the inside of my arm.

"Feeling more comfortable, Belle?" he whispers.

"Yes." So many feelings cascade through my chest. Desire. Anticipation. Giddiness. Since when have I looked forward to a kiss like this?

He drops his head, ever so slowly. Weren't we going to fool around? This feels deeper. But I'm also not panicking and drinking straight from the bottle like I was last time.

The faintest touch of his mustache hits my lips.

"I know we're early, January, but the light's on," Stanford says way too close to the door.

"Motherfucker," Durban growls and steps to the side. My knee brushes against a hard-as-steel bulge behind his zipper.

I blink, my head spinning while I try to remember what the hell I'm doing here. Horses. Riding. I'm not in the tack room to make out.

Stanford charges in and stops, looking left. Then right. He spots us and the corner of his lip curls into a sneer.

January stops behind him, putting her hands on his back. "What's wrong— Oh. Campbell. Durban? Are you riding with us?"

I don't like the way her eyes light up. "We're going over the setup for the reception since there's a chance of rain." I haven't looked at the forecast, and we're way too far out for it to be accurate.

Stanford's sneer hasn't let up. "I would think you've covered that already."

"We have," Durban says. "I like to be thorough." He ends with a heavy note of suggestion.

I bite the inside of my cheek. "You two are early. Did something come up?"

January's lips press into a line.

Stanford shoves his hand into his pocket. "We wanted to get started."

I clap my hands and hop off the counter. "All right. Show me those skills."

I didn't say it to be flirty, but January's pale brows draw together. She's afraid to lose him the way she got him.

I grab Durban's forearm. It's like wrapping my fingers around warm steel. His muscles flex under my touch. "We'll finish this later?"

His dark gaze pins mine. "Absolutely."

CHAPTER NINE

Durban

I'm at my desk when Lane pops in. "Hey, did you get the email—"

"Yes." I stab at the keyboard. I know he expected a reply, but I am cranky that he has to remind me about it. We're testing a new ordering system, and I was supposed to do it yesterday. But I had to leave early in a third attempt to meet with Campbell and do . . . something. Fuck. Anything.

But Stanford Cockblocker Baldwin must watch for me because he keeps dragging his increasingly frustrated fiancée down to the tack room early.

"Bro." Lane pushes all the way into my office and drops into a chair across from my desk. He's in jeans and a white T-shirt with a flannel over it. Standard distillery wear when we all raise cattle on the side. "What's up?"

"Nothing. Just busy."

He takes his black Foster House ball cap off and

flops it on his knee. "You're uptight as hell. Does it have anything to do with you jetting outta here early all week?"

"That's for the wedding."

He rubs the scruff on his chin. "I don't mean to pry—"

"Yeah, you do."

He flashes an unrepentant smile. "How's the wedding going?"

"Good." I have no idea. All I know is that I haven't gotten to touch Campbell yet.

"Sounds like it," he says wryly, then shrugs. "I know none of us cares about what's going on at Hawthorne unless it affects Jamison. And now Campbell too." His gaze is steady on me. "You heading up there early again?"

He's sniffing for information that isn't any of his business. I like Lane, and I've gotten to know him and Cruz well over the last few years, but I keep my private life private. "Not today. It's raining, so I'm sure she'll have to shift to entertaining them all indoors."

"Helluva wedding celebration." He shakes his head. "I'd rather have something like Myles and Wynter. All the Baileys. Family, fun, and food. Then we're done and living our lives."

"Nothing fancy," I agree. "But I might feel differently if I didn't know the couple's trying to justify the hurt they caused or rub it in Campbell's face."

"It's bullshit. How's she holding up?"

I steeple my fingers. "She said Stanford has complained about how big Hailstorm is, being stiff after riding, and almost falling off when he was riding double with January."

"Oof. And he won't give up?"

I shake my head grimly. "Campbell tries to talk to him about taking more time, or giving January her own horse, and they could ride side by side, but he wants his way."

"I'd ask what either woman saw in him, but Cruz and I are here. Proof our dad could talk our mama up one side and down another." He taps his fingers on the armrest of the chair. "Makes me glad to share a last name with Myles. From what I've heard, his dad was a good one."

"You don't have the same— Sorry. None of my business." I stop any personal life talk before it happens, so I won't stomp into someone else's. The town knows the Hennessy backstory and how we were carted off to foster care. They've heard things about my mother, and when they ask for more, I shut it down.

Except when I'm alone with Campbell in a tack room.

"Nah, I don't mind," Lane says easily. "We share the same last name, so if people learn we're half brothers, they assume we have the same dad. But we're brothers from the same mother. Our mess of a mom had a tough life after Myles's dad died. She kept his name and refused to marry our dad. Never did give us his last name, which was one of the few things she could hold over his head."

My phone starts buzzing. Campbell's name flashes on the screen.

Lane pushes up and cocks a brow when his gaze dips to the screen. "I'll let you get that."

"Wedding stuff."

He smirks. "It's kinda like you said earlier—none of my business."

I scowl at his back as he leaves, then answer. "Yeah?"

"Oh." Campbell's husky voice starts a trickle of heat in my veins. "Bad time?"

"No." Never for her. "Why?"

"That's right. You always sound cranky."

"Do not."

"Mm. Sure." That hum of hers goes right to my dick. "Anyway, since it's a rainy day, the Baldwins just want to chill."

"Good. You need a day off."

"You'd be the only one who thinks so."

Who the hell's giving her a hard time now? "Why?"

"The Baldwins want me to earn their money, and I don't need them talking crap about me around town. I do need a successful wedding before anyone else will schedule theirs. I'm hoping to get some smaller things going and do some cross-promoting."

"Do you just go from event to event like that?" The wedding is exhausting her enough, and she's out hustling for more?

"It's like a rolling schedule. I might be working on four or five big events and several smaller ones, but they're all at various stages. And after this, I'll have zero, so I've still gotta get planning, and I finally got a meeting with Bryce."

"You didn't have to agree to go out with him, did you?" I growl. I don't dislike Bryce, but I don't trust him. He's too desperate around women, and he makes stupid decisions because of it.

"No, thankfully, and he didn't ask me out this time."

Doesn't mean he won't try to get with her. "Are you meeting at the downtown office?"

"No, he's at the middle river site today, getting equipment ready."

My warning bells get louder. "And you're going there?"

"Yeah. If I'm whoring for clients, I've gotta go where they are."

"You're not whoring for any goddamn client—"

"Whoa, take a joke, grumpy."

"—and you're not going to the middle river site alone. Why the hell is he even there?" Bryce might be legitimately working riverside, or he could be luring Campbell away, where her rejection won't matter.

"Well, now that you brought it up . . . Can you come with me?"

Astonished, I stare out the glass wall of my office at the pipes crossing over the stills. She's not brushing off my concerns, and she's asking me to go along. She trusts me.

"Durban?"

"I'm here." Still reeling, but here.

"I just know how Bryce is, and I don't want to bug Iverson. Daddy will take it as just another sign I'm not going to cut it in this business or in Huckleberry Springs. So congrats. You're the only other decent guy I know, but you can say no."

The fuck I can. "Want me to pick you up?"

"I can meet you at the distillery so we can talk about how all the Baldwins would like a tasting night." She sucks in a deep breath. "And they don't want you to host it."

"Why the hell not?"

"I believe Pricilla said that you look like you're either going to dump a drink on them or bite their hand."

"I don't bite unless I'm asked to."

There's a quick inhale on the other side, then a frustrated exhale. "I wouldn't know because Stanford is getting jealous. That's the other reason they don't want you. *They* being Stanford."

"That fucker's getting married. What does he care?"

"I think January should be asking him that question, but he's probably gaslighting her. I will happily tell them it won't work out."

No, otherwise it would make Campbell look inept. "We'll make it happen. I'll talk to the guys."

And I'll make plans for Campbell while the Baldwins are busy with their drinks.

Campbell

I greet Clem as I breeze through the Foster House entrance. She's dusting off bottles on display. I tap my shoes off on the rug. It's been raining on and off all day. Right now, it's on.

"Edna was hoping to catch you while you're here," Clem says. She's got Dutch braids in today. It's one of my favorite styles when I'm home, but since I'm technically working and the Baldwins already think I grew up milking cows and yodeling—which sounds fun—I've been keeping my styles chicer.

"Okay. I'll let Durban know I'm here first." I'm two minutes early. I would've been sooner, but I got caught talking to Stanford's grandma about the names of the animal heads mounted in the game room. They have none. Daddy only called his kills "dinner" because they were many of our breakfasts, lunches, and dinners growing up.

"Edna's in the tasting room with him. Go on in."

I keep from sprinting to see Durban. That almost-kiss days ago has taunted me every moment of the day. I think about it at night. What was he going to do? What did he plan? Would my pants have come off? A little dry humping?

Everything I thought of, and it was a lot, sounded amazing. I haven't even done any self-care because I want to experience the explosion he can cause.

Edna's sitting at one of the low-top tables, sipping on a glass of clear fluid with a mint leaf floating inside. She beams at me. "Campbell. Nice to see you again."

Durban's in a chair next to her, his arms folded and his gaze traveling down my body. I'm wearing jeans today to keep from giving Bryce any thoughts that I dressed up for him. I put on a loose vest over a long-sleeved shirt. The rain has kept the day cool.

"Hey, Edna." I give her a quick hug before she can stand.

She grins and raises her glass in a cheers. "Durban's letting me crash your meeting to talk about my hookers."

Durban arches a brow.

I slide into a seat next to him. "Hookers and booze. My favorite combination."

She giggles and pushes up her wire-rimmed glasses. "My daughter told me to leave all the cocktail wordplay alone."

I laugh. Durban's faint smile makes this the best conversation of the week. Other than when we were in the tack room. "I'll think of a title. Do you have a day or time?"

She nods. "Durban here said Monday afternoons are good since the tasting room is closed. Most of my group are retirees. And Clem and Elodie."

"My grandma taught me to crochet," I say. "I picked it up easier than knitting."

"Then you'll have to join us." She pats my arm.

"Mom got frustrated when I'd start so many projects and just leave them."

Edna shrugs and takes a drink. "I don't care if you start a hundred blankets and never finish. It's not about productivity. It's about hookers and booze."

"All right. I'll make sure I'm free." The wedding party will have to accept that I'm not theirs twenty-four seven. "Until then, I'll get it all arranged for you, and I can run a socials page or anything you want to keep your group informed."

"Let me know your rates."

I wave her off. "This is nothing."

"Campbell Joanna Hawthorne, I am paying you." Edna used to volunteer at the school when I was a kid. She downs the rest of her drink and digs a twenty out of her purse. "My ride's here." Slapping it on the table, she rises and shuffles away before I can argue with her.

"She keeps paying." Durban picks up the money. "We save it and add it to her yearly bonus." He stands and digs out a box from a cabinet behind the bar. "Joanna?"

"One of my grandmas." I push the tables in. "Mom was terrified people would call me CJ, but she loved the name Campbell. So she extinguished every CJ she heard. What about you? Where does your name come from?"

"My brothers and I all have family surnames from

Mom's side. Iverson was her maiden name, Durban was her mom's maiden name, and Haven was her grandmother's maiden name."

"Nice to have some family legacy like that."

"I guess," he says noncommittally. "I never knew them. There's a history of running off."

"I'm sorry." I cross to the bar.

"It is what it is."

I slide apart a few of the papers he set on the top. Neat, boxy handwriting fills the page. Some of the numbers are measurements. "What's this?"

"Nothing." He tucks the box back.

I don't know Durban well, but these aren't nothing. I'm being nosy, but I spin a sheet around. Oak-aged vodka, along with lengths of time and amounts for the recipe is listed.

Another piece of paper has a different time for double-barreled whiskey. "Honey infused?"

"Yeah," he says gruffly and gathers them up. He stuffs them in whatever slot behind the counter Edna's money is kept in. "Just what I do when the bar's quiet."

I know he and his brothers work the tasting room, along with the Foster brothers, but they really need to be capitalizing on that. How many office parties would suddenly be scheduled by the women making the decisions? Pictures of them are all I'd use to pitch the tasting room. "Have you done any yet?"

"No."

I wait, but he doesn't elaborate. I shouldn't pry, but there are layers to Durban I haven't seen before, and I'd like to pry them all apart. "Why not?"

He flattens his hands on the bar top and seems to deliberate. "They want to stick to safe products right now. They're afraid that if we weave too far out of the margins, we could damage the whole Foster House reputation. So, we're sticking with tried-and-true blends, and doing single-barrel lines, barrel strength, double barrel, and simple infusions."

"But you want to play?"

"I'm interested in the science of it, yes." His gaze sweeps around the bar, taking in the clean wooden lines of the beams used more for decoration than support. "My brothers and I all own a part of this place. Not the main headquarters, but this site. Foster House Gold. Forty-nine percent owners."

"Forty-nine percent divided by three? So you don't have as much say in how to run the place."

He works his jaw back and forth. "The Fosters don't make us feel that way, and Myles didn't have to sell any part of this at all. He wanted to buy this property straight out."

"Just like that?"

"Foster House does very well. But part of his brand is helping out people like us. Former foster kids trying to make a better life for ourselves. Iverson was in charge of the trust our dad left behind, and we agreed to sell the old mine and any acreage the distillery would need if we could invest back in. Myles did more than that. He trained us. Gave us a profession that won't ruin our bodies, and hell, we even have retirement accounts now. I'm grateful."

"But it's not enough?" I ask softly.

A guy like Durban, who has shelves full of books and sketches out formulations and recipes and woos women with PhDs, won't settle for being the help forever. He might've done it when they had nothing but a tapped-out gold mine, but now this distillery *is* a gold mine, and he wants to take his pick and dig in.

"There are times," he says reluctantly, "when I'm aware that my footing isn't exactly equal."

"Have you told them it's important to you?"

His brow furrows. "There are five of us, six if you count Myles, and we work well together. Their caution is warranted. This space is meant to play, but we have to be smart about it, or we'll go in the red. Ready to go?"

I give my head a quick shake. Message received. Conversation over. "I can drive."

"We'll take my truck."

He rounds the bar and strides out the door. I follow his infuriatingly wide shoulders all the way out of the bar. He's so hot and cold. Mercurial. "I get better gas mileage."

"Most definitely."

I hit the unlock button on my fob. The clouds are giving us a reprieve from the rain. "I invited you. I'm driving."

I start to veer toward my car, parked across the lot from him, but he spins around and blocks my path.

"Driving will distract me." His jaw is hard, and his gaze sweeps around us.

"From what?"

"From not getting to hear you come for the last few days when I fully expected to find out for myself how wet you get."

My mouth drops open, and fire blazes over my skin. That was unexpected. "I can't get a read on you." My body's humming, but there's a whirlwind in my head. "You can be a very confusing man."

"As long as you remember that around you, I'm all man."

More lust pumps into my veins. My skin is too tight, a vault, and only he has the key to open it. Then clarity washes cold through me just as a raindrop splatters my nose. I wipe it off. "That's right. You haven't gotten laid in a while."

"No, but what does that have to do with our arrangement?"

Arrangement. My heart twists just a little. "It explains why you have wild swings. One minute, you're a stone. And the next, you're talking dirty. Sort of."

"I can talk dirty."

Another raindrop hits my forehead. "It's been a while. You might have to brush up on it. What were they saying the last time you were with a woman? 'Show me your totally tubular tits'?"

His eyes flare wide, then he chortles. "I'm not that old. Maybe more like 'chillax and come for me.' "

"Ha! What decade is that from?"

He groans and starts for his truck again. "The nineties, and my dad liked to unwind with TV shows."

He opens the door for me.

"What shows?" I ask as I climb in.

"Anything." He shuts the door and goes around to the other side.

He leaves town on a road I don't normally take. Our ranch is on the other side of Huckleberry Springs in one direction, and the distillery and Hennessy land is on the other. Sy's Water Adventures are on the other side of town.

As he drives, signs point us toward the river site for the midriver adventures. I've gone white water rafting a few times in my life, a couple of river floats even more, but I've never used Bryce's family business. His mom used to run it, and she wasn't as safety conscious in those days. Two lawsuits later, the company was turned over to Bryce. He's not someone I wanted to date, but he's at least more safety conscious.

As Durban drives, I send messages to both Stanford and January about when they want to have a tasting.

Stanford: Tomorrow afternoon. It's supposed to rain again.

I checked the forecast. Cloudy with a twenty percent chance of showers. That isn't exactly worth canceling the archery event Daddy has set up. Now I'll have to reschedule that, which isn't a big deal since the Baldwins are currently the only guests, but there'll be some rearranging with staff.

Me: If it's okay with Foster House.

I could've checked first, but I couldn't resist showing Stanford he's not the ultimate authority. "The couple would like to do the tasting tomorrow afternoon with their family."

A frown pulls at his lips, and his mustache twitches. "Afternoons are our busy time with tours and tastings, but we could start after they have an early dinner. I'd rather have them when they've got food in their stomach."

"I'll let him know." I type out the message and stuff my phone away. We're almost at Sy's.

I'm looking forward to this meeting. I have a good idea, and I think Bryce will work with me even if I don't put out. But I'm dreading walking in there and finding out exactly how much he'll push for, or what he'll want me to trade for his help. He can be questionable, but he's respected my *no*s before.

Durban parks next to a rack of kayaks. Only one other black pickup is in the lot. Any of the seasonal workers must have the day off. We're far enough from civilization and right next to a river in the rain that I'm grateful I asked Durban.

This trip does double duty. I also wanted to get some time alone with him that Stanford couldn't interfere with.

We're here. I'm on. Time to go build my position as event coordinator. I stare at the entrance of the small building and chew on my lower lip. Acid splashes into my throat. I'm probably overreacting.

Durban unbuckles. "I'm going in with you."

"No. No, it's fine." I grip the charm of my necklace. I can't tank one of my few options for work in the community. "As long as I know you're out here, and he knows, I doubt he'll try anything. I don't know if he would anyway, but guys who do that stuff only corner women when they know they can get away with it."

Durban's gaze sharpens.

I give him a tight smile and hop out. "I'm sure it'll be fine."

"Stay by the window so I can see you."

"If I can." A pit in the center of my chest smolders. This isn't like before. Bryce has only ever been persistent. He won't ask me for favors as part of the cross-promotion. He won't corner me between the wall and filing cabinet. Will he?

Stomach acid churns so hard I want to double over. Maybe this wasn't a good idea.

Durban's watching me, and while he's concerned for

my safety, I'm going to look like a fool if I hop into the passenger seat and tell him to floor it. He's going to ask why, and I don't want to get into it.

I suck in a deep breath and enter the office. Shelves to my left are full of sunscreen and trinkets. Coolers filled with water bottles and drinks line the wall. Bryce is at the counter, tapping away on the laptop.

He's handsome in an outdoorsman way. His square jaw and buzz cut match the sunglasses tan lines already forming on the sides of his face. I've never been attracted to him, and that might be because he used to tease me on the playground because I sucked at kickball and football. I told him to get on a horse and we'd see who's better.

I wish I could be doing this meeting on horseback. It's helped me deal with Stanford even though I stress that he'll hurt Hailstorm or January trying to live out my wedding dream.

Bryce looks up and grins. "Campbell. Nice to see you again."

I take a deep breath, and suddenly, I'm back in my old office, another good-looking guy smiling at me, but his is predatory, like he's got plans I won't approve of. Bryce is looking at me like he expected me, like he's happy to see me. But how do I know his intentions are real until it's too late?

My heart rate climbs up so high and hard that my heart might slam right out of my chest. Words echo in my head.

You can go ahead and tell her, but we both know who she'll believe.

Bryce's gaze flickers. "Campbell?"

Your job depends on making me happy. What are you willing to risk?

My breathing becomes strangled. A band constricts around my chest.

You have such pretty lips.

I squeeze my eyes shut. I can't do this. "I'm sorry."

I bolt out of the shack.

Durban

The rain has let up, and I'm glaring at the window when Campbell blasts out of the door. Her eyes are wide, frantic, and she goes in the wrong direction first before stopping short, her head turning side to side like she can't figure out where she is.

I'm out of the truck and by her side in an instant. "What's wrong? What'd he do?"

She's shaking her head. I grip her shoulders and try to catch her eye, but her gaze is darting around and she's gasping for breath.

"Is she okay?" Bryce asks behind me.

"What the hell happened in there?" I holler at him.

He holds his hands out at his sides, his expression poleaxed. "She walked in and then ran right out."

"It's not—" She wheezes in a breath. "It's not him. I'm sorry." Her breathing shudders but grows steadier. She's still not looking at me. "God, I'm so sorry."

I want to rip Bryce's head off, but he's right. She wasn't gone from my sight long enough for anything to happen. Yet there's something about him, or about this place, that caused this. "I got her," I say to him.

He reads into my tone and backs away. "No problem. I'll be right inside if you need anything. Didn't realize you two were together."

I glare at him. Not the time or the issue. He shrugs and heads back to the office.

Campbell's breathing evens out, but a tear streaks down her face. I gently wipe it away with the pad of my thumb. The rain starts again. A soft patter hits the ground and slaps the river's surface.

"I feel so stupid." She sniffs and her gray eyes lift to mine. "I dragged you out here for nothing. And he saw it."

I want to haul her inside the pickup, but just as quickly as the rain started, it stops. She might quit talking if we do too much. "What happened?"

"Nothing. Literally nothing." But she glances away.

"Something did though."

She rolls her lips in and her brows furrow. "Yes and no. It's nothing."

After that night in the bar, I might've believed her bluff. I might've written it off as an impulsive Campbell not thinking about others and doing what she wants. But now I know the alarm-setting Campbell. The woman who's diligently working for her ex and putting up with his pretentious family to prove herself. That girl doesn't do things for only herself.

"Tell me what happened," I say softly.

Her pink tongue flicks out to lick her bottom lip. "My old boss's husband used to do a lot for the company."

A growl rips from my chest.

She nods, her eyes shimmering. "Such a stereotype. I liked him at first. Trusted him. Then his jokes got more uncomfortable and soon he started coming into the office when she wasn't there."

"Were you alone?"

"That came later." A tear streaks from each eye. I cup her face and smooth the drops away.

"Did that fucker hurt you?" I'll go to Seattle right now and find a place to dispose of the body on my way back.

"No. He was insulting. And he was right. My boss would fire me before she listened to how the love of her life kept brushing against my ass, kept pushing how close to stand by me, until he finally cornered me and squeezed a tit."

"Tell me you kneed him in the balls."

"I punched him. Gave him a shiner to explain to his wife, and then I quit. Because I refused to get fired. He was a lawyer and knew how to work the system. They'd run me out of there, and I'd need therapy after." She hooks her hands on my wrists. "Then I went home, prepared to unload to the person who's supposed to be there for me, only to see his bags packed and he tells me he's leaving me for my cousin. The cousin I thought was my best friend, and who I thought moved to Seattle to be closer to me."

She dealt with it all alone? "We need to throw them all in the river."

She chuckles before dissolving into sobs. I pull her into my arms. She clutches my shirt at the sides and cries.

"Fuck them." I want to shout, but I speak softly.

"Fuck them all. Walk away from this wedding and have no regrets."

She shakes her head. "I'm not leaving another obligation." Her voice is muffled against my chest.

"You didn't leave. You protected yourself."

She pulls away and I just want to tug her back into me. How many times has she absorbed blame she didn't deserve? I'm guilty of believing the spoiled girl only cared about herself.

"No one will see it that way, and Daddy would start trouble that I just want to forget."

"They deserve to get taken down."

"I emailed all my coworkers about what happened and left a bad review. He threatened me with a lawsuit and I told him to go ahead. I'm telling the truth, and he should've targeted someone whose family isn't wealthy."

Good for her. I start to smile, but something in her gaze stops me.

She bats away another tear. "Didn't stop him from using his connections. I applied everywhere in Washington, Idaho, and Oregon. Even Northern California. Never heard back. It's why I've gotta make it work here. It's why I can't let more bad word of mouth spread about me. I have nowhere else to go."

This is so fucking unfair. Her old boss should lose her business and get a goddamn divorce. The asshole's behavior should be made public and he should be the one struggling to find work. But that's not Campbell's way. She seems flighty and out of touch, but she's actually alarmingly realistic.

She looks over her shoulder at the office. "I can't go back in there. How embarrassing."

"I can go with you."

Her shoulders hang like she's defeated. "I shouldn't need anyone, and Bryce is going to spread rumors about us as it is."

"Work Foster House in there. It'll explain why we're together."

"Don't you have to get approval?"

"I trust you can figure out a reason that's so good the guys can't refuse."

Her smile is like the sun coming out. "Alcohol and white-water rafting? What could pair better?"

I jut my chin toward the entrance. "Lead the way. I'm not going anywhere."

CHAPTER TEN

Campbell

A day later, I'm back at the distillery for my meeting with all the heads who can make it. They've agreed to meet before the Baldwin tasting. Little embarrassment from my breakdown yesterday lingers, and it's because Durban treated me so kindly. He understood and he didn't argue. Thanks to him, I didn't drag my feet to this meeting today. I didn't even dread facing Durban. He's the support, the reassurance, I didn't get that day I quit and went home to my life falling apart.

Lane's leaning on a railing that circles a mash tank. Durban's standing behind me like he's my bodyguard. Iverson's already done for the day and has given his opinion to Durban, but Haven and Cruz are on either side of me.

"We do a monthly rafting and tasting weekend with Sy's?" Lane asks. Durban doesn't have to tell me that Lane's the unofficial leader. His is the final say. My years in the event world have taught me how to tell who really runs the show. Haven and Durban defer to Iverson, and along with Cruz, they all turn to Lane.

"Yes, that's correct. Rafting first, of course. No alcohol until the outdoor events are done. Rafting and Tasting is the working title." I saved face yesterday with both Durban and Bryce. All it took was having a break-down in front of a man who seems to keep witnessing me at my worst. Crying with the peaceful sound of a flowing river as a backdrop, about things I've gotten drunk over, made me think of how to combine the two, but in a safe way.

To Bryce's credit, he pretended my fleeing from his office never happened, and with Durban there, he was on his best behavior. He was also interested in hosting a company team-building event that included the hot new distillery in the area.

"You've done recruiting events before?" Lane asks.

I nod. "A lot of businesses are willing to host events, but they don't always have the bandwidth for planning and recruitment. That's where I come in. Everything will be done through Foster House and Sy's Water Adventures though, so whoever is your designated contact, they'll sign off on everything for me." I try not to twist my fingers. Durban knows why I don't want my name attached to anything. I need more of a base so my old boss and her husband can't undermine me.

Lane glances at the others but settles his gaze on Durban. "You okay to be that guy?"

I'm afraid to look.

"No problem," Durban says without hesitation.

I twist enough to face him. "I don't want to take you away from your duties."

He shrugs. Crap. Will it be my fault if he gets pigeonholed into PR and marketing and loses the chance to experiment with the products like he wants to?

Wait—I can work with that. "What if you make something special for this group?" I ask.

Surprise lifts Durban's brows. "Like what?"

I think quickly. I don't know much about distilling and timelines, but I also can't have the task getting assigned to someone else. "I don't know. Something you haven't done before that you can essentially beta test on this crowd? Something new."

His focus on me intensifies. "I see." He shifts his attention to the others. "I can do a barrel-aged vodka infusion."

"I say go for it." Cruz checks the time. "The wedding crew is going to be here soon, and then we're on, Haven."

The two leave.

The alarm goes off on my phone. I switch it off. "I'd better get in there too."

I chance a peek at Durban. His dark gaze swirls with something I can't identify. We haven't made plans to do anything during the tasting. Has he lost interest? Did my breakdown yesterday scare him off?

I'm wearing a dress with my ankle boots for nothing. At least I look good, and I'm on the clock, so I follow in the same direction as Haven and Cruz.

The guys are behind the bar, digging out Glencairn glasses and smaller ones that are more like plastic shot glasses. They're murmuring to each other about tasting order and how much each person can get served.

Cars start pulling into the lot. My parents offered a couple of the staff as drivers. It's only going to be the happy couple, Stanford's parents, and some of his cousins. January's parents won't return again until the ceremony, and Sydney told me she was waiting until the final hour to show because of work.

Stanford's got January tucked into his side as they walk toward the entrance. She has her hand lovingly on his stomach, and her face has a flush I know all too well. Freshly orgasmed.

Old tension and crankiness ignite behind my ribs. Stanford's doing it on purpose. All the time we were together, I thought I was in love, when he really just resented me. I was his trophy, and now he's trying to prove he's got a shinier version.

This is going to be a long night.

I greet them all with a smile as they enter, my cheeks starting to ache much quicker than usual.

"Priscilla, hello. Chester, you'll love their lineup."

They both ignore me, and I want to snarl at them, to hold my hands up in claws like I'm going to swipe at them, to do something unhinged to finally earn how they think about me.

Instead, I nod politely to an aunt and uncle I've never met. Then a few cousins of Stanford's. All of them avoid my gaze.

Once they line the bar, I hover at the edge of the room by the door to the merch store. Haven launches into his spiel about Foster House's origins, its goals with whiskey and humanitarian efforts, and then this site, Foster House Gold. Lane's pickup pulls out of the lot. The only staff remaining are the two tasting hosts and Durban.

A wall of caramel-whiskey-scented heat surrounds me and there's a light touch at my elbow.

Durban leans down to whisper in my ear. "Now a good time to talk about the special product just for Rafting and Tasting?"

My hopes take another dip, but chatting about plans is better than standing here like I'm invisible. "Yeah. Your brothers have it handled."

The tasting is supposed to go an hour. He cocks his head toward the door and leads me out. He takes the stairs up to his office, and what he said before about me on his desk runs through my head.

My nipples pucker and heat flushes my body. Is this going to happen after all?

When I reach the top of the stairs, he takes my hand and strums his thumb along the back.

He pulls me into his office and doesn't bother closing the door. "Did you think I forgot?"

"I thought you changed your mind."

"No fucking way." He lifts me to a seat on the edge of his neat desk like I'm nothing more than a doll, and a thrill blasts through my veins. There's a miniature bottle of whiskey on the edge of the desk.

He twists the cap off and sets the edge at my lips. "Didn't want you to miss out on everything."

Not only did he not forget, he planned this. If I wasn't soaking my underwear before, I am now. To mess with him, I lick the rim of the bottle.

A deep rumble sounds in the room. "You're playing with a loaded gun, Belle."

"What exactly is that gun loaded with?"

With another growl, he tips the bottle and whiskey coats my tongue, waking my taste buds. Holding my gaze, he takes a pull, sets the bottle down, and claims my mouth.

I open for him automatically. Warm whiskey trickles into my mouth, and the flavor is softer but richer with him in it. I moan and wrap my arms around his neck. He grips my thighs and pushes himself between my legs, deepening the kiss.

I've been waiting for this. I'm wrapped around him, and he's all restrained power and solid muscle. Caramel and oaky tones hit my tongue with each stroke of his. I'll never be able to see a bottle and not think of how he scrambled my brains with nothing but a kiss.

He pushes my skirt up, but keeps going to brush his fingers over my abdomen. His touch is electric, sizzling along my skin and waking me up in ways I never thought could happen. When he reaches my breasts, I arch into him, breaking the kiss. I need that pressure.

He works a path along my jaw and down my neck. "I know you're going to taste so fucking good."

I take a second to catch on that he's not talking about the kiss. He yanks me to the edge of the desk. His knees hit the floor, leaving his head right where I need to be satisfied.

Windows surround us. Anyone who takes the stairs will see me with my dress bunched around my waist, my knees spread, and Durban between them. My heart pounds harder.

He kisses the inside of my thighs and energy zips from my core and up my spine. "No one's going to see us."

"What if your brother or Cruz comes to find us?"

"They won't." He grips my hips and drags his mouth and nose up my leg. "I want to rip this fucking underwear off."

I picked one of my favorite pairs this morning.

They're lacy and sheer and a poor decision for actual, functional use. They're perfect for a guy to see. Right now, I hate them too.

"But I'm not going to." He pulls the fabric away from my pussy with his teeth and lets it go. I can feel how damp it is on the recoil. I soaked through them before he even put my ass on the table.

He licks me through the fabric and a shudder racks my body. A moan slips out, sounding loud in his office.

He brushes his strong hands up my legs, the calloused, roughened fingertips rasping against my skin. He moves my underwear aside, his hot breath gusting over me. Everything's so sensitized, I'll come from that alone.

"I fucking need this." His voice is ragged, his eyes ravenous when he looks up at me.

"I'm the one who's going to come." I sound breathless.

He brushes his thumb over me, dragging it through my wetness. "Yeah, you fucking are."

He traces the path his thumb took with his tongue, and everything inside me coils tighter. I drop my head back and my knees fall open wider. He reverses his route until he lands on my clit and then he's ruthless. Pleasure courses through my blood, each wave higher than before.

"Oh God, Durban." It's not going to take long. I've been wound up tight for too long. And with each stroke of his tongue, he loosens me up until I'm rolling my hips against him.

I put my boots on his shoulders, keeping the heels from digging into him, but he continues devouring me like it gives him life. Then he pulls back. I whimper from the loss of sensation. I've never been this needy before.

"Are you wondering why I stopped?" he asks roughly.

I nod, and he teases my entrance with his finger. I have to be dripping thanks to how much he's worked me up, but I don't care. I want more.

I try to rock forward, but he stops me with his shoulders.

"I like you like this." He pushes his finger in just a little more, filling me, but not enough. I'm vibrating on a razor's edge of need. Just a little more and I'll splinter apart in the most delicious of ways. "Your eyes are shining and your lips are extra plump. See how your legs are shaking?" He pushes in another inch and it's like he took a tuning fork to my limbs. "You should feel how hard I am."

"Does it hurt?" I roll my hips, seeking more, but he's withholding it. Is this what he's going through?

"Goddamn agony, Belle." His eyelids slide down and he dives back in.

I bark out a cry that I hope doesn't carry down the stairs, but with his finger thrusting inside of me and his tongue lapping at me, I have a hard time caring. The peak is within my reach and he's propelling me there both faster and slower than I'm ready for.

"Durban. Yes. Please, I need—" I catapult over the edge, fracturing apart and exploding outward. I have to bite my lower lip to keep from shouting. I squeak and gasp instead, not at all ashamed of how I sound.

He continues licking and plunging his finger in and out. I rock on the desk, digging my heels into him, stretching the pleasure out as far as it will go, and with Durban, it becomes a long damn time.

I nearly collapse backward, but Durban must sense I've reached my limit. A tumble off furniture will draw attention when the tasting room is right below us.

He shifts my underwear back into place and places a kiss over it, soaking the fabric even more than before. "Just as amazing as I thought." He gently lowers my legs down and prowls up my body.

"Did you? Really think of it?" I brush the spots of dust off his shoulders from my boots.

"If I told you how much, you'd think I was a creep." He wipes off his face with the back of his wrist.

"It's not creepy if it's hot."

A raspy chuckle leaves him. "In that case, morning, noon, and night."

I like that answer. I use the end of my skirt to wipe off any lingering trace of me from his face. The intimacy of the gesture startles me. So does the way he seems to be looking right into me. I want to shrivel against his heavy-lidded gaze, while at the same time, I'm unfurling, ready to be seen for who I really am. Durban sees something else, something not many people take the time to view. I am whatever is convenient for them, but he's taking the time to get to know *me*.

"After I brought you to my house," he says almost hesitantly, "I was a goner."

"I was just a drunk girl." Not my finest hour.

"You were hurting."

I was in a lot of pain that night. The unfairness of it all had crashed down on me and I tried drinking my problems away. I would've made more pain for myself if it hadn't been for him.

Satisfaction hums through my body, echoing loudly thanks to the empty feeling inside me. I liked this. I'd do it again in a heartbeat. Now even, but we don't have the time. Yet that's all it is. I can't have more complications.

He picks up the little bottle of whiskey balancing on the edge of the desk and offers me a drink first. There's less than half left, and I leave some for him. Will I have another chance to siphon some from him?

He finishes it off, and I'm fascinated by the way his throat works when he swallows. Then he props his hands on either side of me. "I'm not going to be able to drink that line again without tasting you."

"I can't believe we did that." We did that during the tasting, with Stanford and his bride and his family underneath us. I'm feeling smug.

"Believe it." His mouth is close to mine again. The whiskers of his mustache tickle my lips. "When's the next shindig?"

A full-body quiver runs through me. "They're taking the weekend to go to Glacier and Stanford wasn't able to justify dragging me along. I told them I need the weekend to set up the cake tasting with Elodie, and I have another event Monday." When a question flickers in his gaze, I brush imaginary dust off his shoulders. "Hookers and Booze night."

"Is that the name Edna's going with?"

"It kind of stuck, and it makes me want to dig out my grandma's crochet hooks."

His eyes soften, and I really like that it's from me. It's not the look of consternation he used to wear around me. "I'm covering for Iverson all weekend, but I'll be here on Monday with Haven. I told Eden I'd help serve her and her friends."

Lucky club.

He rubs the pad of his thumb over my lower lip. Heat coalesces in his eyes. "It's all puffy from biting it."

"You shouldn't have made me come so hard."

He grins, and the urge to take off my underwear and throw it at him makes me grip the edge of the desk. His eyes dance and twinkle, and whatever pheromones he's putting off are stamping themselves into my DNA. Or however that works. His ex could tell me.

That thought dulls my inner glow.

He traces my silver necklace with his fingers. "You're always wearing this. It must mean a lot."

He noticed? "My parents gave it to me in high school. Stanford's mom once told me that I shouldn't wear it or my clients might not think they're dealing with a professional. So I'm wearing it every day until the wedding."

The corner of his mouth tips up. "The quietest of fuck-yous. I like it." He runs his fingertips along the charm. "You need to get back down there," he says. "Every time they make you feel like you're nothing, think about how loud you could've been with my mouth on your pussy."

My belly clenches and I'm ready for him again. Yet as much as I thrill at his words, they're a reminder of what we really are. Nothing but a wedding and a whiskey bargain.

CHAPTER ELEVEN

Durban

Outside Iverson's pickup window, puffy, white cumulus clouds float across the sky. With the Baldwins out of town, Kacey's with her grandparents and Jamison's resting while we meet. So Iverson is driving us to town. Instead of meeting with the guys at the distillery, we're getting out for the afternoon. Normally, we'd do this Monday when we're closed, but Elodie also closes the bakery on Monday and we have to talk to her about some collaboration ideas.

My gaze keeps snagging on the clouds. Plump, just like Campbell's lips after she got done coming. Hot blood starts pumping lower in my body. Her breathy moans kept me up all night. I jacked off in the shower last night, and then I had to do it again this morning.

I'm not looking for another relationship, but I'm beyond ready for exploring Campbell.

There are no wedding activities until next Thursday.

The luncheon. It's taking place in the pavilion if the weather holds out. How am I going to get Campbell alone to take the edge off?

Did what happened in my office help her get through the rest of the tasting?

Haven said the group was uptight as hell until he got some drinks flowing through them. Then they were just obnoxious. He also cited some tension between the couple when Stanford kept glancing at the spot Campbell vacated when I dragged her upstairs and settled myself between her thighs.

A guy could live his entire life in that paradise.

"Hey, buddy." Iverson squints at me before shifting his attention back to the road. "You still with me?"

"I'm right here."

"In body only. Where's your mind been?"

"Lots of stuff in the works." I let him fill in the details so I don't have to lie to him. I'm dreaming of stripping down his sister-in-law and burying myself inside of her.

"The rafting thing?"

"That and the wedding." And how I'm going to get Campbell to myself. Should I tell her to skip underwear before the luncheon?

"Hell of a thing, but I hate to say Campbell might be onto something. William said he hears Stanford and January bickering more."

"How so?"

"Jamison talked to her mom last night, and Christine heard January snap at Stanford. She demanded to know why Campbell has to be at all the events."

"She's the one organizing what they want to do." As

angry as I want to be toward January, a chuckle still bubbles up. "Nothing's even gone wrong."

"All except for a few rain delays that make Stanford scramble to figure out what the hell to do to get close to Campbell."

I sit straighter. We're almost to town, but I need to finish this conversation now. "You don't think she would get back together with him? If he and January don't make it to the altar?"

"Nah. She has more sense than that. More than anyone gives her credit for." He gives me a sidelong glance.

"I give her credit."

"Sure."

I give her more credit now. I want to give her a whole lot more. "Fine. I've seen how hard she works, but you can't blame me for judging her based on some earlier interactions." I blame myself.

"You wouldn't have written off someone you considered more cerebral. You didn't write off Natalie."

"She's older, for one. Finishing her second PhD." She might be done. What do I know about graduate school timelines? The thought tastes bitter on my tongue.

"I know she is. You want to know how I know?"

I shake my head.

"You'll tell me. And if you don't, I'm sure she will."

I kick up an eyebrow. He's never said a disparaging word about Natalie before, and it's not like he's seen her for the last four years. "I knew you didn't like her."

"When you first started seeing her, she was, shit, she was intolerable. So were you."

"Fuck, Iverson. Lay it all out there."

He drives past the businesses on the edge of town.

The mechanic shop across from the small car sales lot. A massage and tanning place. A gas station with a small laundromat attached. We'll be at Dee's Sweets soon.

"Just sayin'. You aren't yourself when you're with her."

I haven't been with her in a long time, and I won't be. I still haven't told Iverson about the breakup and I won't now. He'll be less likely to think I'm messing around with his sister-in-law, and I'll have Campbell to myself.

Of course, I'll also get more time to dwell on what he said. Intolerable? Maybe I was. Having someone like Natalie interested in me after how I was raised? Yeah, I might've overlooked a little. After hearing Iverson, maybe I overlooked a lot.

Maybe that's why I like being around Campbell. We've been underestimated in our lives, and together, we can just . . . be.

When I don't respond after a minute, he only grunts and pulls into a spot in front of the bakery. A familiar blue SUV is parked off to the side. Is Campbell here? I can't see her through the big bakery windows. Lane and Haven are already at a table, a mug of something in their hands. I crane my head to look up and down the street.

Is she at Bryce's downtown office?

"Whatcha looking for?" Iverson kills the engine, peering out the windshield to find out for himself.

"No one."

He cocks a brow.

"Nothing," I amend.

He doesn't make a move to get out. "You've been acting weird lately."

I screw my face up. "You just said I act like an ass

around Natalie, and now I'm weird with you. What the hell, Ivy?"

He holds up his hands. "Got it. Just sayin'. I'm here if you need to talk."

And what would I say? That I don't think about Natalie much because not only does she not want to talk to me, but I'm focused on gray eyes, a husky voice, and plump pink lips? By the way, all I can think about is when I can taste Campbell's soaked pussy again? I'm thinking of naming a single barrel after her hot wet cunt because she's that sweet and addicting, and if I could capture her essence in a spirit, we could make a lot of money, except I'd keep every bottle for myself?

No. A conversation like that would give Iverson a heart attack before he beat the shit out of me for fucking around with his sister-in-law while his wife is trying to finish her at-risk pregnancy. Iverson considers Campbell family, and since he does, so does Haven. I would've been better off thinking of her that way too.

I don't.

With one last glance at her car, I get out. There's no pretty woman with silky chestnut hair anywhere in the bakery. All the rest of the women inside could have pillow lips and I wouldn't notice.

I aim for the counter. A big dose of caffeine might dull the edge my mood is on.

Cruz is at the cash register. I stop behind him in line while Iverson hangs back at the table. A red-faced Elodie is looking anywhere but at Cruz. Her dark hair is gathered back into a loose twist, and she's wearing a frosting-stained apron. Cruz's stance is wide, his hands stuffed in his jeans pockets, but he still towers over her. He's got a black puffy vest on over his long-sleeved yellow shirt.

"So what's the difference between angel food cake and devil's food?" he asks.

Elodie blinks at him like she can't tell if he's speaking the same language as her. Then she turns around to study the menu mounted over the counter behind her.

"I-I don't have angel food." Utter confusion fills her voice.

"You have a devil's food cupcake. Why not angel food?" I can hear the grin in his voice, but Elodie doesn't know him well enough to decide if his teasing is good-natured.

"Angel food is a white cake, but devil's food has chocolate," she finally answers.

"Then why call it devil's food? Why not just call it chocolate?"

I'm about to break in and tell him to order and let her get back to work, but she pushes up her thick-framed glasses. "Um, devil's food is richer than plain chocolate. Along with using cocoa powder for the flavor, I add a pinch of coffee to mine. Increased baking soda makes it fluffier. I don't offer angel food cake unless the strawberries are excellent, and even then, I'd rather make shortcake."

"Why's that?" Cruz asks.

She blinks again. "I like it more."

He chuckles. "Fair enough. I'll take a devil's food cupcake and a lemon-lime soda."

"Put mine on his tab," I joke from behind him.

"We don't do tabs," she says quietly in her firm Elodie way.

"He's being cheap," Cruz says. "Double it and he can have what I'm having, since I've got such good taste."

The guy would flirt with a rock, but he seems unrepentant around Elodie Palmer. He doesn't tease her sister, Clem, quite as unrepentantly, but then Clem is more relaxed around him than Elodie. A brushfire blazes across the baker's cheeks. She rings up his order and serves us the food.

"You've gotta leave her alone," I murmur to him as we cross to the booth the others are in. "She's going to combust or implode."

"I'm going to crack that shell." He gestures for me to slide in beside Haven and grabs a chair from an empty table nearby. "Just watch. Campbell said she'd be right back, and Elodie will talk a mile a minute to her."

I ignore everything he said but one thing. "Campbell was here?" Damn, I missed her?

"For a minute," he says. "She's gotta talk about wedding catering or something."

Lane swipes his finger through the rippled frosting on Cruz's cupcake. Cruz lunges for him, but Lane gets out of the way fast enough.

Lane licks the chocolate off and grins. "Is he still cranking about how he can't wrap Elodie around his finger?"

"Again?" Haven asks.

Cruz scowls and peels his cupcake open. The apples of his cheeks flush. Damn. Does he have a thing for the shy baker, or does his pride just hurt?

"He's charmed the whole damn town," Lane says. "But Elodie gives him the side-eye."

"Smart girl," Haven says and grins when the frown is aimed his way.

"I learn shit when she talks, but she barely speaks around me," Cruz complains.

Their voices turn into a background drone. Campbell

breezes through the entrance, flicking her long, loose hair over her shoulder. She shoves her sunglasses to the top of her head. The way she's dressed makes my mouth dry.

It's warmer out today than it has been. A baby-blue tank top with spaghetti straps hits the top of her jeans, teasing me with a strip of bare flesh across her abdomen. Her hips roll as she walks and she waves when Elodie spots her.

Goddamn, it's like a ray of sunshine barged right into the little bakery.

I miss what the guys are saying, but Cruz is staring at me. His eyes dance and the grin is a warning. Fuck.

He licks all his frosting off the top of the cupcake with one stroke, that infuriating grin still in place.

Campbell sees us and her smile widens. "A meeting of the Foster House minds."

"We have a sweet tooth," Cruz says, smacking his lips, "and a craving that can only be fulfilled by sugar or spirits. For most of us." His mischievous attention is still on me.

She folds her arms, a smile dancing across her pretty lips. "That would make a really good tagline for— I don't know for what."

"Got any ideas?" Cruz asks me.

I shoot him a scowl. "Potato chips."

He snorts and the rest of the guys chuckle, hopefully oblivious to Cruz giving me a hard time.

She stuffs a thumb over her shoulder. "I have to pick up an order for the ranch tomorrow, but I hear Elodie's going to be featuring some Foster House items?"

Lane nods. "Soon there'll be whiskey frosting, cupcakes filled with gin custard, and a vodka glaze for sweet breads. We're collaborating for the street fair in Billings next month too."

"If we need a kickoff event," I say, "we'll let you know." I'll make sure of it. I know she threw out the idea of a special product for the Rafting and Tasting event just for me.

Her gaze warms and a blush stains her cheeks. "I'd appreciate it."

"Yeah, actually." Lane folds his hands together. "That's a good idea. A launch event. When you and Elodie are both free, give us a call."

The delight playing across Campbell's face makes my whole damn day. "You really mean that?" she asks.

"As long as Elodie's on board." Lane glances at all of us. Cruz and Haven nod.

"I'm game," Iverson says. "We're supposed to be the fun and creative outlet for Foster House, so let's do it."

"Absolutely," I say.

Campbell's smile widens. "I'll talk to Elodie and get back to you."

I force myself to keep my gaze on the countertop when she walks away and not on the sway of her hips. Out of the corner of my eye, Cruz smirks and shoves half the cupcake in his mouth.

I ignore him too. Fucker.

Campbell

I'm sitting at a four-top table in Foster House's tasting room, unraveling a row of crochet stitches on my dishcloth. It's supposed to be a half double crochet stitch and not a double crochet, but I got too distracted by Edna's conversation with her longtime friends and the dirty jokes they're telling.

Edna cruises through each of her rows, barely glancing at her square to place a stitch. "Then the young, curvy nurse came out and said, 'I don't know what you're talking about. He doesn't have *swan* tattooed on his penis. It says *Saskatchewan*!' "

The older ladies guffaw, and the one adult grandson present turns beet red, concentrating hard on his blanket. I frown for a moment and exchange a glance with an equally flummoxed Clem.

"Edna," Haven says from behind the bar. "You're going to traumatize me. Each one of you."

Elodie covers her mouth and giggles. When she notices my and Clem's confusion, her face turns scarlet and she intently focuses on the square she's making.

Finally, the punch line dawns on me. Mostly because Edna's talking about how her daughter heard that joke way too young, and then when she learned about puberty and erections, she shouted, "Oh, I get it! Saskatchewan!"

The ladies roar and I start to snicker.

"I can't believe it took me that long," Clem says. She's not making a blanket or dishcloth like me. She brought a crochet kit and is working on an elephant's leg. She peeks around. "Can I confess that my Friday nights are not as wild as this Monday evening?"

"Wild Friday nights are overrated." Elodie says it in such a sage way that Clem and I wait for more.

When she doesn't continue, I shrug. "I have to agree. My last rowdy Friday night, I got drunk and made a fool out of myself. I almost put myself in a dangerous situation too with some of Bryce's seasonal workers."

"That is not your fault," Elodie says, her tone heated. "It's those guys' fault. I bet they thought they could take advantage of you. The fact is, drunk girls should be safe from all that and not blamed."

Clem's dark brows rise. Mine are probably just as high. "Totally agree," I say, "but it scares me to think that I was too tipsy to read a lot of the signs. I think they thought they were helping protect me from Durban at first."

Clem stalls, her mouth forming a troubled line. "Durban's the kind of guy people cross the street *toward*."

Ain't that the truth. "Yeah, but that's because they want to be the ones to jump him."

There's no response. I look up.

Elodie's biting her lip.

Clem screws her face up. "I feel like it's wrong of me to agree with that, him being my boss and all."

"I'm off the market," Elodie says. "So I plead the Fifth."

"I didn't realize you were seeing someone." In school, she was always a quiet girl, but since she moved home, she's been so private that it can be hard to converse with her.

"I'm not." She leaves it at that.

Durban enters the room from the distillery. His dark gaze sweeps over the small crowd, touching on Edna's impressive, colorful stack of skeins, to the table full of goodies that Elodie brought, and finally to us. His gaze warms when it lands on me and we share a secret smile.

From the amused look that Clem and Elodie exchange, maybe it's not so secret.

I almost regret not wearing a dress, but there's no wedding plans today. Just me patiently waiting for Durban to help me unwind. I threw on a loose pink blouse and some gray linen pants, but the heat in his eyes makes me feel like I'm wearing the lacy underwear he spared the other day.

Haven tosses him a rag and comes out from around the bar. "You ladies have a good evening."

"Hot date?" Glory, one of Edna's friends, asks.

"I just had it with all of you." He executes a bow that looks elegant despite his jeans, cowboy boots, and plain black shirt.

A chorus of awws and laughter rings out.

"Take a few cookies," Edna says.

"Don't mind if I do." Haven grabs a few and leaves.

We continue to crochet and chat. Durban keeps us filled on water and mocktails. We each had a drink when we first arrived and then switched to nonalcoholic stuff. One by one, the women take off.

Elodie, Clem, and I are gathering bags of yarn to haul out for Edna when Durban swoops in and lifts almost all of them in one hand.

"Oh, say." Edna sighs wistfully. "There was a time I could do that."

"Gotta let the rest of us shine once in a while." He follows her out. Elodie's the only one who snagged a bag, so she trails after him. If I walk out that door, my night is over and it's only early evening.

"I can stay and help clean up." Clem scoots chairs in.

"It's your day off. Go home. I can do it."

She hesitates. "I would feel guilty, but I think there's

something else you want to take care of." Her gaze strays out the window, where Durban's very fine ass is on display as he loads the back of Edna's car.

"We're colleagues." If colleagues spread themselves out on the other's desk.

"It's best I stay out of my boss's business." She hitches her tote bag full of yarn and hooks it over her shoulder. "Even though I want to know it all."

"There's nothing to tell." There's so much to tell but I have to keep it all to myself. I'm glad I've reconnected with the Palmer sisters since I've returned home. When I lost my job, my fiancé, and my best friend, I also got dropped by a ton of other friends. There weren't enough threads connecting us to survive the severing of the other parts of my life.

Clementine and Elodie are two more reasons why I want to make it work at home. But I don't quite trust them with the agreement between me and Durban. My job and reputation are on the line. So are his.

Or I just want a reason to keep us a secret, to have fewer people giving him their opinions about me, like all of Stanford's friends and family did for him.

Durban enters and our gazes connect. Aware of Clem's observations, I look away.

"Thanks for cutting me loose," Clem says like she doesn't notice. "See you next month, Campbell?"

I nod. "I think Edna's down to make this a thing."

Durban grabs some empty glasses. "I believe her words were 'You could've rolled me in honey and tossed me into a hornet's nest and I'd have still had a good time.'"

Clem's grin is fond. "Nothing scares that woman except for taxes and sitting still. Have a good night."

When she leaves, Durban doesn't move. "You don't have to help clean up."

"No, it's . . ." Oh. Doesn't he want me here? He did say that our arrangement is just that. He's helping me de-stress and get silent, orgasmic revenge on Stanford and January. His interest in me doesn't go beyond that. "Okay. Sure. Thanks again."

"Do you want to stay?"

"I've got other things to do."

"We all do. But you already put in the time and effort to set this up. You don't have to keep working." He tugs out a chair with the toe of his boot. "Sit."

Since I don't want to go home and hear my parents chat about wedding logistics and the ranch operations— if they're even home—I do as he says.

"What do you want to drink? Another limeade?"

The tasting room serves vodka mojitos, but I almost prefer the mock version. I get in less trouble that way. "I've had a lot of sugar. I need something more solid."

"Like a good steak?" he asks as he rounds the counter with an armload of glasses.

My stomach rumbles. Elodie's baked goods are to die for, and the load of bread I bought from her is on my passenger seat, but a well-seasoned steak would hit the spot. "I could grill one when I get home, but Daddy hates it when someone else uses his grill."

"I'll cook you one." He pauses while filling the drawer dishwasher like he can't believe he offered.

I can't either. "That's not necessary."

"You got other plans?"

"Avoiding anything related to the wedding."

He smirks. "Let me finish this, and you can follow me to my place."

"Your place?" I ask, feigning ignorance to hide my racing heart. "You live around here?"

Humor fills his eyes. "It comes in handy when I bring drunk girls home."

"Mm. It's a rampant problem."

He shoves the door closed. "It's only happened once, but she was polite enough not to vomit at my house."

I wince and he starts chuckling. An evening that should've been my most humiliating, and we're laughing about it. I'm not proud of myself, but looking back I can't think of a better way it could've turned out.

CHAPTER TWELVE

Durban

We decide to eat on my porch. The cozy setting evokes
a lot of expectations I had for this house, and it's tying
my insides into a pretzel.

It's only a meal, I remind myself for the hundredth
time. As I grill us some rib eyes, she sips on ice water
and I nurse a whiskey neat while we chat about the
crochet club, my house, and the origins of the gold mine
and how it landed in Hennessy hands.

"Your family has deep ties to the land," she says as I
set down our plates of steaming meat.

I nod. "Dad was really proud his family was able to
buy it from the mining company. He always said our
roots don't run deep; they make up the earth."

"The whole town is glad it stayed in Hennessy
hands."

"That's good to hear." Smiling, I tuck into my food.

We finish our meal in companionable silence. Two hungry people who seem to enjoy each other's company.

My throat thickens each time I think about how much I'm enjoying myself. How often I wish it would happen again and again.

I push my plate away and keep my attention focused on the trees making up my backyard.

"Everything okay?" she asks quietly. She's just finished her meal, and I haven't said a word for several minutes.

"It's just hitting me," I answer honestly. I'd never talk about this, but for some reason, the words rush off my tongue. "When I built this house, it was for friends and family. But other than my brothers, you're the first visitor I've had."

Her lips part. "Wasn't Natalie—"

"No." Not for lack of an invite. I could figure out logistics, but she never did. "I always went there. She hasn't been back since this was getting built. Haven and I flipped a house to help us with income until the renovations were done and the ranch was fully operational. I haven't even been in this place three years. Haven and I are usually at Iverson's, since that's where the shop and everything is for the ranch. So we gather there, and I get to hang out with Kacey."

"You wish it was different?"

"I feel like I'm borrowing someone's happiness." I can't believe I said that. She's going to think I'm pathetic, getting nothing but some frequent-flyer miles out of a four-year relationship.

"I know what you mean," she says quietly. "This wedding is hard because it's what I wanted, but also because it means it's just going to take longer for me to get there. I want a family, but I also want my person. Someone who's just for me."

A cavern in my chest echoes her sentiment. I thought Natalie was that person, but my life is no different without her. "Do you feel like you wasted those years?"

She chews on the inside of her cheek as she thinks. "I didn't then. Now, it feels like it." She rises and gathers our plates. "Stanford's taken up too much of my thoughts lately. I'm going to clean up since you cooked."

My kitchen is just off of the porch, but it feels like she's running away. I grab our glasses and silverware and follow her inside. "Grilling is nothing. It's a treat to do it for more than one person."

"I appreciate it." She loads my dishwasher and I hand her what's in my arms. Straightening, she peers out the window over the sink that looks onto the deck. Her full lower lip sticks out. "Did you grab everything?"

"Yeah?" Why would that upset her?

"I was going to do it. Like I said, you cooked."

"I don't mind," I say carefully as the crease between her brows deepens.

"Or you don't think I'll get back to the rest. I do . . . eventually." She hip-checks the door closed.

"I believe it." Most of the time, my house doesn't feel lived in. Seeing signs of her doesn't bother me, but she's worried it will. Has someone made her feel bad about it?

Wasn't I that guy? Holding her time blindness over her when she's trying to do better—ignoring that there may be legitimate reasons for her tardiness. I'm not doing that to her again. It's just a little clutter.

This thing between us is about helping us through tough times, but I can build her up too, just like she did for me with Rafting and Tasting. "So you need to believe *me* when I say it's fine. Is there something else bothering you?"

She barks out a laugh and heads out to the deck. "Until the wedding is over, that answer will always be yes. I have the cake tasting with Elodie on Wednesday. It's going to be a whole spectacle. They want a cupcake tower, a cookie cascade, and then a five-tier cake—with each tier being a different flavor." Throwing her hands up in the air, outrage furrows her brow. I want to smooth out the lines only because I know she's bothered. "There aren't going to be that many guests. Five tiers?"

"Each a different flavor," I echo.

"I'm trying to give them realistic expectations. They think because Elodie runs a small bakery, she has nothing better to do but make cupcake towers and play with flavors. And because Elodie's Elodie, she's going to do it. It's going to be the best, but I'm going to be so upset for her because the couple isn't going to treat her like she deserves. They aren't treating anyone like they deserve. And they get away with it!"

Her chest is rising and falling and color leeches up her neck. She weathers how the couple and their family treat her without complaint, but the way they *might* treat Elodie has her incensed.

I slide my hand around her neck. "They won't walk all over Elodie. Know why?"

She gazes up at me with those wide gray eyes. I have her pinned between the table and me. "Why?"

"Because you're going to talk circles around them until they feel like dumbasses for disagreeing. Just like you did with Chester. Like you did at the tasting room. You're good at your job."

"You mean that?"

I stroke my thumb up and down her neck, her warm, soft skin sliding under my touch. "You're excellent at what you do, and you need to start calling them out on their bullshit instead of absorbing the blame."

"I'm paid to tolerate their blame."

"It's not right." I tip my head closer to hers.

"You're in customer service." Her voice drops lower. "You should know about pleasing the customer."

"I don't give a fuck about pleasing anyone." I skim my lips over hers. "Just you."

"This isn't . . ." She swallows and I keep a good inch between us. "This isn't part of our agreement."

"You're stressed."

She nods, and her eyes shimmer. "I got myself all worked up."

Fuck me. She's worked up in all the wrong ways, but I know all the right ones. I tsk. "There you go. Seems you need some relief."

"Durban?"

The nervous thread in my name gives me pause. "Yeah?"

"Is it only our agreement? Like . . . friends with benefits?"

The corner of my mouth tips up. "Are we friends, Belle?"

Her breath gusts across my chin. "Something like that."

I had a benefits-only relationship for the last four years, even if I didn't know it at the time. I should run. I want more. But I want Campbell, and without this wedding or the pressure it's causing, there wouldn't be an us. I wrap my other hand around her waist. "Do you want me to relieve your stress?"

"I want . . ." Her heavy-lidded gaze strokes over my face. A light breeze ruffles her hair. "You."

She's bold, honest, and vulnerable when she says that. It's my undoing. I lift her to the counter and position myself between her legs. "I want you spread out beneath me and at my mercy." Her lips puff apart and I claim them, sweeping my tongue inside. She doesn't taste like whiskey tonight. Crisp water and my cooking. A possessive part of me rears up. Damn right her flavor comes from me caring for her.

I break the kiss to lift the shirt over her head. I push her back until she's sprawled on the tabletop so she's ready. My next favorite meal. I bunch it up and slide it under her head. "Does that flush when you get angry cover your whole chest when you come?" I trail my fingers down her neck and over her sternum, stopping at the lace border of her bra.

Birds sing in the distance. It's wide open out here, yet we're more isolated than we've ever been. I finally have her all to myself.

She bites her lip. "Only when I come really hard."

"Is that a challenge, Belle?" I slide the cups of her bra down until her rosy pink nipples pop free. A groan rips from me and I cup one breast, rolling her tight peak under my fingertips.

"Just an FYI. I'm ready to come really hard." She sounds breathless, and she arches into my touch.

"You can be nice and loud here." I unhook her bra and drape it over the chair. Thank fuck her pants are easy enough to slide off. She lifts her legs for me.

If I stopped to appreciate the beauty of her spread

on the table with her hair fanning around her, I'd be captivated. Enthralled. My very own whiskey siren, tempting me away from the careful plans that keep me isolated and alone.

"You're so fucking beautiful." I lean down and put my mouth right where the wet spot on her underwear is. I lick out and taste her through the fabric.

"God, Durban." She groans and rolls her hips into me.

"I'm only getting started." I peel her underwear down. She plants her heels on the edge of the table and I push her knees apart. She gets fucking wetter the more I look. I drag a finger through it and her whole body trembles. "This pretty pink pussy of yours is all I can think about."

She tenses like she's going to get self-conscious and close her legs. I don't bother sitting. I stoop down, bracing a leg behind me, and lick through her soaked seam.

"Oh God!"

"Be fucking loud," I say over her swollen clit before I claim it as my own.

Her moans ring through the trees and she buries her hand in my hair. She tugs at my scalp as I feast. I push her legs up farther, opening her completely to me. I want her powerful orgasm. I want to see her flush. I want to sink into her when she's spent and ready for me.

Need pounds at my temples. I force myself to ease back. She releases my hair and meets my hungry gaze.

"Are you going to let me inside of you tonight?" I push a finger in so she knows what I mean. Her tits rise and fall, her pearled nipples straining for the sky.

"I can't wait," she says on an exhale.

I push another finger in. My erection is digging into my zipper, but I welcome the pain. I'd shoot my load with no warning otherwise. "Do I have to go get condoms?"

Her eyes widen. "You don't have any?" I thrust in and out and her eyes go hazy. "How does that feel so good?"

Because it's me. I don't say that. It feels heavier than this moment. "After you come, I'll tuck you into my bed and get some."

"I'm—I'm on birth control, and after . . ." She rolls onto her elbows and rocks herself into my steady thrusts. "I was tested."

"Me too." On some level, I guess I assumed my previous partner hadn't been waiting for me.

"Then—oh, God." Her head drops back. "Take me without one."

I'm supposed to wait. I'm supposed to take my time. But I straighten and yank my fly open with my free hand, stroking in and out of her while I do it.

She sits up higher, her gaze going from my crotch, where I'm wrestling my shirt out of the way one-handed, to the other hand pumping in and out of her.

I free my dick.

She gasps. "Is there anything about you that's not impressive?"

I look down. My cock soars past my open fly but gets crowded by my shirt. I rip the damn thing over my head and drop it at my boots.

She's swaying into me, urging me to go faster, all while eating up my torso with her gaze. "I want to touch you."

"Later." It's my time to indulge in all those fantasies that have haunted my dreams day and night.

I shove my pants down farther. Cool air caresses my dick, giving me a modicum of control. My fingers are dripping but I continue prepping her. I won't last long. Not with the sexiest woman laid out for me, making those noises I can't get enough of.

I stroke a thumb over her clit.

"Yes," she groans. In her need to get closer, to get me to go faster, she's worked her ass down to the edge of the table. I'm so fucking close to paradise. But I don't move.

I carefully insert another finger, pushing all three into her tight channel. Her mouth drops open and she sits up higher. The angle's changed and she can't rock against me as easily. She's at my mercy. But I'm completely at hers.

I circle her nub, and a full-body quiver runs through her. Her breathing is speeding up, and she's close. I'm fucking close too. I remove my hand, instantly missing her heat. She hisses and arches, like she's seeking me. I'm going to give her what she wants, what I need.

Notching myself at her hot entrance, I go rigid. The pleasure ricochets through me like a pinball. "Fuck, you're tight, Belle."

She grips my shoulders and we both watch as I push in. I ease out and sway forward, her juices coating me. I push in farther. "Your greedy little cunt is taking me so well."

Hell, I don't talk like that. But she's not fazed.

"You fill me so good. Like I've always wanted."

Pure satisfaction overwhelms me. No one's satisfied her like I'm going to.

I bury myself to the hilt. She wiggles, adjusting to my size, clenching around me like she's demanding my release. It's hers. All of this, everything I can give her, is hers.

"Watch me fuck you." I pump into her, bracing my legs and clenching my ass cheeks.

I take her in. The pink cheeks. The flush developing on her chest and cresting up. The wonder and lust in her eyes. My pace increases. My peak is way too fucking close. Her walls flutter around me, but she's languid, enjoying the fuck.

I never thought that moment in the storeroom would bring us here. I've stroked myself off to her moans so many times. Imagined how hot and wet she'd be around my cock, and here she is. My real-life fantasy.

I lift her hand, curling mine around her fingers so only her index and middle fingers are free.

I suck them into my mouth, the salty-sweet flavor reminding me of her pussy. She whimpers.

I release her and continue thrusting. My damn eyes are going to cross if I have to hold back anymore. An entire electrical storm is waiting to unleash at the base of my spine, but I'm not coming without her.

Her tits are shaking with my thrusts, like a wave rolling through her body, from her pelvis to her shoulders. She's even wetter than before and the smack of our bodies fills the air.

"Show me how you touched yourself that night."

She eagerly does as I ask, and fuck if that doesn't make me almost immediately nut.

"Oh God." Her moan fills my ears. All of my senses are focused on her. The tips of her fingers graze me as I propel in and out. Her moves get jerky and her cunt grips me tighter.

"So. Fucking. Good," I grit out.

She spasms hard around my dick and then lets out a cry. "Yes!"

Fuck, she's coming. Ecstasy courses through my veins, coming from right where we're connected. My guards slam down and my climax roars out of my body with a shout.

"Fuck, Belle. Fuuuuck." I spill inside of her, the first time I've done that. Everything's more intense. My climax, the squeeze of her around me, and the slide of my cock inside of her.

When I finish coming, I sag over her, propping myself on my hands by her head. I dip my head and lick a path up her neck. "You're blushing."

She shivers under me and a lazy giggle leaves her. I grin.

Running a finger down my cheek, she stops by my mustache. "I love this dimple."

"Ugh." I tip my forehead to hers. "I used to get teased so much for that in high school."

"High school kids can be mean."

"It was my brothers."

She laughs and closes her legs around me. "Now what?"

"Now I take you to bed and we keep doing this all night."

Her brows lift. "You can go again?"

My dick is still half-hard inside of her and need is knocking at my temples. "It's been a long time and you're a sexy woman."

Campbell

. . .

I had no idea sex could be like this. I had no idea being with a guy could be this easy. Yet he's so hard.

I brace my knees into the mattress as I pump up and down on his magic cock. The thing never goes soft, and the sense of power I get from looking down and seeing him hard for me yet again is heady. I don't want to give this up.

"You're a goddamn mess." He nibbles along my collarbone. We're in the middle of his bed. All his covers have been pushed to the edge. The sun has long set, and we just got out of the shower.

"You make me that way," I gasp. I'm going to be raw in all the best ways in the morning. I'll walk all day with a secret chafe between my thighs. I have whisker burn there too, along my stomach and across my breasts. It's like he marked me with his own special brand.

He nips at the sensitive skin at the base of my neck. "You take it so fucking well."

I thrive on that praise and I can't explain why, but it's coming from Durban, and I like hearing it.

"Fuck, Belle." He grips my hips and grinds me into him. "That greedy cunt of yours is going to ruin me."

"Good. Because you've wrecked me."

His grunt is full of male satisfaction.

Every time I lower myself on him, he fills me so completely, I can't believe he fits. His dick is as big and proud as he is. I have this man all to myself tonight. I haven't asked to stay over, but he tossed my clothes on the dresser with his when we entered, and he hasn't told me to have a good night yet. We've barely disconnected since we started.

I stuff my hands into silky hair and tip his head back. His dark eyes bore into me, full of lust and something I'd like to call affection. I'll take him not being annoyed with me. Although if he fucks like this, he can be irritated all he wants.

He thrusts his hips up. "That look." Grunt. "When I'm deep inside." Grunt. "Gonna be all I see."

There've been times when I can't figure out where I stop and he begins.

I'm so close to my peak, and I can't believe I can physically orgasm again. I cover his mouth with mine, and he invades me with his tongue, plunging and licking with the same precision he thrusts into me with. He roams his hands over my body, palming my breasts and rolling my nipples between his thumb and forefinger.

The pressure builds to a breaking point. I'm going to explode or implode; I can't tell which. A dam bursts and ecstasy steals my breath. I take his, not letting him go as I come.

I swallow his groans and growls, and he takes the whimpers strangling my throat. Our frenzied kissing slows down to a lazy version of what we were doing before. He holds me to him, and I don't want to leave the cocoon he's made.

Eventually, I place a final kiss on his lips, then lay my head on his shoulder. "You're a beast in bed." I sound sleepy.

"It's your fault." His voice is a deep rumble. "I dissolve into a lust-filled beast around you."

"It's not me. It's never been like this."

He pulls back and studies me. "It's not usually like this."

Disbelief makes me scoff. "You're telling me that you haven't left a string of deflated women behind in bed?"

"Every guy would like to think so, but I've topped out at two in a row. Maybe three times if you span the whole twenty-four hours." He rubs his hands up and down my back. "You and I have this crazy chemistry. We both needed this release."

Disappointment crowds my afterglow. Stupid agreement.

Gently, he pulls out of me and rolls me onto a pillow. "Wait here." He bundles the blankets and drapes a few on the bed, his arms and abs flexing in the shadows. Then he goes into his connected bathroom.

I'm not going anywhere. I have to come to terms with my newfound Durban Hennessy obsession and how I hate that what we have is temporary. I did need this release, but I would've been fine. I wanted him. I feel like I *need* him.

I'm falling for him.

So hard.

A pressure lands on my chest, and I curl up with a soft comforter the same shade as the beams overhead. I inhale through a straw. I can't be into Durban Hennessy. I spent years in a relationship with a guy who thought he was better than me. I can't want that again. But Durban hasn't acted like that since he hauled me out of Bootleg.

I also spent years with a guy who didn't really want me, and the motivation might be different, but Durban doesn't want me. Not really. Sex is different from a relationship, and his type is a brainy woman. I'd never make him happy.

He returns with a warm, damp towel and gently wipes me off.

Gah, I'm in too deep. "Thank you."

"Anytime. Don't move. I'll be back to make the bed."

I can just enjoy this, right? He takes the pressure off, and in doing so, he's showing me how high I should be setting the bar.

He prowls across the bedroom in the shadows and lifts that boyfriend bar even higher. He slips the sheet over me, then each of his three blankets. He crawls in next to me.

He hasn't officially invited me for a sleepover. "If you want me to go—"

"No. Let them wonder where you're at."

"It'll be my parents wondering." I sit up. "Shit. I should send them a message. They alerted the sister brigade last time."

Sliding out of bed, I try to grab the top blanket to wrap around myself.

He holds firm. "If I get to watch you walk naked through my house, I'll make you breakfast in bed."

I release the blanket. "What if there's crumbs?"

"I'll lick them off you."

"You drive a hard bargain, Hennessy." Grinning, I find my phone in the kitchen, send the message that I'm staying with a friend, and then I climb in the bed.

I roll to my side so I can see his profile. He's got an arm slung behind his head. The top of the comforter rests across his abdomen. This all feels so normal my chest aches.

What would it be like to go to bed with him every night?

I can't go there. I just got over rejection and heartbreak.

"I have to get up for chores in the morning," he says,

turning his head toward me. "So don't leave before I can make us some eggs."

"I prefer muffins, actually."

He flashes a smile. "I can make muffins."

I laugh. "I'm just kidding. I would offer to cook, but I make a mess."

"You keep warning me," he says wryly.

"It irritates you."

He shifts his position to face me. "When I thought it was because you were so self-centered that you don't think twice. But I know better now."

Pleased, I smile. "My college roommate used to get so upset with me because I joked that I needed two to three business days to wash my dishes. I had to get a single dorm room until I got an apartment."

"You're aware, and I think that's half the battle. The cowboys in the bunkhouse were some nasty guys."

"I have a feeling you're super fastidious. This house is unreal."

He's quiet for a moment.

"Did I say something wrong?"

"There's nothing else to do and no one to dirty it up."

There's an emptiness in his tone. He's not just getting laid, he's getting company. That's his part of the arrangement. "I can get you a medium-sized dog."

His chuckle is deep and pleasing. "So it'll either be a chihuahua or a Great Dane?"

"The guy at the rescue swore up and down Coal was a medium-sized dog, even after I commented about how he looks like a yellow Lab. But he had those big eyes and I just knew Kacey would fall in love."

He curls a piece of my hair through his fingers. "Maybe I should get a dog. You can pick it out."

"You'd trust me after Coal?"

"He's quite the guardian. And a giant teddy bear. You did good."

Stunned, I don't say anything. He's been so supportive through the whole wedding business, but a dog has nothing to do with our agreement. "Are you serious? You want a pet?"

"He's going to be a working dog, but yeah, I'd like the company. I have two weeks before I can get a kitten."

"You should take two," I say sagely. "Double the mousers and they can keep each other company when you're not here."

"Is this that peer-pressure thing I heard about growing up?"

I laugh lightly, but his words don't settle quite right in my brain. "You didn't get peer pressured?"

"We would've had to be around peers."

"Oh." I don't know what to say to that. He's alluded to what his upbringing was like with his mom, but no details, and I don't want to be nosy.

"Mom left us alone a lot." His voice is wooden, like he's put distance between himself and the memories and he doesn't want to close it up. "We worked a lot, taking side hustles when we were too young to be officially employed. Then Iverson got a cheap pickup and lawn mower and we did lawn care. School was . . . a blink. We did what we had to and left it behind."

"Your mom wasn't around?"

"It was better that way. She liked to party. Liked to be the center of attention. Men's attention." It's dark, but I can see a corner of his jaw clench. "She liked to spend money too, and she tried to take ours."

"That's awful." No wonder the brothers do everything together. They worked at Daddy's ranch as a unit, and while Daddy will never give them that much credit, he never had more reliable or knowledgeable employees. Mom said it plenty of times since the brothers quit. Then the Hennessys bought into Foster House Gold together, and they all run their ranch as one.

"We learned the hard way that we can't have her name on any account with us."

"Oh my God. So you had to start hiding your money?"

He continued to play with the ends of my hair. "Yep. Got pretty creative. Helped that we were all taller than her. Lots of high places. She had a type though—ranchers, and that came in handy too. Lawn care as three teens only pays so much."

"Is that where you learned your skills?"

"Caring for horses, cows, whatever. They'd pay us, and long after Mom dusted them, they'd still hire us. It's how we got connections to keep working in the industry after we all turned eighteen."

"You went right to work?"

"I did, yes." He goes quiet, like he knows what I'm asking. The root of his admiration for his ex was clear. Someone he thought should be so far above him finding him worthwhile.

"Iverson took a few classes, but it was more money and he was still caring for us. Then I graduated and worked more so he could finish his degree, but as soon as Haven was done with high school, Iverson dropped out and we all took off."

No wonder he waited for Natalie. She's everything he wanted to be and she was attracted to him. It must've hurt him so much when she told him he couldn't understand the pressure she was under.

I hate her on principle, but he's probably still in love with her. A guy doesn't wait years for a woman to just be over her. I'm a rebound. I'm not someone he'd run after or wait for. If she were to appear in town, he'd probably forget my name.

My throat burns and heat pricks the backs of my eyes. I'm mourning something that hasn't happened.

He releases my hair and pushes the strands behind my ear. A tender action that chases away the sadness. I'm just going to enjoy my time with him. The room is quiet. Cozy. My eyelids grow heavy.

"Sleep tight, Belle," he murmurs.

I will now.

CHAPTER THIRTEEN

Campbell

When I wake, Durban's gone, just like he said he'd be. He also said he'd cook breakfast, and there's a delicious sweet smell permeating the air. It's like I woke in Elodie's bakery.

I roll out of bed and stumble into the bathroom. There's a hurts-so-good stiffness in my muscles, and the chafe between my legs only reminds me of every delicious thing Durban did to me. But as much as I liked the orgasms, our pillow talk is something I'll never forget.

I push my tangled hair off my face. I don't have anything to tie it up with. A new toothbrush and comb rest on the counter and my heart melts. Durban's going to make someone a good partner someday. I just don't think he wants to be mine.

Shaking my head, I clean up and brush my teeth. I'm not in a place to make major future decisions. I've known Durban for years, and I've never thought he was a bad guy. Just a judgmental prick. After one night of sex, I'm wishing for more?

To be fair, he's outshined all of my exes. Most definitely the last guy I dated. Durban just set the bar in the stratosphere.

When I'm done in the bathroom, I toss on my linen pants, skip the underwear until I get home, and then put my bra on. The Dee's Sweets sweater I wore when I was here before is draped across his heavy wooden dresser. I toss that on and bury my nose in the collar. Hints of caramel and oak.

I'm leaving his bedroom when I snap my fingers. Straightening up, I return and make the bed, wipe down the sink, and evaluate my efforts. I'm not going to be a whirlwind in his safe space.

A puppy will do that. Was he serious about me finding him a dog? He's getting kittens. As if I need more fodder for my imagination, a big Durban cuddling furry little creatures adds to it.

I grab my phone. The screen lights up with messages.

Stanford: Hey, where are you?
Stanford: Campbell. Where are you?
Stanford: What's on today's agenda?
Stanford: Are you taking ANOTHER day off?
Stanford: Make sure to adjust the invoice.

What a dick.

I roll my eyes and shoot him the schedule for today, which includes another training session with him and January on Hailstorm, and a casual family meal—no bar service. Tomorrow is the tasting with Elodie in the afternoon. After that, they're going to Banff through next Monday.

I can't wait for them to clear out of the lodge again.

Me: I've attached the schedule for today and tomorrow before your foray into Canada.

In the kitchen, the sweet smell gets stronger, but I can't find anything on the short island cutting off the dining area from the kitchen. Nothing on the rest of the counters. I run my fingers along the smooth countertop.

Is this marble? Granite? It's expensive, whatever it is. The backsplash resembles the rock from the mantel, and wow. The man's got good taste. And from what he said, I'm the first woman to enjoy it.

Take that, Doctor-Doctor Natalie.

Did he get up in time to bake?

On a hunch, I open the oven. A gust of warm air bathes my face. Inside are a half dozen berry muffins. A grin stretches my mouth wide.

My phone buzzes. I close the oven and check who it is.

Stanford: We're changing the time for lessons today.

I growl just as Durban enters from the laundry room. He cocks a brow.

I forget the text and take him in. He kept his cowboy boots on and they give him that rolling swagger I admire. Then there's his tight black shirt and green flannel with the sleeves rolled up over it. As always, he fills out a pair of blue jeans in an obscene way. His hair is smashed down around his head from the hat he must've worn while doing chores. The look in his eyes is smoldering. It says that he knows what I look like naked and how I sound when I come. All true, but his gaze heats like he wants to do it all again.

The guy is insatiable.

So fucking hot.

I toss my phone on the counter. "Stanford wants to change the schedule." I cross my arms. "He's pissy because I'm not at the lodge to wait on him hand and foot."

"Then he can suck it." He crosses to me and plants his mouth on mine. The mint on his tongue is the same as mine. I wrap my arms around his neck, desire kindling in my belly. If I was wearing underwear, I'd dampen them again.

My body is primed for him. That look is all it takes, and I'm ready. Will it ever be like this with anyone else? Do I want it to be?

My phone vibrates against the counter, and keeps going. Someone's calling.

He releases my mouth and I peek at the screen. Stanford.

"Ugh. He can wait."

A mischievous gleam enters Durban's dark eyes. "Answer it."

"It's fine. I'm not at his beck and call." I am, but I can take a few bucks off the invoice. Durban will make it worth it.

The phone keeps vibrating. He turns me to face the counter and grips my hips. Tingles explode between my legs. My ass is right against his crotch. He reaches over me and taps the answer button.

My mouth drops open. "Wha—"

"Hello?" Stanford snaps. "Campbell."

The waistband of my pants slides down my hips, and I suck in a breath. Durban hisses. He's discovered I'm not wearing underwear.

"Hello?" Irritation is ripe in his voice.

I can't believe Durban answered. "Y-yes?"

My pants pool around my feet, and Durban nudges my feet farther apart. Hot hands land on my bare skin and skim to the front. My eyelids flutter.

"Where the hell are you?" Stanford asks.

Durban's fingers tighten on my skin and a low growl only I can hear emanates from him. He strokes his finger through my pussy lips and I jerk. I'm so sensitive from last night, but I'm primed for another round.

"I'm . . ." What was my excuse again? "Billings. I'm in Billings."

"With who?"

Durban moves my hair to the side with one hand, the fingers of his other hand slicking through my pussy and grazing my clit. I vibrate with need. I rock back, bumping against the hard ridge behind his fly.

What'd Stanford ask? Oh, yes. "Um, a friend."

"Who do you know in Billings?"

Durban skims his lips over the nape of my neck. "Tell him it's none of his goddamn business." He speaks low, but I can't promise Stanford didn't hear it. The stress of dealing with Stanford and his controlling ways is no competition against what Durban's making me feel.

I'll use it, just like I'm supposed to. "Your message said you wanted to change the . . ." I bite my lip to keep from groaning. Durban and his wicked finger circle my clit. I'm so fucking wet, a drop runs down my thigh. "The training. You want to change the time?"

The drag of Durban's zipper is loud in the room, but I can't summon enough concern about Stanford hearing it.

"Are you alone?" my ex asks.

None of his business. "What time would you like to meet?"

The broad head of Durban's erection prods against my cunt and I tip forward, giving him more room to work.

"Noon," Stanford snaps.

I hiss as Durban enters me in one smooth thrust. My body clenches around him, greedy and wanton. "T-tight turnaround." God, I sound like I'm out for a run.

Or like I'm getting fucking while trying to act professional.

Durban strums my clit while steadily pounding in and out of me. This isn't some marathon sex session. I'm going to come in record time, and it'll be while Stanford's listening if I don't get him off the phone.

"I can do one." The last word comes out on a whimper.

"Are you okay?"

"Just getting ready for the day."

"A bit late in the morning, isn't it?"

"God, yes." My cheeks burn. I'm right at the peak.

Durban keeps the pressure on my nub, but he brings me against his chest, with his hand at the base of my neck. "Don't let him hear you come." His hot breath tickles my ear, and it's like there's a power line between my earlobe and pussy. "That's for me alone."

"I'm paying you for a full day," Stanford insists.

Durban's grinding into me, his grunts quiet.

"I'm doing my job." I gasp, fighting to get this last sentence out before I hang up on him. I'm soaked and the suction between our bodies is growing louder. "My contract doesn't give you access to me for the entire twenty-four hours of the day. If you'd like more time, you need to talk to January first."

There's a sharp inhale.

I suck in another breath. My whole body is tight, my climax hammering to break free. "See you at one."

I slap the phone just as a "Yes! Durban!" rips from my throat. Pleasure rams into me and my legs go weak. I shudder through my orgasm.

"Fuck, Belle. So fucking good." He releases inside me, filling me with heat. He rests his head on my shoulder, his hips kicking with small spasms. "So fucking good."

When logic returns, I check my phone. Good. I hung up correctly.

What would I have done if Stanford had overheard? It's none of his concern and he wouldn't know who I was with—except I screamed *Durban* while I came.

Okay. Our secret deal is still intact. My ex might be suspicious, but my sex life won't be the talk of the wedding, which probably would make them think I'm terrible at my job for some messed-up reason.

Durban lays another kiss on my nape. "Is he always that fucking rude to you?"

"Lately, yes. He's getting worse."

Durban pulls out of me. Before he tucks himself away, he squats and lifts my pants back into place. "He knows you were fucking someone."

I adjust the waistband. "I don't think so. I didn't sound normal, but—"

He zips himself up. "A man's going to remember what you sound like when you're about to come." He spins me around to give me a lingering kiss. "I'm never going to forget."

He doesn't have to. I could remind him for the rest of our lives.

Where did that come from?

My very real desire for this to be more. I push my hair back. I'm getting way ahead of myself. Wedding first. Then, maybe . . . No impulsive moves. I'm sticking to the plan. "You made muffins."

"I'm going to make some eggs and bacon to go with them." He checks the clock. I have a couple of hours before I should be back at the lodge to get ready for lessons. "Training is going to be stressful after that call."

I frown. "Yeah. I guess Stanford's not getting laid enough to reduce his stress."

"It's the quality, not the frequency."

I run my hand down his hard chest. "Good thing you've got both covered."

"You're going to be wound up after the lessons."

I bite the inside of my cheek, hope surging. Is he asking what I think he is? "Yes. And after the cake tasting."

"I don't want to fall down on my end of the bargain."

This time, the sting of being reminded of the bargain isn't there. Is he using it as an excuse to spend more time with me? "You'll be in this big house, all alone."

"Seems I should have some company tonight. And you should work off some stress."

A grin breaks free. "I'll bring a change of clothes this time."

"You can keep skipping the underwear."

CHAPTER FOURTEEN

Durban

I drum my fingers along the bar top. The last of the tours for the day are done. I've cleaned up everything. Haven's coming to work the bar for the evening. I can go home and get something ready for dinner. Dee's Sweets is closed, but Campbell's enduring the after-hours cake tasting with Stanford and January. Campbell said it makes the couple feel special, but also protects Elodie from any public rudeness from the future Mr. and Mrs. Baldwin.

I'm antsy. I want to go home and watch Campbell walk into my house like she did last night. We made chicken alfredo together and she told me how the training went. Hailstorm can get stubborn with Stanford, but at least Stanford didn't drop January. The swoop-and-grab is still clunky and Campbell worries for their safety, but Stanford refuses to drop it.

Lane enters instead of Haven. He's wearing black

slacks and a half-buttoned white shirt. If he wore a tie while he was at the headquarters in Denver, it's long gone.

"How was the drive?" I ask.

He shrugs. "It gets old." Shoving a hand through his inky hair, he sighs. "Makes moving sound like a good idea." He crosses to the bar and sits on a stool.

"Want a drink?"

"Gimme a finger of that ninety-proof whiskey we bottled last month."

I don't grab a glass. The cask was bottled, but Lane hasn't approved it for sale. We're sitting on it. "You're not sure about it."

"It's . . . subpar."

The Golden Nugget is one of mine, and it's a rye whiskey. "It's for mixing."

"Customers won't know that when they buy it. We need to release products that stand on their own. Foster House is known for whiskey. We have more leeway with vodka and gin."

I stomp down my frustration. We've had this discussion several times over the years. "It's a good whiskey."

His jaw hardens. "It's not good enough."

I leave him and go to the storeroom. I grab a bottle of Golden Nugget. I don't pour him a glass. I make a Montana sunrise. Whiskey, lemonade, huckleberry syrup, and grenadine. Just to rub him the wrong way, I add a cherry and a small umbrella.

His expression is unimpressed. "You know how much I like cherries."

"A bunch of cherry fiends around here," I grumble and drop in two more.

He uses the thin straw to stir it, then takes a sip.

Rolling the drink around on his tongue, he furrows his brow and swallows. "Damn, that's good flavor."

"I know." I'm newer to the whiskey world. I've been drinking it a whole lot longer than I've been making it, but I know the science. I know I can create some amazing products.

"Use that for Rafting and Tasting." He takes another drink while my optimism takes a dive.

"We talked about something new, and I was going to do a vodka infusion." Campbell set it up so I can do something new. She threw me a bone in front of all the guys, and she didn't have to. She has faith in me without knowing what I can do. "It's summery."

He shakes his head. "We need to move all the Golden Nugget."

"And we will. In cocktails. How many festivals and street fairs do we have set up this summer? Our presence at those shouldn't be to move product on shelves. Maybe we start offering exclusive event lines."

Interest lights his eyes. Lane's good at the business end. He learned everything about running a national brand from his brother. But he's too pragmatic when it comes to Foster House Gold's goals.

I should be the realist, but Campbell handed me an opportunity after hearing only once that I wanted more of a creative role. I'm not wasting her faith in me.

Lane nods thoughtfully. "What kind of vodka infusion for the rafting gig?"

"It's summer. It's Montana. Huckleberry mint."

"Tourists will eat that shit up."

"Hoping they'll drink it up."

He tilts his head. "I didn't peg you as the outside-the-box thinker."

"It's not outside the box. I've studied what other distilleries do, especially those in the state and Wyoming."

"Our competition."

Previous conversations with Campbell run through my head. Her experiences could come in useful. "And our colleagues. We should work on some promotional events with them."

He takes a slow drink, his gaze shrewd. "You have some good ideas. Your girl too."

"Who?" I know exactly who he means, and I like how *my girl* sounds.

He gives me a flat look before he shakes his head. "I underestimate you. I need to quit doing that. I keep thinking you're a quiet cowboy that got dragged into the distilling world." He blows out a breath. "I'm just a mechanic cosplaying as a businessman."

"Didn't you cosplay as a cowboy first?"

He lets out a short burst of laughter. "Didn't feel as unusual of a transition."

"Guess we're all just trying to figure our shit out."

"Yep." He slides off his stool, goes to tug his shirt sleeves down, seems to realize how disheveled he is, then scrubs a hand down his face. "How's the wedding prep going?"

Fucking fantastic. I get to bury my head between Campbell's legs each night. "Straightforward."

"The couple's not causing any trouble?"

"Campbell's been managing it."

"She's good at what she does."

I nod. She's very good. The girl I thought was wrapped up in herself is the best listener I've ever met.

After we sate ourselves on each other, we talk. At night, in the dark, I tell her stuff I've never shared. Is it the temporary nature of our relationship, or a real connection?

I think I know, but I wasted years on someone I thought I was in love with. I don't want to change what we're doing. In a little over a week, the wedding will be over and then what? Waiting two weeks is a drop in the bucket compared to my dating history, but I don't want to dive in further than Campbell just to find out only one of us is thinking about a possible future. I'm not going to make the same mistake twice.

Campbell

I stop at home to pack a bag for tonight. I have another weekend off before the week of wedding festivities really takes off. I made it this far, and other than a few annoyances, it hasn't been that bad. Stanford's parents have transitioned to treating me as the event planner. Now that I'm not trying to trap their son in a marriage with a girl they think isn't good enough for them, nor am I trying to win him back, they're happy to ask for my travel recommendations.

As for the couple . . . They oscillate between sucking face where everyone can see and bickering where they think no one can.

We've taken a break from the horse lessons. Stanford can finally get January on Hailstorm, but January's shoulder is getting wrenched out of its socket, and I'll have a heart attack if my cousin breaks her neck. I do not like worrying about her.

I talked them into using two horses. January will have to figure out her dress situation, but I convinced them of the photo worthiness of a shot of them both riding into the sunset.

Then I took an antacid.

Time to figure out another dream wedding. I'm no longer sure I can get married on the ranch after this.

I'm just leaving my bedroom with a small overnight tote bag when the front door opens and closes.

Mom rushes down the hallway. She jumps when she sees me, throwing her hand on her chest. "Campbell, ohmigosh. Did you hear?" She rushes past me, her cowboy boots clicking on the hardwood floor.

"What's going on?" Did the wedding implode? My hope skyrockets. If I don't have to go through next week and it's not my fault, that would be a real dream come true.

"Jamison's in labor."

Happiness fills me. "Oh! That's awesome. Do they need help with Kacey?"

"I'm meeting them at the distillery and picking her up so they can get to Billings. Haven's watching her."

"Not Durban?" He said he would be there all day, so I stayed at the guest lodge to go over inventory with Chef before January's friends and cousins start arriving next week.

"He's doing the evening chores, and there's a heifer with a hoof issue in the barn he's checking on."

"I'm around all weekend if you need help with Kacey."

She shakes her head. "Not right now, but I promised her Auntie and Nana time this weekend." She stops and blinks at me. "Are you going to Billings again?"

A tendril of guilt slides across my conscience. Everyone thinks I have a beau in Billings when the only time I went there was to recruit the wedding band. "I'll be coming and going."

She arches a brow. "Is it getting serious?"

My evenings this week have been some of my favorites, and I'm fighting off the fantasy that it could turn into something real. He hasn't said anything to give me the impression he wants more than sex. "No. Not after Stanford."

"I don't blame you. Will you be home Saturday?"

"I'll make sure I'm around." I'm about to turn when she grabs me into a big hug.

"I like having you around." She's still squeezing me. "If only Avery would move closer, but with you and Jamison back in town, I don't have to ration my days off to go see her and Thea."

I hug her back. "I'm glad to be home."

Just not in this house, but a place of my own will happen soon. After the wedding, I'll have enough to look for my own place. Jamison told me it's dismal out there unless I build. Huckleberry Springs is an old town and the houses reflect that.

Durban's sprawling but cozy home flashes through my head. His place is so gorgeous.

She releases me and I almost go reeling. "Be safe."

When she's out of sight, I pull out my phone. I have a text waiting.

Durban: I'm at Iverson's. Let yourself in.

Campbell: Need help?

He's probably already done.

Durban: No, just gotta doctor a hoof and I'll be there.

Campbell: I'll work on dinner.

Warmth curls through my belly. Let myself in? Don't mind if I do.

I stop in town and pick up some fruit and veggies from the store, and then I take the back roads to Durban's. I don't want anyone in our business. These quiet, intimate, steamy nights are just for us, and if we're exposed, they might stop. No one's going to think I'm making a smart decision when it comes to men while I'm in the middle of this wedding, and I don't want to get questioned.

I don't want Durban to get asked about what he's thinking. He might realize he's wasting his time on me.

I drive to his house, loving the view more each time I make the short trip.

I park in my usual spot on the concrete pad in front of his garage and let myself in just like he said to. I drop my groceries on the counter and deposit my duffel on his precisely made bed. The nightshirt I forgot is neatly folded on the pillow.

The corner of my mouth lifts. He didn't have to text me to tell me that I left a mess. Sometimes he leaves my nightshirt where I drape it, and sometimes he cleans up without holding it over my head. There's no condemning statements like Stanford used to wield.

I picked up the kitchen. You're welcome.

Why can't you take five minutes to look behind you?

You'd forget your head if it wasn't attached.

In the kitchen, I look through his fridge. We talked about spaghetti last night and there's a pound of hamburger waiting. I can wow him with my grandma's homemade meatballs.

Ten minutes later, four rows of three seasoned and rolled meatballs are on a pan. I'm humming to myself when the door opens from the garage.

I wash my hands with my back to the entrance of the mudroom. "He-ey. I hope you're ready for some balls."

"Can't say they're my taste," Haven answers.

I bark out a cry and whirl around, spraying water across the counter and floor. "What is it with you guys and sneaking up on women?"

He's grinning like I robbed a bank and he gets the haul. He leans against the doorframe and crosses his arms. Like Durban, his biceps bulge in his gray Bootleg Tavern shirt. "Hi, Campbell." His smile weakens. "What a surprise."

"Hi, Haven." I hastily grab a paper towel and dry my hands. My cheeks are burning, and for some stupid reason, I want to cry. Will Durban be upset? No one's supposed to know. What if he's embarrassed to be sneaking around with me? He's going to care what Haven thinks.

"Nice balls you got there, but uh, what's going on?"

The oven beeps and I wince.

"Does Durban know you're here?"

"Yes." I scowl. Does he think I'm a hungry stalker?

"Well, that part's a relief."

Is Haven's disapproval going to end everything? If I have to finish this damn wedding after getting rejected by Durban, that's just a cruel joke.

He pushes off the doorframe. "Don't let me stop you. Durban owes me a meal anyway."

He crosses to the sink and I scoot over. I can't help the feeling that he's going to kick me out despite being here with his brother's approval. We've always had a good relationship, but that was before Haven realized I'm sleeping with his brother.

"Need some help?" he asks as he scrubs his hands. "Might as well put me to work."

I'd rather have him busy than asking me more questions I don't have the answer to. "Do you want to chop some veggies for a salad?"

"I'm allergic to them," he says soberly.

"Which ones?"

"All of them."

Laughter bubbles out of me. He's joking with me. That's got to be a good sign. He won't tell Durban he's made a bad decision, right?

He dries his hands. "I know my way around a salad, and as long as you don't make me eat it before the meatballs, I'll chop away."

My smile dims and the relief pushing through my panic stalls. "Are you okay with this?"

"Not gonna lie, I don't like cheating."

I jerk my head back like he slapped me. "They broke up."

Astonishment passes over his face. "No wonder I caught him whistling when he was doing a wash the other day. He can actually get on with life." Why wouldn't Durban tell his brother about Natalie? "You two seeing each other?"

"Sort of, but we're not telling anyone," I admit and try to get over my confusion. Is he hoping Natalie will return, or that I'll just be a good but forgettable time? "I don't want to disrupt the wedding, but this is . . . helping me get through it."

He studies me for a moment. "Did you think I was going to run you off?"

"I'm not exactly his type."

"Clearly you are."

I open my mouth. Shut it again. I'm not prepared for that response. "Natalie is—"

"Kind of insufferable."

Why does a thrill soar through me? I could take flight from it. "She is?"

"Trust me. The breakup is good news. Private fucker didn't share it with me though."

Durban is a private man. That clears my cloud of insecurity, just a little.

"She's his Stanford," he continues as he digs through the grocery bag of produce I bought. He pulls out bananas, sets them aside, then lines up the head of lettuce, tomato, and cucumbers. "No kale? Or what's that purple shit?"

"Arugula."

He shudders. "I might actually eat this salad." Pulling out one drawer and then another, I give up waiting for an answer and slide the meatballs into the oven.

When I turn around, he's got a knife and cutting board out. "Natalie is a super nerd, and don't get me wrong, that's fine. But she also has this tone when she talks to Durban." He swirls the tip of the knife in a circle. "And she would rarely speak to me and Iverson. Durban was like her little cowboy fetish or something. So trust me, I'm glad to see that he's moved on. Finally."

"Even if it's to me?"

He frowns and slices through the tomato. "What's wrong with you?"

All the excuses that Stanford gave me pile into my brain. "I'm impulsive. Messy and forgetful. I can't hold a job and had to come home to work for my parents."

"Aw hell, Campbell, that's just being normal."

Again, I'm punched with the urge to cry, but not from fear. I want to shed tears for that young Campbell who felt so alone and misunderstood. "If I had more Durbans and Havens surrounding me, I might have fought both times I was unfairly terminated."

He stops slicing and frowns at me.

"Both times?" Durban asks from the mudroom.

I whirl around to see him in the same spot Haven was in when he first busted me. The panic from earlier resets. Shit, shit, shit. Haven's cool with us, and the apprehension of Durban's reaction was forgotten.

It comes roaring back and tears poke the backs of my eyes.

He doesn't bother taking his boots off. He closes the distance between us and grabs my shoulders. "Hey, it's okay. We're here now. What happened?"

It's me he's worried about? Not his reputation or what his brother thinks? "No, it's not that. I'm over that." He doesn't let go and he's looking at me like he doesn't believe me. Right. I only told him about the one time. "Um, so, I legitimately got fired from my first job out of college because I was always late. Fair. Then I got a job at a senior center, a bougie one. My boss was cutting our hours for bullshit reasons. Like, oh, 'that was training and it doesn't count.' Or she'd demand we be twenty minutes early, but we couldn't clock in, yet she put us to work. That's like, a couple hundred a month!

When I confronted her about it, she fired me and made up complaints from the residents."

"You didn't kick her ass?" Haven asks.

I shake my head. "I was, um, dating Stanford and he thought I should get something better, and I didn't want my parents to know I'd lost another job."

Anger etches Durban's hard features. "You didn't lose it. She should've been fired."

"I was a girl with a lot of resources but no support."

"The resources were conditional," Haven says as his knife steadily clicks on the cutting board. "We know all about that, don't we, Durban?"

He grunts and pulls me into him. I soak in his heat and the faint hints of hay, dirt, and animals.

"You aren't mad?" I ask against his brick of a chest.

He pulls away. "Why would I be?"

I slide my gaze to Haven. "He thought you were cheating and I told him about the breakup."

Durban's features turn pinched. "About that. Thought it might help hide how Campbell and I are sneaking around through the wedding. Don't want to worry Iverson and Jamison."

There's that disclaimer again. I have to forget about how my feelings are growing and enjoy my time.

"Haven can keep his mouth shut." Durban looks over his shoulder at his brother. "Since we're feeding him."

"My lips are sealed." He mimics zipping his mouth shut. "Your girl asked me if I'd like some balls. She didn't specify and I almost turned her down."

"I didn't know it was him coming into the house."

"I'm hurt. I thought I was the only one sneaking up on you." Durban grins and gives me a kiss. It's way more chaste than it would've been were we alone, but I sink into him.

"Hey," Haven says, but Durban doesn't break away from me, "did you hear I'm going to be a favorite uncle again?"

Durban smiles against my lips, and I laugh. If this could be my every Friday night, I'd be a very happy woman.

CHAPTER FIFTEEN

Durban

Since Iverson and Jamison are still in the hospital waiting for the new arrival to show, I bring Campbell with me to do chores Saturday morning. She's wearing jeans and boots and a little pink top that makes me want to park this pickup in the nearest opening between the trees.

She hangs back with the horses while I take a round bale out to the cows. By the time I return, she's picked the fresh eggs, topped off the chicken feed and water, and is in the barn with the kittens. She's sitting on a square bale of hay, cross-legged, with little kittens crawling all over her and the mama cat sprawled at her side. Even Coal ditched me to hang out with Campbell.

I find an empty five-gallon pail and turn it over. As soon as I take a seat on it, two little kittens make their way to me, little tails straight in the air. I pick one kitten up while the other claws its way up my jeans. Mama Cat sees me and comes sauntering over.

"She likes you," Campbell says. Her long hair is hanging out the back of the Hawthorne Guest Ranch ball cap she retrieved from her car before we left.

"She knows I feed her." I rub the cat's cheeks and she swipes all around my legs. The kittens are sniffing me and I give them pets too.

"She's a good mama."

She is, and she's getting fixed next month so she can be a spoiled barn cat. "I have a soft spot for good mamas."

Campbell strokes a hand over a blissfully sleeping kitten. Both of our phones vibrate at the same time. I take mine out.

Iverson: It's a boy. Tavis Hennessy.

A delighted gasp leaves Campbell. "A nephew! That's going to rock Jamison's world after bossing two sisters around all her life."

I chuckle and tuck my phone away. I'm elated for my brother, and I can't wait until I get to meet the little guy. But right now, I'm more than a little grateful to have a mostly normal morning with Campbell where I don't feel like we're sneaking around.

Having dinner with Haven last night was more fun than I thought it'd ever be. Campbell put Haven to work and talked to him like a friend. For a while, I didn't think he'd leave, and I honestly didn't mind. We were chatting about the ranch, laughing about some of the wild cowboys we worked with and where they are now. Campbell shared what it was like growing up as a Hawthorne with the whole spread of the ranch as her backyard. Privileged but protected. And we talked about what it was like to work for her dad. Hard damn work, but the job was stable.

I might not be looking for another relationship, but last night resembled what I wanted from one.

"Iverson's been looking after rowdy boys for a few decades now." Mama Cat decided the dog would make a better bed and trotted over to him. "A son won't faze him after me and Haven."

"You guys don't seem rowdy. You seem very, very serious."

"Not that serious."

She laughed and one of the kittens jerked awake. "You are definitely the most serious."

"I wasn't always." I like her laugh, but the thought that she thinks I'm the least exciting of the bunch bothers me. I'm fun, dammit.

"Hmm, not so sure about that." A smile still plays along her lips. "I think you were always the voice of reason. Who's that character? Jiminy Cricket?"

"He was the conscience." I'm sounding less like a thrill by the second. At least I can rock her world in bed. A little scrape of longing scratches the back of my throat. Before Natalie, women often moved on because I wasn't the rough and rowdy cowboy they wanted. That's why being with Natalie was a reprieve. She sometimes joked about how I should send her cowboy videos instead of dick pics, but she mostly liked that I listened to her.

I listened, but she didn't often reciprocate. I saw it as a sign that she wasn't with me just because I could rope a steer. Our worlds didn't overlap, but she assumed I couldn't know enough about hers to have an opinion on it, and I didn't realize that until I'd wasted so much time.

A pit smolders in my gut.

"What are you thinking about?" Campbell's scratching under the tiny chin of a tortie. "Did I insult you?"

"No." A foolish feeling slowly sinks in. I'm being sensitive. "I was just thinking that you're right. I'm usually the one telling everyone what won't work with their plan or the execution."

Her pink lips turn down. "There's nothing wrong with that. Avery was Jiminy Cricket for us. Sometimes, I joke that's why she moved so far away. She'd had enough of our shit."

"Would you have come back if you didn't have to?" I like where I live. Do I want to see more of the world? Maybe. I've seen the bad parts and that's enough for me.

"I missed home. And since Jamison defied Daddy's rules about dating his employees, he's lightened up a little. I think he realizes that we can take care of ourselves. I mean, he raised us to." She sighs. "I just didn't think I'd be able to do what I want here. Planning my ex's wedding wasn't it, and I'm not sure if I can make an entire living doing event planning for rural communities, but I'm going to try."

"You'll get more work after the wedding."

"You think so?"

"I know so."

She bites back a smile, her white teeth sinking into her lower lip. "Okay, Mr. Know-It-All, what's something Foster House can do for the wedding that would double as marketing?"

I narrow my eyes at her. She's still gnawing on that lower lip, and I'm tempted to take over for her, but we're talking about her work. "I feel like you already have an idea."

"I do." Her grin breaks free and it's an arrow to my goddamn heart. "I'm sure it's way too late to do anything about my idea, but I thought those little single-serve bottles would make great wedding favors for the reception."

"How many would you need?"

She rolls a shoulder. "Fifty would be enough."

I do some quick calculations. That's no amount at all. "If I give you some spirits for the bride and groom to choose from, we can bottle them this week."

Her eyes flare and she sits straighter. "Really?" She hugs the cat closer to her. "I wasn't even going to ask. I could put them on all the tables after the meal is served."

I laugh. "When it's too late to say anything?"

"She won't be able to without looking like a dick. Everyone's going to be gushing about them and she'll have to eat her irritation. Then it's all done and I don't have to talk to either one again."

"Deal, but put the blame on us. We'll call it Chapel House. I'll run it by the guys, but it's such a small batch, it won't be anything. Haven can make a quick label for it in minutes."

"Chapel House." The awe in her voice nestles around my heart. I could trick ride around her and she wouldn't blink. I'm just doing my job, and she's impressed. "What kind of whiskey will it be?"

I know just the barrel to take it from. "It'll go well with the vanilla bean in the wedding cake. I'm aging it in an ex-sherry barrel, hoping to bring out the apricot and almond."

"Oh, yum." She sounds like she means it instead of tuning me out.

"Regardless, it should be a nice mix of fruit and spice. I'll save you a bottle."

"I'm taking you at your word." She stretches her long legs out and disrupts the sleeping creatures on her lap. They hop off and lope to snuggle with Mama Cat and Coal. "What do you do on a lazy Saturday?"

Nothing this special. "I usually go to the distillery, but Lane and Cruz are getting everything done today. They wanted me to take this weekend off because of the wedding next weekend, and then Mae Bailey is coming to town Monday. They want to get everything ready to show off to her even though she's seen the distillery already."

Her brow furrows. "I know that name." She snaps her fingers. "Copper Summit Bourbon. She was your foster mom."

Pleased she remembered when I haven't talked about Mae a lot, I nod. "She's disappointed to miss the monthly crochet club."

"I'll get her the dates. The weather's nice and Edna will make her a bestie in no time. Do you get to hang out with her?"

I've seen Mae a couple of times since we opened the distillery, but this time, she's staying for a few days with Lane. "Lane wants to plan a get-together at the tasting room. He'll haul some grills in and whoever can show is invited."

"Good. She should see that not only can you make some good spirits, but you're a beast at the grill."

I laugh, but she's right. I want to see Mae and show her that we turned out okay. Three months with the

Baileys was a blink, but it was needed after losing Dad. "You're coming too, right?"

Surprise lights her eyes. "Like I just happen to show up? I know Haven knows about us, but he also knows the arrangement."

The goddamn arrangement. I just want her there. I want to introduce her to Mae. My mom isn't in our lives, and I don't even know where she's living anymore, but Mae's arrival is creating that same sensation. That *I want you to meet my mother* sensation. Which is crazy. Campbell isn't my girlfriend, and Mae's not my mom.

How do I get Campbell to the gathering without revealing ourselves? "You're doing work for Foster House. Therefore, you're invited."

Her pleased smile turns wicked. "Stanford is going to be so irate I have plans for Monday."

"He's going to make you give him a discount." My blood boils. That fucker should pay her for every second of her life he wasted.

"And then January will stew about why he's so uptight about it. She so deserves it." She unfolds her legs. "Okay, Jiminy, what do you do for fun on Saturdays?"

"Work." But I've never had a whole day to kill with her.

"You haven't always worked. What'd you do before, when you had time off from the ranch?"

"Fish." I haven't been out since the ice and snow melted. "There's a spot not far from the distillery. It's land we made sure to keep out of the deal so we could preserve our secret spot."

"What if I'm horrible at fishing?"

"You don't have to catch anything to fish." I'd rather have her with me.

"Is your spot top secret?" she asks in a husky voice.

"Not if you keep talking to me like that. I'll show you where it is and all the things we can do there with the privacy."

"Sounds like we have another deal."

Campbell

We went fishing both Saturday and Sunday. Now it's Monday morning, and we're out fishing again. I have an afternoon date with my mom and Kacey. Jamison and Iverson returned home yesterday with Tavis, so my parents are keeping Kacey until closer to the wedding to give my sister and Iverson a chance to rest.

I wade out of the water. No wonder the brothers wanted to keep as much of the land around this stretch of the river theirs. The water swings wide around a curve and bubbles over rocks, making it the perfect fishing spot. There's enough shore to pack some chairs and a blanket and have a picnic. Or maybe a few orgasms before casting a line, as we did on Saturday under the clear blue sky.

Durban exits the river next to me and we pack up our poles and waders. We didn't have much luck today, but neither of us was trying to catch anything. I like it out here, and I like that he wants to be here with me.

Things feel a lot more serious after the weekend, but tonight will take care of that. I'll arrive separately to the distillery and pretend to be nothing more than an occasional event planner for the company and Iverson's sister-in-law.

And after tonight, I'm going deeper into the wedding activities.

"Penny for your thoughts?" he asks as he gathers our supplies in his arms.

"I'm caught between hoping that Stanford and January smoothed some things over while they were in Banff or that they decided to cut their losses and cancel everything."

We start hiking toward the pickup. He took an off-road route that didn't include parking in the lot of the distillery to get here. I wish we could just strut onto Foster House grounds and wave to everyone we know.

There I go again. Unrealistic expectations.

"You're less worried about your reputation?" He lets me go ahead as the path narrows until we reach the clearing the guys made when the renovations were being done. They didn't want customers to see them leaving the trees with fishing gear.

"More like I'm tired of being scared of what other people think." I'm tired of bearing the responsibility. Why is it up to me whether or not my uncle signs over his share of the land? Daddy and Rayburn should just duke it out. I flash Durban a grin over my shoulder to keep that resentment from showing on my face. "Though you seem to have accepted me just fine."

He continues looking right through me. "You're surrounded by support."

In a way. It's one thing to have people around who can doctor me if I fall off a horse. It's another to be put on one I've never ridden before and told to win the barrel race.

If I was bolder, I'd march into the guest lodge and announce that I quit. I know I have the right to, but I can't. I have to finish one job. I have to show my family I can do it. And maybe I want to prove to Durban that I really am the girl who has her shit together—maybe not two PhDs together, but I can at least finish a job.

After he brings me to his house and I get my stuff and my car, I go to my parents' place. Mom and Kacey are in the kitchen, making the goodies we're having with our afternoon lemonade.

Mom grins. "Back from Billings already?"

"With your friiiieeeend?" Kacey says in a singsong voice.

That's my sister coming out of that little mouth. "Yes. I'm back. Let me get a load of laundry started and I'll be right out."

I'm unpacking when my phone goes wild.

Stanford: Where are you?

What now? Instead of replying, I call him.

"What the hell, Campbell?" he answers.

"Excuse me?" I'm off the clock, and I don't need to take his attitude.

"We're supposed to have riding lessons."

"Not today." I put him on speaker and pull up my calendar. Nothing for today.

"I messaged you."

He did? I check, and yep, some texts came in midmorning when I was fishing with Durban. "I didn't have a signal this morning."

"Where the fuck were you?"

"Excuse me?" I say again.

January's voice sounds in the background and a horse whinnies in the distance. They must be at the barn. How does his bride feel about him raging to his ex that she stood him up? Except I didn't.

"Gimme a minute," he snaps at her. "Campbell, we have three days to get this ride down correctly."

Normally, I'd get all flustered when Stanford gets bossy like this. He reminds me of Daddy and how I felt like I was always letting him down. "If you're using two horses, it won't take long and we have times scheduled on Tuesday and Wednesday."

Hailstorm would get treats and wouldn't have to listen to January and Stanford snap at each other. The other trail horse, Clyde, will be good for January.

January's voice rises in the background, but I can't make out what she says.

"I said gimme a minute." He's speaking through gritted teeth. I don't have to see him to know.

He's going to have a runaway bride before he knows it, and as much as I'd love to sit around and laugh at their fate, I have stakes in this wedding too. There's no way I'm going to let my ex rob me of another five days of sneaking around with Durban.

Oh, and the land deal.

"Stanford, do you mind putting me on speaker?" I can feel his argument coming. He's wound up and he lashes out like a snapping turtle. "Then you don't have to explain it again to your bride."

I purposely use the moniker to remind him that if he's going to walk down the aisle in front of his family and not look like the loser who cheated on his ex, then he needs someone at the end of the aisle waiting for him.

"Fine. You're on speaker." God, he sounds like a spoiled kid.

What was I thinking when I ignored every red flag he waved? "How about I call Grady and see if he can spare someone to take you two riding? You know Hailstorm. Clyde is his brother. Just as mellow. Just as treat driven. January will enjoy the ride and maybe you two can have some me time before the festivities this week really kick off."

He huffs but I hear a murmur of approval from my cousin. It's not just Stanford's reputation on the line, or mine as a professional. January needs to prove to her family that she's not impulsive like me.

"If there's no problem with that, I'll go ahead and call Grady." The foreman is fed up with the bride and groom, and I won't be there to buffer. I'll owe him one. "Once I get the okay, I'll send you a message. And if for some reason it doesn't work out, then might I recommend a romantic walk down to the pond?"

"Ooh, that sounds nice," January says. "Let's do that instead."

Stanford did that walk with me when I first brought him home. It's when he told me he loved me. Now I can see that he was manipulating me because he'd been an ass earlier that day and I'd told him to go back to Washington if he didn't like my home. I'd fully planned to break up with him when I returned to Seattle.

I can't see his face, but the base of his neck is probably pulsing. There's likely a subtle flare in his nostrils. I smile smugly. He can't manipulate me when the love of his life is hoping for a romantic walk.

"Go have some one-on-one time," I say with an exorbitant amount of cheer.

"Thanks, Campbell," January says a moment before the line disconnects.

Either she hung up on me, or he did, but it doesn't matter. I was able to avert an argument that could prevent them from getting to the altar, and I thwarted Stanford's controlling ways. I have five more days with Durban.

I never thought I'd look forward to this week, but here I am.

CHAPTER SIXTEEN

Campbell

Five hours and a tea party later, I'm late. In my defense, Kacey insisted she help me make the salad I brought to contribute to the food trough. I couldn't say no, and rushing a four-year-old doesn't go well. Then we decided to make brownies, and before those were done cooking, she wanted to try another kind of tea. I told Mom to save the kitchen mess for when I'm done here.

Durban and I didn't talk about where I'm sleeping tonight, and I don't want to invite myself over, but also, another trip to "Billings" might rouse more questions than I can answer.

I pull into the distillery parking lot. All the cars and pickups are lined up at the edge of the lot by the trees. My stomach is pitching as I park. I shouldn't be nervous, but I've never had to pretend I haven't tasted every inch of a guy in front of those he cares and trusts the most.

Which also means that he doesn't want those closest

to him to know about me and him. Yet he invited me, and isn't that as confusing as it is endearing?

I suck in a deep breath as I get out of my car, grabbing the bowl of food I brought. I know why we're a secret. We have a good reason. I can't stifle the part of me that wants him to announce us as loud as possible and damn the consequences, but that's a me problem.

He didn't react when Haven busted us, but one is different from all. And he did swear his brother to secrecy.

I start for the crowd, my nerves cranking tighter. I could use a sounding board, but Jamison is still resting after having a baby, so I'm not bothering her with this. Besides, she'd feel obligated to tell Iverson, and then where are we? If Durban hasn't talked to him, I'm not going to spill the beans.

I could call Avery, but she's utterly pragmatic, and I don't need to hear that I'm setting myself up to get hurt.

People mill around tables that have been pulled out of the tasting room. Guys hang out around a grill. There's nothing but tall men in tight shirts with rugged facial hair. Did they multiply?

Durban breaks away from the group by the grill and walks toward me. The tangle inside my belly loosens, and my body warms, like it's getting ready to feel his hands and mouth all over me.

"Hey." The sun makes his dark eyes glitter.

"Sorry I'm late."

"I'm just glad you're here." He says it like he means it. There's no censure. I try to be on time, but I took a gamble today for my niece, and he's not hanging it over my head. I could get used to this.

I tap the top of the bowl. "Kacey wanted to help me with this. We had a tea party today with Mom."

His eyes warm, and I really like when that look is aimed at me. "Sounds like a fun afternoon."

"Well, you know. It was a long drive back from *Billings*."

The warmth in his gaze turns to heat, and I'm caught in the inferno. Flashes of last night, the whole weekend really, make my skin tingle. "I hope the trip wasn't boring."

"It was the mellow de-stressor I needed." Definitely not a lie. I handled the wedding couple and had a fun afternoon. A ton of orgasms helped, but also a weekend of hanging out and talking with Durban. I brandish the salad. "Mom wouldn't let me come without making sure I have something to offer. It's a chop salad. Kacey wouldn't let me touch the brownies we made because she wants to bring them home to her mom and dad."

The way his features soften at that sends my insides all wonky. Each of my ovaries is pointing toward my biological clock and tapping its heel.

I've long wanted what my sister has—a career and a good man who treats her like a princess—so much that I tolerated an arrogant, controlling man to get there. After the breakup, the importance of quality in a partner became crystal clear.

Durban would make a good dad. He'd be practical and understanding and— I cannot go down that road. Not yet. I need one win before I risk getting turned down by someone of his caliber.

"Didn't think we'd have veggies otherwise?" His dimple makes an appearance, and it's like my very own first-place ribbon. Not many people make him smile wide enough to show it.

"Definitely not Haven."

"No. He always brings a dessert. The guy lives in fear that there won't be any."

I scan the crowd. "Did you hire a lot of new people?"

Myles and a tall, bearded man I don't recognize are standing by Lane, Cruz, and Haven. Edna's chatting with an older woman who's pleasantly smiling and nodding. An icy blond is with Clem and another woman with red hair.

He points to the man next to Myles. "That's Tate, Mae's oldest boy." He swings his arm to the redhead. "His wife, Scarlett, and next to her is Myles's wife, Wynter. She was just a little older than Kacey when we were there." He reaches out like he's going to put an arm around my shoulders, but he drops it. "Come on. Let me introduce you to Mae. She's talking to Edna."

As we walk by the group of guys, Haven lifts his chin. "Nice of you to make it back from Billings to join us."

I hold back my smirk. "The getaway was nice."

"Only nice?" Haven's grin widens. "That's disappointing but not unexpected."

I laugh at the absurdity, but I peek at Durban. He's shooting Haven a playful glare.

Myles steps forward. "Campbell, this is Tate, Mae's oldest."

I shake the older man's hand. His smile is congenial, and I'm instantly at ease around him.

"She's the planner for the Baldwin wedding." Durban's standing closer than a guy I just work with would normally, but I don't mind. I like that he can't seem to help himself. "And our Hawthorne Ranch liaison, who's also a Hawthorne."

"We're hoping she'll help us brainstorm." Lane opens the lid of the grill, and the meat inside captivates all the guys.

"Me?" I ask, surprised.

"Not many other event planners in our network," Haven says. "And Durban says you're good." His grin widens.

Out of the corner of my eye, I see a muscle flex in Durban's jaw, but I don't look right at him. My blush will rage if I do.

"I'll introduce you to Mae," Durban says and steers me away.

When we reach Mae, she asks if she can hug me, and when I say yes, I'm embraced by the startlingly strong woman. She wrangled three young Hennessy brothers in addition to many other kids.

She chats with me for a few minutes about my job, delighted to hear about what I do. Her attention is solely on me, and there's no sense I'm falling short of whatever she expected. Meeting Stanford's parents was the opposite of this. Their looks were full of judgment, and anything I said or did only added to it.

I can't ever meet Durban's mom or dad, but this introduction feels like more. It's like he's showing me off to someone important to him, even though she only filled three months of his life.

She's not his mom, I'm not his girlfriend, and he hasn't told me he wants anything different. This is just another dream of mine that is going to go to someone else.

Durban

When I pull into Iverson's, Campbell's car is there. I didn't intend to come at the same time she's visiting, but I like the happy accident. She didn't come over last night after the gathering. Another night in "Billings" would make it too hard to explain.

The way she laughed with Mae and joked around with the guys left me wishing I could put a hand on her lower back or hook an arm around her shoulders. Myles and Tate are happily married, and the other two Foster brothers don't seem to be into Campbell, but I wasn't feeling territorial. I just wanted to show her off as mine.

I can't be falling for her this fast. I thought I was into Natalie after a couple of weeks with her too. Then she moved away, and what bloomed from our long-distance relationship was a deep appreciation for her brains and ambition, and a vast overestimation of how important I was to her.

With Campbell, everything is moving at lightning speed, yet I don't know if I'm the only one in the storm. How do I know when it's too fast?

I don't need to. The wedding is Saturday. Stanford and January are supposed to leave Sunday morning, and I can't have Stanford getting his underwear in a twist, obsessing over his ex, and making his bride run to her parents. When the land is officially signed over to William and Christine, then I can talk to Campbell.

I get out of my pickup.

Iverson meets me outside. "Finally going to meet the big guy?"

"I can give you more time."

"Nah. Jamison is going stir-crazy. She was going to make rounds if you didn't get down here soon." We walk toward the house. "We would've been at Foster House yesterday to see everyone, but we both fell asleep when Tavis was napping."

"Too bad you missed Mae."

"Nope." He opens the door for me. "Jamison made sure I called before they all left town, and they stopped by."

I step in and am enveloped in cool air. It's warm enough outside to run the AC, but there's still a tinge of sunshine and huckleberry blossoms. I follow the cloud to the main area.

My gaze goes right to Campbell. She's standing in the middle of the floor, rocking back and forth with a bundle in her arms. The blanket is blue and light brown, and a tiny mop of dark hair sticks out. She's smiling at our nephew, then she looks up.

My world stops spinning.

She's so damn beautiful, my chest aches with a yearning that's as plain as a billboard. I want this. I want her.

But not too long ago, it's what I wanted with another woman. Am I rushing things? Is my midlife crisis making deals with a pretty young woman and dumping all my upended hopes on her?

That's not fair to Campbell.

A light smile plays across her lips. "Durban. Long time no see."

It's felt like forever. "Nice you could make it to the party last night."

I pry my gaze off her and the Tilt-A-Whirl it creates in my chest.

Jamison is curled into the corner of the couch. Her hair is in the messiest bun I've ever seen, there are bags under her eyes, but she smiles like she's exactly where she wants to be.

Kacey's sitting on Avery's lap in a recliner, poring over her cardboard books. Avery's watching me with a blond brow cocked. Thea's sprawled on the floor at Avery's feet, her short dark hair sticking up in all directions.

I tip my head to them. "Avery. Thea. How was the drive?"

"Long," Avery answers, her gaze jumping from me to Campbell.

Shit. Did everything I was thinking play across my expression? "You staying for a while?"

"Yes." Avery's eyes flash. "We're moral support only. I'm not attending the wedding."

Thea tosses her arm in the air, giving a thumbs-up in what must mean solidarity. "Team Campbell."

"Me too." Kacey puffs her lips out. That's my girl. "I don't like Stan."

Campbell beams. "I have the best posse in the world, but you guys need to go to the wedding so you can tell me how awful January looks and how tacky Stanford's outfit is. He's going with a tux, refusing to wear the crisp black jeans and white dress shirt that January wanted him to wear."

"Is it bad I was worried I'd miss the train wreck?" Avery asks.

Thea sits up and crosses her legs. "I don't want that wedding to be a hot mess, for your sake," she says to Campbell, "but I want January to be a hot mess."

Tavis squawks and squirms. Campbell adds a little bounce to her side to side. "You want that too, don't you?" she coos. "That's why you're my favorite nephew."

"Until Durban or Haven give him some competition," Jamison says with a yawn.

Avery cocks her head, her sharp gaze pinning me like a bug on display. "Planning to give Tavis some competition, Durban?"

Thea taps Avery's knee. "That's intrusive."

"Sure is," Avery answers, but her challenging stare remains on me.

Campbell has rocked herself so her back is to her sister. Her flushed cheeks are on display, and her gaze is darting everywhere but me.

I might've been bowled over by baby fever, but she's not. Why would she be? She's not even thirty, and she's kick-starting a brand-new career. I'm seeing things that aren't there again.

"No baby making is going on," I say. I hold my hands out and close the distance between me and Campbell. "Mind if I hold the little guy?"

Her blush deepens, but she lets me take him. He's a warm weight in my arms. The smell of baby powder mingles with Campbell's summery scent. That's stamped into my midlife-crisis brain now too.

Fuck. All the sex is scrambling my brain. I'm conflating it with the wedding festivities, and my mind is taking off on a tangent. I hold Tavis and remember his sister at this age.

"Ready for the luncheon tomorrow?" Campbell asks

me. Just when I can't believe that she's brought it up in front of her family, she wiggles her fingers toward them. "They were going to boycott that too, but January was upset."

"She'll have no one at her precious lunch," Avery says snidely, "while Can't Stanford will have a full house."

"January will die thinking about how Campbell would've filled that pavilion," Jamison pipes in.

"I need to be in on all this drama." Thea puts her hand on her chest. "I, for once, will not be causing the family drama."

"I'll be there," I say and stuff away the dismay that I might not get Campbell alone like I thought. We're so close, and she'll have too much family there. But my gaze collides with hers, so she knows that I won't just be hoping for sex. "Team Campbell."

CHAPTER SEVENTEEN

Campbell

I'm standing in the pavilion with a sister flanking me on each side and Thea circling us like a bulldog. January called Jamison and invited her to the luncheon. She practically begged her.

Mom's avoiding her sister-in-law. Every time the woman comes close, Mom unapologetically darts in a different direction. Mom's taken to standing by me, since my aunt keeps a wide berth around me.

I love my family.

For the millionth time, I peek over my shoulder at the handsome bartender mixing a cocktail for one of January's childhood friends. The woman's flirting with him, but his expression is impassive as he rattles the metal shaker. As if he senses my attention on him, his gaze slides over. Like every other time, he gets the barest hint of a smile. The girl across from him probably can't tell. But I know, just like I know it's for me.

He's been making me feel like the sexiest woman alive. I'm in a subdued gray dress with white trim, sandals, and my sunglasses perched on my head. I'm not a guest. Avery and Thea are dressed like they're going to the derby, minus a fascinator, although Thea's cowboy hat could almost count as one. Avery's taller than me and Jamison, her wedge sandals boosting her even higher, and her linen baby-pink romper shows off her tan and her highlighted hair.

Thea always shocks me with the way she can style her hair to make her cheekbones and eyes intimidating. Maybe I should cut my hair short. Wear a power romper. Then maybe I would tell off someone who screws me over instead of absorbing all the blame because that's what I've always done.

Jamison pushes at her boobs. She's wearing a maternity dress she had for Kacey and flip-flops. She's dressed for comfort and gives zero fucks. "I can't believe how fast these things fill up."

Iverson's at my parents' house with Tavis. It's not a long drive, and if he needs to bring my nephew here for some food, Jamison can ditch this show and nurse in the lodge. So far, she's sticking it out.

Staff dressed in black polo shirts and black jeans bustle into the pavilion with wagons of food they wheeled from the lodge. Chef is probably in his element, but stressed at serving so many people so far from the kitchen.

I glance at the sky. It's beautiful outside. No chance of rain. The logistics would've been hell with a thunderstorm, but it's not fair that cloudless skies and perfect June temperatures are forecasted for the next several days of wedding festivities.

So far, the couple's time at the Hawthorne Ranch couldn't have gone smoother. I'm the only wrench in their plans, and that's self-inflicted. I can't be blamed for that without them seeming like the villains they are

"I'm going to make you sit." Mom cups Jamison's elbow and glances at me, Avery, and Thea. "You guys coming or are you going to chat for a while?"

Thea dips her head. "I'll come with you. We got dibs on the table in the back, right?"

"It's our assigned spot." January's family is supposed to be up front. Sydney hasn't arrived yet, but that sister drama isn't mine. Other than my aunt and some cousins from her mom's side, January has no other family with her.

Avery and Thea exchange a look.

Thea shoves a thumb over her shoulder. "I'm gonna go sit."

I'm alone with Avery. Warning prickles over my skin just as Avery crosses her arms.

"You and Durban?" she barely asks as a question.

I stiffen and hug my tablet to me. "I don't know what you mean."

"I mean the way he undresses you every time he lays eyes on you. Or how you blush when you two exchange a look that would give Mom a heart attack. I bet if I check him out right now, he'll be focused on your ass."

"There's nothing going on."

She stuffs her hands in her pockets and casually turns around, putting her back to everyone else. Her gaze lifts to Durban for a second. "Yep. You've never been able to lie well." I scowl at her, but she only shrugs. "I can ask him."

"Stop it," I hiss. I've lost this game before it even

started. Avery's cunning and observant, and she won't drop something when she thinks she's right. "We're just using each other, okay?"

Her eyes go cold. "He's using you?"

There are times I appreciate her older-sister protectiveness, but not today. "We're using each other. I've been so wound up with this whole month-long wedding celebration, and he just got out of a long relationship."

"And you two are in a situationship of your own?"

I nod, but there's a tug on my heart. "I'm not romanticizing it. When this wedding is done, he'll move on, and I'll have a business to build."

"What the hell does that mean?" She flicks her narrowed gaze to Durban and back to me. Growing up, people used to think Avery was the quiet, timid one. She's blunt and takes no prisoners, and she's only gotten worse—better?—since moving away from Huckleberry Springs.

"It means that we're friends with benefits," I say quietly. Almost all the guests are seated, and the staff is starting to pass out the starter salad. My stomach rumbles.

"You used to irritate the crap out of him." She taps her chin. "That's why I always suspected he wanted to fuck you."

"Avery!" I snap my mouth shut. That came out way too loud.

January focuses on me like she has laser vision set for destruction. Her mouth forms a flat line. She scoots back and primly walks toward us. I hold in my groan, but Avery doesn't.

"Is everything okay?" she asks with a polite smile, her head tilted like she's talking to a kid.

"Of course." I make sure my grin is a thousand watts. The staff is approaching with the carts full of the starter salad. "You're going to love the salad. Strawberries are super sweet right now, and Chef sources the spinach from a local greenhouse that gets an early start."

January considers me. "It doesn't feel polite to eat when all of my guests aren't sitting."

My facial muscles strain with the effort of holding my smile. "Avery was just taking her seat."

Avery flings her ponytail over her shoulder and gives my arm a squeeze. "Brides, am I right?" she mutters. She gives January a patronizing pat on the shoulder. "Relax and have fun. It's your big day." She says it with false excitement.

I want to both laugh and cry. January's eyes shimmer. Avery never could stand her, and I was surprised Avery was on the invite list at all.

January sniffles, and my shoulders drop. I *am* the planner. I'm cursed with professional pride and the urge to fix this. She's a client, and she wants a good start to her happily ever after. Just because I don't have one isn't her fault. Well, technically, it is, but she saved me from Stanford, and no matter how much she loves him, their marriage is going to end in her heartbreak. Stanford will take care of himself.

What should I tell her to make her feel better that doesn't sound like I approve of this marriage? "It's very considerate of you to include Jamison."

My cousin gives me a self-deprecating shrug, like it's the least she could do when in fact it *was* the least she could do. "I want my dream wedding to be perfect, and that includes having the most important people around me." She shoots me a supportive smile. "Feel free to enjoy some leftovers when a seat opens up. I'm sure there'll be extra plates on the cart and some water glasses left untouched."

As she sashays away, my temper rises until my heart beats around my skull. I tried to help her feel better, and she turns around and demeans me?

I'm not touching any damn leftovers or unused water glasses.

Two days.

Two more days.

I just want to tell her to kick rocks—right up her ass and out that smug expression. I did once, and that's how I ended up planning her happy day. January can be petty, but I never thought she'd stoop to this level. Was our whole friendship a lie?

Leftovers. Spare water.

My heart rate soars. A blood vessel in my head is going to pop if I stand here much longer.

I suck in a few deep breaths before I cross to Mom and touch her shoulder. "I need to dip into the lodge for a bit. I'll be back before the meal's done."

Avery and Jamison frown at me. If Mom senses something's wrong, she doesn't stop me, only nods and shoos me away.

My face is hot as I pass Durban. I refuse to look at him. I've talked to him about all of this, but now's not the time. Maybe tonight, when it's dark, and we're alone, I can spill my heart out about how much this moment hurts.

I'm across the lawn and in the lodge in record time. I head straight for the meeting room. It's dark, and I leave the lights off when I enter.

I'm about to shut the door when a big body comes through. "What's wrong?"

"Durban," I whisper-shout, whirling around. "You can't be here. You have to serve cocktails."

He comes in and closes the door. The light is off, but sunlight pokes through the slats of the blinds at the window. His face is carved from shadows, and my stomach somersaults. I could stare at him for an eternity and never get tired of the view.

My dull headache infringes on my admiration of him. I prod my temples with my fingertips. This wedding is messing with my head. I want what January has. I want Durban. I'm ready to throw myself down the aisle at him. Miss Independent right here.

How can I trust my feelings when I spent so long with a guy who was very wrong for me? I had no idea my best friend would bury a knife to the hilt in my back.

"Thea jumped in for me," he says. "Claimed she was ready to punch the snotty bride and that she put herself through college bartending. Avery's distracting your mom from going after you. I told them I had to grab some supplies from the bar in here."

Good. Everything is taken care of. My family and Durban have my back. "I was so tempted to quit on the spot. She purposely insulted me, and that's what hurts the most." I squeeze my eyes shut and suck in his caramel-and-oak scent. My hormones are programmed to relax around him. Tension melts out of my body to the point where I'm just tired. "I've taken so much shit from employers that I didn't deserve, but standing up for myself cost me every time." I fold my arms and lean my butt against the table. He's between me and the doorway, like he's buffering me from the world.

"You can quit." He brushes the backs of his fingers down my cheeks, and I soak up every millimeter of his touch. "You can tell her and Stanford to go to hell, and we'll support you. Your dad will support you. The town will support you."

I blow out a heavy breath, but turn my face into his hand. "I'm so close to the end. I can't let her ruin this for me. This is the only way to cut my uncle out of all our lives. If I wreck his daughter's wedding, he'll never let the land go." I inhale a lungful of air, steeling myself to go out and face the crowd. "I'm going to finish this. I'm going to help this ranch. I'm not going to be the drain on this family."

He's even closer now. "You're too damn good for this wedding. Your whole family is." He pauses and screws his face up. "Your immediate family."

Our bodies are lined up. I slide my hands around his shoulders. "I feel better now. Because of you."

"I didn't do anything."

"You made me feel less alone." I know my sisters and Mom are out there. Jamison, Avery, and Thea will throw down with almost no notice, and Jamison would do the same and calmly go nurse Tavis afterward. But I can't have that. I can't be the cause of more drama.

"I'm here for you. All weekend."

And after? I'm afraid to ask. Two more days. That's all. Three, if I wait for Sunday to see if Durban is still interested in me.

What if he wants to be done with me? Or keeps me at a distance and keeps what's between us to just sex?

Preemptive hurt rises up like smoke. Would I go along with it just to get more of him? Put up with the bare minimum when I know I want more? I've been down that road.

The wedding hasn't even happened yet, and Durban's here with me now.

I want to push my hands through his dark locks, but he's combed his hair nicely. If he'd worn his cowboy hat instead, he would've stolen all the attention from the groom.

It's why I suggested he doesn't wear it when he's working. A wedding planner has her pride.

He places his mouth on mine for a slow, searching kiss. I take it further, licking across the seam of his lips. It's like I flip a switch. He clamps me harder against him and opens for me, tangling his tongue with mine in a slow, sensual dance.

The ridge of his erection presses into my belly. I don't have much room between him and the table, but I claw at the waistband of his jeans. I need him to hold up his end of our agreement now. I need him to drain this stress from me, to squash these hopeless and hopeful thoughts playing tug-of-war in my head.

He breaks the kiss like it's the last thing he wants to do. "Are you sure?" He's got his hands on my waist, stroking my sides with his thumbs.

I'm one hundred percent certain I want him. Beyond tonight, but for now? Yes. "Can you be quick?"

He scoops up the hem of my dress and drags my underwear off. I step out of them, but I wouldn't have cared if he ripped them off.

"Hold this," he says about the fabric of my skirt. He shoves my panties in his pocket and finishes freeing himself. Then he hitches me on top of the table and skims his hand over my thigh, sweeping up to my pussy. Pleasure ripples from every point he touches.

"I need to get you ready," he says roughly in my ear.

"I'm ready. Just fuck me."

He lets out a combination of a growl and a grunt and thrusts inside. Suddenly full, that pressure I wanted him to drain is gone, replaced by him and increasing satisfaction. I smother a cry against his shoulder but immediately grind against him. I need more, and I need it fast.

He pumps into me, long and slow at first, until I grab his ass and urge him to go faster. And faster he goes. "Do you need it hard, Belle?"

"God, yes." I widen my legs. The edges of his fly cut into my thighs, but I relish the bite of pain. With each shove in, he rubs against my clit, and I edge closer to the top of my peak. Almost there. "Harder."

The cords of his neck strain as he hinges his hips back and forth. "Hold on tight."

I release his butt and grip the edge of the table. He slams into me. Withdraws. Rams in again. Over and over until he's grunting with each breath.

My mind is blissfully empty. I can think of nothing but hanging on. I careen through my crest, coming harder than I thought possible. My body clamps on to him so tightly, I don't know how he keeps moving. I clamp my legs harder around him.

He grits his teeth through a roar, coming with me, and plants both hands on each side of me. When he slams his mouth to mine, I nearly topple back.

Two seconds later, he's pulling out of me and tucking himself back into his pants.

My heart rate hasn't slowed down, but it's for a

different, more climactic reason than when I walked in here.

"You okay?" he asks as he helps me put my feet solidly on the floor.

"Much better." I'll go through the rest of the night on a post-coital cloud. I straighten my dress and give his pocket a pointed look. "Um, my underwear?"

The corner of his mouth lifts. "I'm gonna go ahead and keep these." He wraps an arm around my waist. "And you can be distracted from everything going on out there by my cum running down your thigh."

Durban

Iverson tosses a square bale of hay into the back of the trailer hitched to the side-by-side. We're behind the barn, finishing morning chores. His horses are lined up at the fence, their tails swishing, watching us.

"Last one," I say as I fling mine in.

He swipes the back of his wrist across his brow and rests a gloved hand on the edge of the trailer. "How'd last night go?"

"Fine." He continues to watch me. The back of my neck prickles. "What?"

"Jamison said you couldn't keep your eyes off Campbell. And then you two disappeared during the meal."

"I had to restock," I say as boringly as possible. Like I didn't have the hottest quickie of my life and become that pervert who won't give a woman her underwear back.

"You came back with one bottle."

Damn. I hoped no one noticed. I shrug and take my work gloves off. "That's restocking."

"Something you want to tell me?"

"Nothing to share." I'm not the only one involved. If Campbell wanted Jamison to know, she would've told her. Either she was keeping her sister from worrying, or she flat-out didn't want to tell her.

He narrows his eyes, studying me even longer. "Haven told me."

"That cocksucker!"

Iverson stabs a finger in my direction. "I knew it! What does he know that I don't?"

I snap my mouth shut. Haven didn't say a thing, and I fell for it. Iverson outsmarted me.

Hurt passes through his eyes. "I know I've had stuff going on, but it's not like you can't talk to me."

I puff out a hard breath, drop the tailgate of the trailer, and prop an ass cheek on it.

"Natalie broke up with me."

His cheek twitches, but he holds his reaction in well. "And Campbell is the rebound?"

"*No.*" Is she? I've never needed a rebound relationship, and maybe at first I was only looking for relief, but Campbell's always been more than that. "We didn't want you to worry, but we didn't want anyone to know. Haven caught her at my place and said he wouldn't tell. It's just . . . She was stressed about the wedding, and I was frustrated about waiting for Natalie only to be dropped right before she finishes her degree."

"Damn." He shakes his head before narrowing his attention on me. "You miss Natalie?"

I miss Campbell. I haven't thought about Natalie,

but I lift a shoulder so it doesn't seem like I'm panting after Campbell when she's vulnerable.

A flicker of disappointment lights his eyes. "Can't help taste," he mutters.

"I don't miss her," I say, irritated that he assumed my silence was about my ex because why wouldn't he?

He takes off his gloves and slaps the side of the trailer with them, shaking his head. "I thought it was weird that you and Campbell were working real well together when you could hardly tolerate her."

I didn't know her. "We get along just fine."

He snorts. "With your clothes off."

We didn't need to be naked last night. But all those times talking with her, in the dark, in the barn, and eating together, I was stripped down more than I've ever been. "It's just until the wedding's done. Then we're going to concentrate on our work."

"What about work do you need to concentrate on?"

"Getting taken seriously."

"We do take you seriously."

"No, you and Lane take the bottom line seriously, but this whole endeavor was to push the limits of spirits. Right now, we're pushing mediocre."

His brows shoot up. "Damn, Durban. Tell me how you really feel."

"We need to really unleash our abilities, and then we need to show them off. We need to enter more contests, win awards, and create buzz. We need to make the bottles that sell at estate auctions for thousands because that would mean our reputation is that well known and respected."

Iverson doesn't immediately respond. He swats his gloves against the trailer a few times. "We're working on

Rafting and Tasting. Then there's the street fair in Billings."

And Bozeman and Helena. "We need more. We need to expand."

He slides his gloves back on. "Maybe you could talk to that event planner you're sneaking around with and see if she has any more ideas."

"I will." Relieved my interrogation didn't last long and he didn't berate me for fucking his sister-in-law, I push off the tailgate of the trailer and walk around to the driver's side. Time to get this day going. Excitement's starting to build at the thought of discussing another project to work on with Campbell. It means working together more after the wedding. It means watching her blossom and thrive.

"Durban?"

The hesitant expression on my brother's face isn't one I've seen before. He's the guy we go to for everything. Our leader, and not just because he's the oldest. Because he's always taken care of us. "Yeah?"

"Relationships . . . can be . . . more."

"What are you talking about?"

He doesn't get into the side-by-side but continues to shift uncomfortably. "It means, fuck, I don't know. You waited for Natalie for years, and she only tossed scraps to you, and now you're limiting what you could have with Campbell to the wedding."

"That's all we've talked about," I say stubbornly, embarrassment coagulating in my chest. She hasn't said she wants more with me. "We have an agreement, and I'm not adding to her stress."

"You want more though."

"It's only been a couple of weeks."

"You stayed loyal to Natalie for years after only a few months."

A blob in my chest starts to pulsate. "Exactly. I'm not making that mistake again." I start the engine, and it whirs to life. I'm done with this conversation.

Iverson doesn't move. "You weren't the one that made the mistake."

I stare ahead, fighting off a case of heartburn that feels a lot like yearning. I did make a mistake—with Natalie and, worse, when I judged Campbell. Add in the mess of a relationship Campbell just got out of, and she'll probably want to be left alone after the wedding. If she does keep me around, it'd be for the orgasms. As much as I could lose myself in her forever, sex isn't enough. Waiting on her for years wouldn't be enough.

I want all of Campbell, and I'm too much of a pussy to ask her if she wants the same. "Campbell and I think each other is fine for a good time, and neither of us has expressed wanting more. It's as simple as that."

CHAPTER EIGHTEEN

Campbell

I'm in the meeting room, which has become my makeshift office during the final days of this event. It's also functioning as storage for the decorations that'll go in the pavilion tomorrow. I've had sketches and diagrams sent to the staff. My notes with Chef have been triple-checked.

I can't wait until I can dig into a big event that doesn't have me feeling severed and sewn up with each step of the process.

Reclining in the chair right beside the spot Durban fucked me on last night, I take a deep breath. I can't believe we did that. I risked getting discovered, and from the way Jamison was side-eyeing me the rest of the night, there's a lot of suspicion. I could barely look at Durban until the luncheon was done. I didn't miss the way January glared at me either.

I don't know what more she wants. I'm giving her

the wedding of my dreams, and if she thinks I'm sneaking around with Durban, so what? She should be relieved I'm not trying to steal her man. She can have him with a bow on.

I swipe a hand down my face. Time to go get the pavilion prepped. I rise, gather my stuff, and shut off the light. Oh, right, my headphones are charging. I need music to do my admin stuff, or my mind wanders. I dig those out of the wall, and I'm walking toward the door when voices make me stop.

"I don't know why you insist on having her at the dinner." As if I conjured January, her voice snakes into the meeting room.

"Keep your voice down, Jan." Stanford has that tone, the one that used to make me feel so small. He could always put me in my place so effortlessly. Instead of January's very justified question, he turns it around on her.

Hasn't she told him she hates that nickname?

"Well, then answer me," she replies almost as loudly as before. "You're surrounded by guys. I'm not allowed—"

"Did I come to your quaint luncheon?"

I almost snort. January's gathering had four courses. Yes, they included a spinach salad, tiny sandwiches, veggies with some fancy marinade that Chef was excited to try, and mini pastries, but it was an experience. I made sure of it. Just like I'm putting on the most masculine stag party, or whatever Stanford and his buddies are calling it. His prime rib dinner with four different sides and a pistachio-cream-filled cannoli from Dee's Sweets is going to be so good, the whole wedding party is going to talk about it for years.

Chef's making a plate for me to eat before the dinner begins, so I don't miss out. No leftovers for me.

"I know, but it just seems like you're making this about her and not about us." January's whining now.

"Aw, babes-a-million, you know it's only about us. You wanted our wedding here."

I hold back a gag on babes-a-million. How did I not see that as red flag number twelve? *It's because you're one in a million, babe.* I roll my eyes at his excuse. Maybe his other exes and I can form a babes-a-million club.

I will January to see that he's turning this argument on her. Once her eyes are opened, she won't be able to unsee it. I still care for her, but also, I would love for her to ditch his ass.

Successful career, successful wedding. If I repeat that enough, I'll make it through tonight and tomorrow.

"I wanted the wedding here, but I didn't want her to plan it." January sounds so pouty my lower lip sticks out for her. "She's gotten fired twice."

I bristle when he chuckles.

"Thankfully, she can pull her shit together for us." He says it so smoothly, I almost miss the insult. Bastard. "Tonight, I'm hanging with the guys as a big thank-you for coming out to Nowhere, Montana, with us. My dad and I are going to celebrate that we'll no longer have to waste time bumming around this big, boring state and can finally get back to civilization. Then tomorrow? Tomorrow, baby, you and I are going to say our vows and we're going to become one."

"You and me," she says in a cringey baby-girl voice

There's a loud smooching sound. "Us. And you're going to show me that new lingerie you bought just for tomorrow night."

"What if I give you a preview?"

My gag reflex is going to revolt if I keep repressing it. The kissing sounds grow more frequent and somehow deeper. Gross. What if they come in here and know I was listening?

I'd be mortified and look like a pervert. Clothing scrapes along the wall, and adrenaline pours into my veins. I am not going down for eavesdropping when I was in here doing my job.

Thinking fast, I stuff my headphones on and rub my eyes. Then I rush out and pull to a stop when I see them. Stanford yanks himself off her, his eyes hooded and his lips glistening.

Again, gross. I used to be into that. Before Durban, with his dark eyes and the way his mustache marks me like I'm his property.

"Ohmigosh," I say and fake a yawn. "If you need the meeting room, it's all yours."

"Were you sleeping?" Amusement dances across Stanford's face.

"It's going to be a late night and a long day tomorrow." I smile primly when I see the judgment in January's eyes. "Since I get breaks, you know, legally, I took a siesta. Well. See ya." I start walking away.

"You heading out to the pavilion?" Stanford asks.

"Yep." I don't stop.

Their voices fade behind me. I push out the door by the kitchen and round the back of the lodge to head toward the pavilion. Staff is already treading back and forth, getting the tables and chairs cleaned and set up. There won't be any decorations but the big, boring Montana landscape. Stanford thinks it's good enough to impress his buddies. I think it's the perfect decor.

Durban would too.

My belly flutters. He's going to be here soon.

"Hey, Campbell, wait up," Stanford calls from behind me.

I'm tempted to sprint. I don't slow. "How can I help you?"

"I need to talk to you about tonight and tomorrow."

"Okay." I wave to the sous chef, hoping that's enough to dissuade Stanford from whatever he wants to say.

"Privately."

I go rigid and come to a stop twenty yards from my goal. "What's up?"

He looks around. "Here?"

"I don't think it's a good idea for us to be private."

He has the grace to look chagrined. "I want a different bartender."

"Excuse me?" Does he think he can ban Durban? It's Stanford's wedding, but damn. I'm not a miracle worker. And I need Durban around for my sanity. If I have to stand in my little corner tonight and watch Stanford drink and boast for hours, I'll lose my shit on the bride and groom so fast.

"Durban Hennessy. He's not allowed here."

I bark out a laugh. "Be serious."

"I am."

He is. Shit. Stanford is going all alpha male, and it could tank this wedding. I can't think of me, or he'll sniff that out. I'll appeal to the common sense I hope he has. "Do you think bartenders grow on trees?" Maybe that's not the best tactic. "You hired Foster House to provide a wet bar. Iverson just had a baby and he can't pull himself away, and the other three have to run the distillery while Durban is here."

"Then swap him out."

I cross my arms, trying not to make it such a defensive stance. My anger writhes to get out, and I struggle to contain it. RIP my professionalism. "You want to play dictator with who serves the drinks, you're going to realize they don't care, Stanford. You need them. They don't need you."

He lifts his chin, the picture of arrogance. "I do not need them."

"And all the people that January told would be treated to a rustic Montana experience, from the food to the drinks to the people who produce and serve them? What is she going to tell them?"

His expression ripples with displeasure. The cracks are visible. It's working.

"It'd be embarrassing." I shrug, like, *what can you do?*

"I don't want him serving," he reiterates.

"What's the real problem? Does January resent his presence?"

"She said you two were unprofessional yesterday."

She can suck it. "What did she see?" He cocks a brow, but I continue the stare-down. In the name of irritating him more, I fiddle with the horseshoe charm on my necklace. "What does she think we're doing?"

He works his jaw back and forth. "You're fucking him."

As often as I can. "Say I am. Was it in front of guests?"

"Was it during the luncheon?"

"Was what? Restocking the bar? Or getting my head in a better place when your bride and my former best friend invited me to sit at someone's dirty spot and eat any leftovers available?" I press my lips together. I'm not going to make this any more personal; otherwise, I will be the reason for it and the blame for it. "I would hope even you can see how far out of my way I'm going to be professional. I'm not the one who betrayed someone who trusted them without question. I'm not the one who planned a wedding at the home of the person they betrayed. And I'm not the one holding the family's legacy over their head to pull off a hiccup-free ceremony."

His jaw gets harder with the more I say. I've pushed him too far. I've hit his pride and that of his bride.

"This could very easily be a train wreck," I say in a gentler voice. "It's up to the three of us to show everyone else that the atmosphere is celebratory."

He's softening, then his gaze lifts over my shoulder, and fire flashes in his eyes. "He's here."

The hot brush of Durban's gaze caresses the back of my neck, and a sensuous shiver traces over my skin. I melt against his invisible touch, and Stanford's shrewd gaze latches onto whatever dreamy expression has plastered itself across my face.

To keep that professional front up, I dig out my phone. "Right on time. Early even. Excuse me while I catch him up on how the rest of the evening's going to go."

I ditch Stanford, but I have to make a hard decision, and it's right when I could use Durban's special stress relief the most.

Durban

· · ·

Campbell's wringing her hands, and from my periphery, I can see Stanford mean-mugging me. He knows we're having sex. Well, he suspects it. But the bottom line is that he's upset, and we're facing down the last twenty-four hours.

She's giving me that worried look, the one that says she's scared I'll be disappointed. I am. Who wouldn't be if they were told by Campbell that they shouldn't touch her tonight? She's also fretting about my reaction toward Stanford.

I lean on the makeshift bar I'm going to stand behind for the next five hours until eleven, when the guys will all go to their rooms for a night of sleep before the big day. No hijinks allowed. While I might like the plan, I would bet January set the curfew. She doesn't want to be in her room, being a good little bride and not seeing the groom the night before the wedding, but she also doesn't want to be made a fool. There's no way she's giving Stanford a green light to spend the night away from her when Campbell's in the area. If January truly fears that something could happen, then she doesn't know her cousin very well.

Campbell would never betray her like that. I have that misplaced loyalty in common with Campbell.

Campbell flutters her fingers in the air. "I know it's not fair, but I don't dare leave the pavilion or he might come looking for me."

He could try. He'd be stopped. I lean closer to her, not in an intimate way, but like we're discussing how many drinks to serve each of the groom's party. "Belle, it's okay. I'm not going to get you in trouble, and as much as I'd like to be the thorn under that man's collar, I'm not messing with his night." I maintain eye contact so she knows I'm serious. "Because it would mess with you."

Finally, her shoulders relax. "Thank you."

"There's nothing to thank me for. You asked me to be professional."

"Believe me, I wish I had the guts to be unprofessional."

"There's a lot riding on this." A lot that her parents should stand up for and not her alone. William has been doing what he can to take the pressure off. All of the staff of Hawthorne Guest Ranch has, but the vast majority is on Campbell's strong shoulders.

I only admire her fortitude more.

"I need a drink to kick this party off," she mutters. She props a hand close to mine on the portable bar top and one on her hip. To anyone else, we're shooting the breeze, and she's telling me to water down the liquor to keep these guys from getting out of line. I already planned to do that. I brought the lowest-proof spirits with the most flavor and chose the manliest cocktails that make a guy not realize how much nonalcoholic stuff is already in there. I basically do the opposite of what Silas would do at Bootleg Tavern.

I put a plastic glass on the bar top. Her gaze drops to it, then lifts to me.

The ice bucket was dropped off just as I arrived. I dig out two round balls—Chef made sure even the ice was fancy—then I grab a bottle of cucumber-and-jalapeño-infused vodka. "This is new."

Interest shines in her eyes. Much better than how fraught she was minutes ago.

I pour a small splash. She won't want to drink a lot, and it's not enough for anyone to find reproachful if they see her having a drink. Then I fill the cup with club soda and add an umbrella left over from the luncheon.

She takes a sip, and a little one of those moans I love slips out. "Ohmigosh, that's refreshing."

I grin, proud as hell when infusions are the easiest thing we can do. "We're going to use that for the Rafting and Tasting event next month with the huckleberry mint."

"Your idea?"

"I get to do stuff outside the box and customize each event we do. Iverson also suggested I speak with an event planner and come up with more ideas."

She takes a drink and looks around before leaning in. "I heard you're sleeping with one."

I lean closer. "Belle, we ain't sleeping."

She giggles, and the happy sound draws attention. "More events?" She's in business mode. Relaxed, but her brain is whirring. "What do you have planned already?"

"The bigger street fairs."

She takes a drink and plays the liquid over her tongue. I know just how it'd taste if I kissed her— refreshing, just like summer. "What about a smaller, more targeted craft fair, like food crafts?" Excitement flares bright in her gray eyes. "Local one. A Huckleberry Springs street fair during the height of tourist season. All local vendors."

"I like it. We can bring the people to us. I bet you could even pull it off this summer."

Her pleased smile curls right through me. "On a smaller scale. I'll reach out to Elodie, and— Oh! You know what you could do?" Her thrill grabs Stanford's attention, and I don't have to do anything to rub it in his face. She's living her life right now, doing a job she enjoys, and it's getting under his collar. "She's doing the Billings street fair. What if she uses some Foster House spirits in her goods, and you guys cross-promote each other? Each booth can send people to the other."

Damn, that's a good idea. She came up with it that quickly? "I'll talk to the guys and we'll link up with Elodie. Then you can work on the fair."

Her grin turns triumphant, and warmth infuses my insides. I put that there, and it wasn't because of sex. "And you can use both events, should they happen, as reasons to try something new."

How did I ever think Campbell was selfish? She makes things happen for others. She's always thinking of them. "You're pretty amazing, you know that?"

She takes another sip of her cocktail and casts her eyes downward, as if the attention is too much. "It's just part of the job."

"No, it's much more than that."

Her blush is going to make everyone think we're fucking, and we are, but in this moment, her flush is because someone appreciates her.

I don't want to be just another person in her life who makes her feel alone. When this damn weekend is done, I'm dropping my heart at her feet. If she wants to kick it, I'll deal with it. But if she wants to just let it stay there, in her vicinity, I'll be happy. Because Campbell Hawthorne is a girl worth waiting for.

She sets the drink behind the bar, in the corner of the workstation, and grabs her tablet. "Can you keep this safe while I double-check everything?"

"Yes." Before she leaves, I almost grab her wrist, but that might put the tension back into her shoulders. "Campbell?"

She spins around, and the skirt of her dress swirls. She's got her tablet tucked into the crook of her elbow, and she hugs it closer. Intelligent. Competent. Sexy as hell. I thought I had a type, but it's her. Just her.

I do the same surreptitious look she did earlier. "I'm not leaving you alone tonight. I'll walk you to your car—and all the way to my place." I lower my voice for the last part. "And you're going to wear that Dee's Sweets sweater of mine and nothing else to bed."

A grin spreads across her face, like the damn sunrise just for me. "Promise?"

"Fact."

CHAPTER NINETEEN

Campbell

I wore my most comfortable cowboy boots since I didn't want to show any more leg than I had to today, but after hours, my feet hurt.

Durban hasn't cracked a smile once all night, even when Daddy ordered a drink. Neither of them looks like they're enjoying their night. Durban at least comes off as sternly professional. Daddy's red face makes me question if he's got heartburn or if he's having a heart attack. As for the rest of the crowd, they seem to be enjoying themselves.

Stanford's cousins from the East Coast and the friends of his I had a hard time tolerating when we were together dutifully ignore me. When my back's turned, it's a different story. Murmurs ignite and the spot between my shoulders burns with their stares, but I haven't overheard anything, and that's fine with me. I don't know what narrative Stanford and January spun, and I don't want to. I can brush off the furtive looks that turn innocent when I'm close, but if that's the worst, I'll chalk this up to a successful, if frustrating, evening.

There's been plenty of shitting on Montana. The guys joked about how they were surprised the lodge doesn't have outhouses, or why they didn't get full-body long johns, the kind with the flap in the back for taking a shit, when they checked in. I'd be insulted, but my imagination created a humorous image of all these boastful men in onesie pajamas. Then I tried picturing Durban in a pair, and my mouth went dry. His muscles would only complement the style.

The sun has set, and most of the light in the sky is dying. The bug netting was lowered a couple of hours ago. It's almost ten thirty, and many of the guys are filtering out. Stanford sees them all off, casting glances toward Durban and my dad. My uncle was one of the first to leave. Seeing how well the wedding is going off seems to give him the same heartburn/heart attack appearance as Daddy. A vine of satisfaction winds around my heart. If my aunt and uncle dislike Stanford and have to eat their emotions the entirety of the marriage, that's a small but sweet revenge.

"Go ahead and call it a night, Stanford," Daddy says gruffly. "I'll make sure everything's wrapped up."

Irritation ripples through Stanford's glassy eyes. "It's early. There wasn't enough planned for tonight."

I bristle against the censure. There were free drinks, free food—five courses—cards for poker, and a blackjack table in the corner. It was all funny money, but with the firepit and even more free booze, what did he expect? "I could've busted out Twister."

Durban snorts behind me, and I repress the urge to

share an amused look with him. My ex grinds his teeth together so hard I can't believe I don't hear his molars crack.

"Eh," Daddy says, rising and slapping Stanford on the back, rightfully defusing the situation when we're so close to the finish line. "It was a groom's dinner and not a bachelor party. The difference isn't just strippers."

Stanford rolls his eyes. "Listen, about tomorrow, I know Jan wants me to ride up, but I'd like you to bring the horses to us right after we say our vows, William."

I frown. That would mean Daddy would miss the wedding. Not a hardship for him, but inconsiderate all the way around.

Stanford tugs at the collar of his gray dress shirt. "I'm not smelling like a horse when I say my vows. There has to be some sophistication at some point." Without waiting for Daddy to answer, he starts for the path. "I'm going to check on my bride and turn in."

"Good idea. Tomorrow's going to be a long day." Daddy waits for Stanford to step off the pavilion platform. "And the first day of the rest of your life," he calls.

There's a stutter in Stanford's step, and Daddy's laugh is silent, but his chest is shaking. "If that gives him a hitch in his giddyap, then there's trouble in paradise." He circles a finger at Durban. "Pour me the strongest thing you've got, Hennessy. I know there's something hiding back there." Daddy blows out a breath. "Pour three of 'em. We deserve it."

He hobbles off to talk to the few staff members loading carts and cleaning out any remaining dishes and garbage. The chairs will remain out, and the tables will get wiped and hauled out tomorrow when it's daylight.

When the last of the staff clatters their carts across the yard, Daddy takes a seat. I sit across from him, and Durban puts a glass with a finger of what I guess is whiskey in front of each of us. He settles down next to me. The night is warm, but I soak up his heat.

Daddy takes a big drink, downing half of what's in his glass. "Good stuff," he says on a sigh. He holds up his drink and rotates it, letting the amber liquid catch the light. "I had no idea you boys could do more than cowboy."

"Daddy!" How can parents say something so instantly mortifying?

I'm not touching Durban, but I can guess how tense he just got.

Dad shrugs. "They were good cowboys. Damn good." He lifts his glass like he wants us to clink ours against it.

"I'm not toasting that," I say tightly.

"It's all right." Durban raises his glass and gives me an encouraging smile. "How 'bout we toast to being underestimated. I'm guilty of it too," he says softly.

I warm inside. He means me. I clink my plastic cup to theirs. "That makes all of us."

I grin at him, and his eyes twinkle. I want to say more, but Daddy's watching us. Smiling at my dad, I take a drink. Maybe soon I'll have something to tell him.

Daddy polishes off his whiskey and slams the cup to the table. He heaves out a weary sigh. "This wedding, kiddo . . ." Rubbing his hand over his mustache, he shakes his head. "We should just cancel it. Bow out and tell my brother to take it somewhere else."

Hope surges inside me and crashes just as quickly. He would do it. I wouldn't even have to beg. So I need to be strong enough to see this through, all the way around. The ceremony. Keeping my fling with Durban a secret. Maintaining my professionalism. "There's too much on the line. I can do this."

"You shouldn't have to," he grumbles.

I lift a shoulder. It's been a long evening of watching my ex boast about himself and listening to him trash many of the things I love. Strain has sunk into my muscles like I soaked in it. "One more day. Maybe I should plan a spa day for Sunday."

"For the whole week," Daddy says.

"And the next weekend." The corners of Durban's eyes crinkle with his sort of smile. He flicks his gaze toward Daddy and back to me. "Go somewhere by yourself. No exes allowed."

By myself. Ouch. He was saying that for my dad's benefit, right? Does Durban want this thing between us to be nothing but a fling? Something to bridge the gap until he finds another uber-smart woman who gets his science jokes.

"Tomorrow is gonna be a tough one." Daddy scoots his chair back. Fatigue lines his eyes, and even his mustache is drooping. "Honestly, I expected this to be worse. January could've been more of a bridezilla, and the silver spoons could've been even bigger pricks."

"They're still pricks." Durban glowers at his cup.

"Yeah." Daddy stands and stretches. "But after tomorrow, my brother can be a prick without his name anywhere on this property. Thanks to Campbell." I flash Daddy a wan smile. He cocks his head toward the screen. "Let's head out. The staff is going to flip this in the morning."

"Go on, Daddy. I need to review tomorrow with

Durban in case it's too chaotic to touch base before the reception starts."

He pauses, looking at me and then outside. The lights around the lodge illuminate much of the yard, but the pavilion is an oasis with a gravel path lined with temporary solar lights.

"I'll make sure she gets to her car okay," Durban says. The man made me a promise and he's going to keep it. For me.

I'm falling so hard for him. It's more than how he makes me feel physically. He takes care of me. We might be trying to hide our fling, but he's still watching out for me.

My heart swells so damn big in my chest when I take him in, reclining in his chair with an ankle kicked over his knee. His hair is still neatly combed after a busy night of filling orders and getting talked at like he's a posable mannequin. A situation like that is his hell, but he played the game because I asked him to.

Daddy's waiting for me to give the okay. I get up and round the table to give him a hug. "Good night."

He squeezes my ribs. "I'm proud of you, kiddo. Say the word, and I'll abort this thing."

Word.

Word, word, word.

My time with Durban would also be up. The chaos that would ensue if the wedding got called off? I'd lose track of Durban, and then what? I call him? I look at my phone every three seconds waiting on him? I go into the distillery like an obsessed fan and do the walk of shame out if he rejects me?

Ugh. The wedding has to be a go. "It's fine. Love you. Say good night to Mama for me."

He gives me another pat before he ducks out of the netting and takes the path to the parking lot.

I don't return to the table. Durban tracks me as I wander around the pavilion.

I trail my fingers over the nets. Stanford demanded that Daddy spray for bugs, but my ex didn't get his way. My uncle even tried to strong-arm Daddy, but he wouldn't budge. I can still hear his growl. *We work with the land, we don't fight against it.*

The legs of Durban's chair scrape against the wooden floor. "This place is going to be transformed tomorrow." The steady thud of his boots sounds behind me, growing closer.

"Tomorrow, there's supposed to be a breeze the perfect strength to keep the bugs away." A perfect day for my cousin's big day. The netting will be rolled up and unnoticeable. I tread toward the front where the band will be set up for the reception. "There'll be a flower arch in the shape of the ranch sign you drive under when you turn down the driveway." I stop exactly where the couple will stand. "White draping, white roses, with blush roses as accent."

"You have good taste."

My smile is sad. It's going to be so beautiful. But it won't be me enjoying it. "The chairs will all have matching accents on the backs. And a white satin runner will go from here to where the groom will dismount Hailstorm after he rides in like a white knight. After the vows, he'll throw his new bride up on Clyde, and he'll get on Hailstorm, and they'll ride away." Right in front of me. Because I'm relegated to the back corner.

"Maybe Hailstorm will have diarrhea."

I laugh. "Maybe, but there'll still be the reception to get through."

"Where will the dance floor be?"

I hold my arms out and spin. The tips of my fingers brush against the hot skin of his arm. "Right here. And she's going to dance to the song I told her I wanted to dance to with my prince when I was five." I stop and drop my arms.

He digs out his phone. "What song is that?"

" 'Can't Help Falling in Love' by Elvis Presley. My parents danced to it at their wedding. They said no one could believe Daddy didn't have something by Garth Brooks, but Daddy's a romantic and he and my mom love that song."

Durban's staring at his phone, tapping into it as he wanders to the nearest table. Is this another thing he thinks is corny?

Heat pricks the back of my eyes. Another shard of my childhood wedding dream cracks into smaller pieces. Tomorrow is going to be beautiful.

The first piano notes of a familiar song ring out from his phone.

Stunned, I stand in place while he prowls toward me.

"This song?" he asks.

"This one," I say softly.

He pulls me close to him with one hand around my waist, and he takes my other. We start a slow two-step.

"She won't be the first one to dance to this here tomorrow night," he murmurs. "It'll be one thing she can't take from you."

If I hadn't fallen hopelessly in love with him already, that would have pushed me off the cliff. My entire heart is at his booted feet. "Thank you."

I rest my head against his shoulder, and we dance. His heart beats a steady rhythm under my ear, making a special remix just for me with this song. The crickets and the frogs around us harmonize. It's a sound that won't be replicated tomorrow. The band won't sound the same, the nature sounds will be different, and the couple up here dancing will not be us.

I cling tighter to Durban and let him spin me around our makeshift dance floor.

Durban

I park in my garage. After the song played, I killed the lights in the pavilion and steered her right to her car. Then I followed her to my house, counting off each mile. The short drive felt ten times longer than normal. After that dance, after watching her all night and having her close, I have to get my hands on her.

She parks behind me, gets out, and strides toward me. I open the driver's door, and as soon as she crosses the threshold, I hit the button to close us into the garage. She stops by me, her long hair over one shoulder, glowing under the light above us.

"Come here, beautiful." I tug her toward me. Campbell makes me an impatient man.

She grins and steps out of her cowboy boots and right onto my lap. I lean the seat back as far as it'll go and leave the door open to make room for us. There's a bed not far away, but she's on top of me right now. This is perfect.

She leans over me, her hair forming a curtain around us. The way she wiggles every time she moves finishes the job of making my erection rock hard. She pauses and gives me a sultry smile before grinding against me. The heat of her pussy is dulled through our clothing, but it's still there, teasing me, driving my desire higher. I'm ready to tear our clothing off and drive into her, but she leans forward, looking beyond me into the back seat.

A ragged groan rips out of me when she plants her chest on my face to reach over me. I don't waste a moment. I grip her sides, slide my hands up, and pull down the collar of her dress to plant a kiss between her breasts. Her chuckle ripples through her and into me. The little silver horseshoe necklace slips out of her collar.

She settles back onto my lap and brandishes a small single-serve bottle of whiskey with Chapel House on the front. The party favors.

"Shit, I forgot to haul those in." I was too focused on getting Campbell to myself.

"You can bring them tomorrow. They're going to be given out at the reception anyway." She studies the label. "This is the single-malt one that you thought would go well with their vanilla bean wedding cake, right? Notes of fruit and spice?"

Touched, I nod. "You remembered."

She looks at me like, *of course*. "You said it was aged in an ex-sherry barrel. You were hoping to bring out the notes of apricot and almond. Did it work?"

It has a complex flavor profile that'll be lost on the couple, but I'm damn proud of it. I think it's perfect for our Chapel House line. "Why don't you see for yourself?"

Surprise lights her eyes moments before heat darkens the gray in her irises. "I'd rather taste it on you." She drapes herself over me and slants the bottle over my mouth. "Open up."

Fuck yes. I do as she orders. A splash of whiskey hits my tongue. I roll it around, holding her gaze, loving how heat and lust shines in her eyes just for me. Notes of vanilla, cherry, and almond fill my mouth.

Mimicking what I did the first time I got to taste her, she takes a sip and fuses her lips to mine. I open, then she does, only letting a trickle of warm whiskey into my mouth. A guttural growl leaves me.

Whiskey will never be good again without the flavor of Campbell on it.

I wrap an arm around her and hug her closer, delving into her mouth further. I stroke against her tongue again and again. The thrust of my hips against her shifts her up and down against my chest.

Gripping her hair, I break the kiss and tilt her head. Need pounds through me, punching against my zipper. "Drink."

She dumps the rest in her mouth, maneuvering the bottle until it's empty. Then she smashes her lips against mine. The whiskey mingles between us, our tongues clashing. I claw at her dress, but when my fingers graze her waist, I stop.

"Christ, Belle." Arousal pumps hot through my veins, and my discovery is going to burst every vessel. "No underwear? All fucking night?"

"Yes. Just in case, but I thought it was a lost cause." She rocks her bare pussy against my erection. Her heat seeps through my denim.

I trace her lips with my index and middle fingers.

They're plump and wet just like that sweet sex of hers rocking against me.

She flicks out her tongue to lick the tips. I groan and put them in my mouth, wetting them, then I slide my hand between the two of us. There's nothing softer or sweeter than Campbell Hawthorne.

My other hand is still tangled in her hair. I draw her face closer to mine. "I love how wet you are for me. So fucking hot and needy."

"For you."

I circle her clit, and she goes liquid against me, an illicit moan leaving her.

"It's never been this way before," she says, all breathy.

Can it be this way forever? I claim her mouth before something like that leaves my mouth, and we have to stop to address it.

She reaches between us and works the button of my jeans open. I lazily stroke her swollen clit, and she rocks against me. We're each doing separate actions, but we're moving in perfect harmony.

I think I'm in love with this woman.

It's too soon. I haven't known her long enough. I can't be.

She frees my dick, and it crowds out the questions. It's just us in the cab of my pickup. Just us for tonight. As she grinds back and forth against my fingers, she pumps my erection in her hot hand. I'm going to come way too damn fast if we keep doing this. We have the whole night, but I also need to make sure she gets enough rest for tomorrow.

I abandon her clit, and her eyelids flutter. She rises,

ready to sink down on my cock and take it all, but I grasp her wrist.

"Feel how wet you are for me." I line my fingers up with hers.

Her breath wafts over me in a whiskey-scented cloud, but she touches herself, and I feel her doing it. Blood hammers through my erection. It's fucking throbbing, but I have to steal these moments.

"Oh God, Durban."

"Stroke yourself, Belle." I move her fingers in circles.

Her lips part and her eyes fall shut. "Yes."

I can't wait any longer. I ditch her clit and guide myself inside her body. Sweltering heat hugs around my dick, gripping and demanding. "Keep stroking yourself," I order and thrust up.

She cries out and slams down as I'm rolling up for more.

"God, yes." Her hair's in my face and tickling my neck, but I don't care. I put my hand back on hers and help her rub her clit. I need her to come with me.

"Touch yourself," I say, even though she hasn't stopped. "Feel me driving into you."

"So good," she groans.

"You fit me so well. Fucking perfect, Belle." I lean up to catch her lips again.

Planting my heels, I change the angle to drive into her. She fists her free hand in my shirt just as her body clenches mine. Fucking finally.

"Come for me, Belle."

She tears her mouth from mine to cry out. A flood of heat blooms between us, and I let go with a roar.

How can this feel so damn good? There's nothing like it. There's never been anyone like her. I pump, the length of my thrusts shortening. I spill inside of her, and she takes it all. She wrenches her hand away, and I clasp it in mine. Shudders run through her, and I'm still spasming, my hips jerking.

Then we fall still. The garage is quiet with only our breathing making any noise.

I cup her face and run my thumb over her lower lip. "I'm going to take you inside, fuck you one more time, and then you're going to bed and getting a good night's sleep."

She wraps her long fingers around my wrist. "Thank you for taking care of me."

"Anytime. I'll get you through this wedding."

Her gaze traces my face. There's tension returning that should've been fucked out of her. She pushes up, and I slip outside of her warm body. She scoots back, and the horn honks, blasting off the walls. A yelp shoots out of her, and she jumps, her head hitting the top of the cab.

A shocked look crosses her face. I can't sit up or I'll knock her around some more. "Damn. You okay?"

She sputters and dissolves into laughter. I chuckle, and it grows. Her mouth drops open, and she's laughing so hard she collapses on my chest. My dick is tucked between us, getting jostled around by the way we're shaking. Yet I don't make a move. I could so easily lift her hips and slide into paradise. I could watch her mirth change to fiery passion. The blush on her cheeks wouldn't fade. But there's not a thing I'd change about this moment—unless she hurt her head.

"Are you all right?" I manage to get out around my laughter.

She loses it even more, going silent with how funny

she finds the situation. She buries her face in my shirt. "That"—breath—"scared the shit"—a gasp—"outta me."

My cheeks ache from smiling so hard. What a ridiculous moment, but I'm pulled under even more. The sex is amazing, better than I ever thought it could be, but talking with her formed a connection I didn't think was possible. Now that I know it is, what am I going to do about it?

CHAPTER TWENTY

Campbell

It's morning, and my face is pressed against the shower wall. Warm water rains onto my skin as Durban's driving into me from behind.

I could use this kind of wake-up each morning.

His punishing grip is on my hips, but I love the bite of pain. I hope there are marks when he's done, so I can wait in the back of the pavilion with his brand on me. While the couple is dancing during the reception, I'll remember last night and how tenderly Durban held me as we danced.

"*Yes*." I'm almost there. He hasn't played with my clit yet, and I haven't been bold enough to touch myself. It's like he's on a personal mission to get me off without any other stimulation outside of his cock.

It's working.

He tips my ass up until I'm on my tiptoes, but I'm

wedged so tightly between him and the shower wall that I wouldn't fall if my feet lifted off the ground.

"You're getting close," he growls in my ear. "I can feel you fist me with your cunt."

"Oh God, yes." Tension coils hard inside my belly. Compact and pulsating. I'm ready to blow as if last night was nothing but a primer.

What we did in the pickup changed me. I've never been so close, so in sync with a guy. Then he said he'd get me through the wedding. When he fucks me like this, I can't contemplate if that's all he wants. He's got me out of my mind, and that's just where I need to be right now.

He bends his knees and slams into a spot that shatters my world. My cries echo off the walls. The pleasure is blinding. I have to squeeze my eyes shut and let myself go. He really is the only thing holding me up.

"This's right." His hot breath gusts across my ear. "You'll feel me inside you all through the ceremony." He pumps into me, and my orgasm doesn't stop. "And all through the night."

I want to feel him inside me forever.

Warm water hits my skin and drips into my open mouth, but I drink it down, gasping and swallowing through the detonation that was my climax.

"Fuck, Belle." He rams into me one last time, melding us together as he spills inside of me. I can feel my pussy flexing around him, keeping him as close to me as possible.

"Goddamn, Belle. How does it get better every time?" He rubs his hands up and down my sides, finally concentrating on my hips. "Shit. Your skin's turning red."

"Good." I give him a lazy grin over my shoulder. "It'll be perfect under my very functional dress tonight."

His returning smile is sly, and he grabs a washcloth. The way he cleans us both up is another turn-on, making the fading thrum between my thighs gain strength.

Will I get this again?

This can't be the end of hanging out with Durban at his house, waking up to him, slow dancing under the stars. He has to feel this too. I'll keep my hope stoked all day so I have the guts to talk to him after the reception is over.

He shuts the spray off. Steam fills the bathroom. After we dry, and I'm dressed in my clothing from last night, I finger-comb my hair out. My parents won't be home when I go change and do my hair, so I'm not worried about explaining where I was. They might think I left early to prep for the ceremony.

I squint into the foggy mirror. Am I passable if my parents are home after all? I'm not sure what I'd tell them about who I was with. Pleading the Fifth might work. I'm an adult. But I was also last seen with Durban, so Daddy might jump to completely accurate conclusions no matter what.

Then what would I say?

Daddy, I love him, but I have no idea if he feels the same way. Give me another twenty-four hours, and maybe I'll know. Wait until your brother signs off on the land so the bride and groom don't get upset that I literally fucked around during the events I planned for them.

"Hungry?" Durban asks, twining his arms around my waist from behind. He's in jeans and a shirt, and his hair is spiky from the shower. I like this unkempt side to him. I'm the only one to see it.

"Yes." My answer comes out softer as doubt about our future sets in. I lift my chin. It's the last day. I'm not wavering now. "But I'll grab something at home. I don't dare be late today of all days."

January wants me on hand once she and the bridesmaids start getting ready. I want to be across the state. Across the country. Best I can do is across the lodge.

He eases back and spins me around. "I can make a quick breakfast."

"No, it's fine." I flatten my hands on his shoulders. "I appreciate you taking care of me these last few weeks."

Uncertainty passes through his dark eyes. "No problem. It's been . . . fun."

My nervous giggle echoes loudly in the bathroom. "Is that what it's been?"

"It's been—"

An annoying chime starts in the bedroom, and I groan. "That's alarm two. I think I missed the first one."

I peel myself away from him and rush to grab my phone off the nightstand on the far side of the bed and silence the alarm.

He steps out of the bathroom, the towel still around his shoulders. His hair's not combed neatly to the side yet. "Do you think after the reception we can talk?"

My heart creeps into my throat. I really do need to get going, but I can't leave this hanging. Does he sound hopeful, or is that my wishful thinking? "About what?"

He's hesitant, his jaw working. "Our arrangement."

I rise on my tiptoes like anticipation is lifting me on a butterfly's wings. "Yes?"

His brows are drawn together, and he stuffs his hands in his pockets. That's not the stance of a guy ready to confess his love. Another buzzing fills the room.

"It's mine." He picks it up and does a double take at whatever's on the screen. His expression goes blank, and he clicks the button on the side to silence it.

My third alarm goes off, and another awkward chuckle leaves me. I'm entering mindfuck territory, and I have a job to do today. My personal life needs to take a back burner. Today, I'm going to be there for my family in a way I never have been before, and I can't do that if I'm late yet again. Besides, a ping comes from his phone. Whoever is trying to reach him is tenacious.

"You can take that. I really have to get going."

"It can wait. I'll walk you out."

And confuse me some more? Turn my hope all topsy-turvy? I can't handle that before walking into January's wedding takeover. "It's fine. I can pick up my stuff before I go." I left a mild whirlwind of towels in the bathroom.

"Leave it. You don't have time." Another ping and his cheek twitches.

I hope everything's okay. Perhaps it's Iverson, and he's too uncomfortable to answer while I'm here? I take him up on the tidying offer and scurry toward the door. Wedding first. Talk later. It's been my mantra for enough days. I don't have much longer to wait.

I almost blow him a kiss but that seems like something lovers do. *Official* lovers. I throw him a finger wave and rush out.

I push my damp hair back and duck into the mudroom. Where are my boots?

Right. They're still in the garage. My cheeks flush at the memory, and I bite my lower lip when I smile. I nailed my head and we both laughed. It was silliness I haven't experienced with a guy, and it was with Durban, of all people.

I carry my boots in so I can go out the front door. When I have one almost on, I huff out a breath. My phone. I left it in the bedroom. Ditching the boot, I rush through the house. The bathroom door is closed and his scruff trimmer is running.

Just as I grab my phone and turn, his phone screen lights up from where he must've tossed it on the bed. My horseshoe necklace is lying next to it. Crap. Did I really forget that too? Regardless, Durban's got my back. Smiling, I lift it, trying and failing not to look at the screen. The chain stays dangling between my fingers. Two missed calls from Natalie and two texts.

Natalie: Can we talk?

Natalie: I got offered that job in Bozeman.

Horror flushes through my body like a frigid autumn drizzle, and I curl my hands around my necklace. He's been talking to Natalie?

She's moving to Montana?

Are they even broken up?

My gut says yes, he wasn't lying about that, but embarrassment nearly chokes me. I'm so foolish. I got my hopes up, and he was just biding his time until Natalie graduated. And of course, she realized she fucked up because he's an amazing guy. Here I am, a hopeless romantic. Who else would take an agreed-upon fling and make it into a fairy tale without the guy ever knowing?

His trimmer clicks off, and I jolt. I spin and sprint to the door on the balls of my feet, trying to be as quiet as possible. I was made a fool of once, and I won't let it happen again. I can leave this arrangement with my head held high.

He told me once that I shouldn't be blamed for taking a man at his word, so I won't. The tears gathering in my eyes say otherwise, but I blink them back as I slip out the door and run to my car, boots in my hands. I've got a shit show I'm in charge of, and I'm going to do a damn good job of running it.

Hot tears roll down my cheeks, but I'm going to exit this situation with my head held high. Once I'm behind the wheel, I punch out a text to Durban. My heart breaks with each word, but it's done.

I reverse and drive away from his place for the last time. I won't be planning *their* wedding.

Durban

I walk out of the bathroom. The engine of Campbell's car fades. I should've walked her to her car, given her a goodbye kiss, and pumped her up about the rest of the day, instead of cleaning up the towels, but I didn't want her to worry about them.

I can't believe I almost made her late by talking about us. Today will launch her career and help her family, and I almost made it about me.

My phone pings, and then starts ringing. Shit. I don't know what Natalie wants, but we have no business together anymore.

I don't look when I answer. "Hey, we do need to talk, and it's about you not calling."

"Whoa," Haven says. "I can send smoke signals, but it takes too long."

"Shit. Sorry. Thought you were Natalie. She's been trying to call."

"Why?"

"Good question."

"Okay," he says, like he wants to stay far away from the situation. "Do you have time to lend a hand? I've rounded all but one asshole steer that got out. He thinks he's outsmarting everyone when he's dumber than the rocks he thinks he's trapped in. We need horses and ropes to get him out."

"Yeah, I can be there in ten." I hang up and see more notifications.

I hit Campbell's first and read it three times, my stomach sinking lower each time until it slams to the floor.

Campbell: In case tonight's too hectic, I wanted to say thanks for everything. You fulfilled your end of the deal. No more cleaning up my messes. See you around.

What the hell? Thanks for everything? See you around?

The back of my throat burns. She's done with me?

A ping sounds just as another message from Natalie appears. Why the hell is she trying to get a hold of me now? I need to figure out my Campbell situation. The Natalie one is done.

Natalie: We should talk.

Her timing sucks, but then it always did. Just another thing I ignored when I was with her. I read her earlier messages. She got offered the job in Bozeman, and thought I'd care? A missed call too? Why the hell has

Natalie resurfaced? Is she missing how she strung me along until I was no longer convenient? I told Campbell once I wouldn't do that to someone. I know exactly how it feels.

Does Natalie have some sixth sense that I'm moving on? We're over and have been for weeks. She breaks up with me and then contacts me, like I should be diving for the phone? I deserve better than that.

After being with Campbell, I can look back on my relationship with my ex and see that it was one-sided. I put in all the effort, and that's not what I want. I deserve to have someone champion me as much as I support her.

Grinding my teeth together, I punch out a message.

Me: There's nothing to talk about. We're done.

Natalie: It was a stressful time, but it's over now.

It sure as hell is.

Me: So are we. Don't call or text me anymore.

I stuff a hand through my combed hair. Does Campbell mean what she said?

Fuck. I've got a brother waiting and a steer to rescue, but I'd ditch them both to talk to Campbell.

I'll see her at the reception. I can't intrude on her day. We'll have plenty of time to talk after her job is done and her uncle signs off on the land.

My gaze lands on the bedding, and something tugs at my brain. I frown, waiting a beat. The necklace. I need to bring that with me to return to her. I found it on the bathroom counter and laid it by the phone so I wouldn't forget.

It's gone. Frowning, I search the blankets, growing more frantic by the second. It was right here. I didn't move anything but my phone, and it's not like someone else could've taken—

Shit. Did Campbell come back for it when I was in the bathroom? Did she see the messages? Does she think I'm getting back with Natalie?

The pit in my gut knows she saw them. Every word. She practically gave me her blessing. *Thanks for everything. See you around.*

Goddammit.

CHAPTER TWENTY-ONE

Campbell

"And now I'm a bad sister!" I draw in a shuddering breath, but I collapse my face into my hands. I'm sitting on the edge of my bed, and I just want to crawl into the corner.

"You are not a bad sister." Jamison pats my back. Tavis is sleeping in his car seat through my breakdown, and Kacey's with Iverson. "I'm glad you called me. I would've kicked your ass if you hadn't."

I was sobbing so bad by the time I reached town, I doubted my sunglasses could hide my ugly cry. My attempts at holding on to righteous anger didn't work, and I dissolved. At the turn to my parents' place, I called Jamison and got out the gist of what had happened. My silver chain is back around my neck. The damn thing saved me from future heartbreak, but it's not helping the hurt right now.

"I bet she's gorgeous." I've said that three times already.

"You're a hottie, so quit with that."

"I bet he was so happy when he saw her call." And relieved when I left. The tears well up again. "Ugh." I swipe at the mascara running under my eyes.

She bats my hands away. "I think we'll have to start from scratch."

"Perfect. I'm going to tank this ceremony before it even starts."

"You are not going to tank it. That's up to January and Can't Stanford."

I wipe my hands down my face, inhale, hold it for four seconds, and blow out for five. I do it again. I've had the worst morning, but I haven't come all this way to be a quitter or let another guy derail my plans. "Okay. Time to get me fixed up."

Jamison pulls the stool away from my makeup chair and plants it in front of me. "I'll get you ready. You talk."

"I already told you everything."

She returns with a few makeup wipes and sits. She's in leggings and brackets my knees with hers. Her over-sized shirt looks more comfortable than my charcoal-gray skirt and baby-pink blouse. It says I'm a professional and clearly not a guest.

A crease forms between her chestnut brows as she dabs at my streaked mascara. "You told me his ex called and texted, which basically confirmed that you two are messing around, since you've been avoiding me."

"It's been a day since the luncheon."

"A day and a half," she mumbles and dabs at my face.

I manage a half smile at her disgruntlement. She probably got the details from Avery and was leaving me alone until after the wedding. Too much was left for after the wedding, and now it's all fizzled out like a dud firework. The fuse was lit, but nothing blew, leaving too much disappointment and fear to bother trying again.

"I fell in love with him."

She drops her hand, her amber eyes shimmering. "Oh, Campbell. I'm so sorry." Resting her warm fingertips on my knee, she keeps the makeup wipe crumpled in her palm. "But you don't know that he was happy to see Natalie. That man tracked you the whole time at the luncheon. He was a hungry cougar, and you were an itty-bitty bunny."

I sniffle. "It was just sex." Toe-curling sex. Back-bending sex. Eyes-rolling-to-the-back-of-the-head sex.

She snorts and tosses the wipe to rip open a new one. "Listen. I try not to think about my siblings getting down and dirty, and that includes my in-laws, but if Durban is anything like Iverson, there's no 'just sex.' "

"It clouded my thinking."

She resumes smudging around my eyes. "Is that all you did? Really? *Just* sex?"

"There were sleepovers." The tears threaten to crowd again, but I don't want to undo Jamison's cleanup efforts. "We made meals together."

She meets my gaze before returning to her task. "It'd make sense if he developed feelings too."

"What's four weeks with me compared to four years with her?"

"You could say the same about you and Can't Stanford, yet here you are. In love and worried Durban doesn't feel the same. What if he does?"

"He doesn't, or she wouldn't be telling him that she was offered a job in Bozeman." Familiar humiliation burns much deeper this time. "Do you think he's been talking to her the whole time?"

"Do you think that he has?"

"Sounded pretty friendly," I mutter.

She sighs and rises to cross to my vanity. Rooting through the scattered vials and tubes, she shakes her head. Tavis stretches, blinks, and drifts back to sleep.

"I don't know Durban that well." She turns around and taps the mascara against her fingers. She's in full big-sister mode with her mouth set, ready to talk sense into me. "What I do know about the brothers is that they're close, and they're a lot alike. They aren't players, and I always thought that was surprising. Iverson limited things to just hookups, and the other two were the same, until Durban met his ex, and it was like the long-distance thing saved him from having to endure hookups. But even before that, all of them were very careful about not having accidental babies or about leading women on. You know why?"

I look at my hands twisting in my lap. "Because of their mom."

"Yes. And that caution spreads to love. There's a reason Iverson was thirty-eight before I fucked his brains out and changed his mind."

"TMI." I fake a gag.

She only laughs at me. "But you know, I sometimes wonder if our connection would've lasted if there hadn't been a perfect storm. He got the offer on the land, and he and Durban and Haven were starting to look ahead, and they didn't like what they saw. No retirement, living in the bunkhouse, and only a lot more hard work. Then I came home, and Iverson couldn't get away from me."

"You made sure he couldn't."

"I was doing my job. It's not my fault I had to have meetings with him," she says innocently, then comes to sit beside me. She bumps her shoulder against mine. "What I'm trying to say is that Durban is probably in his head, wondering if what he feels is too soon, or if it's even real. Four years is a long time to just get dropped." I nod since my experience was five years. "He doesn't want to do the wrong thing and risk it all, but he's probably at the point where he wants more. He wants what you two have. Compare that to what he had with Natalie, and it's got to pale in comparison."

Sadness swamps me, and I blink back tears. Maybe mascara is a lost cause today. "I have no idea, but I do know one thing. I'm not going to be that unsuspecting girl again while a guy fools around behind my back."

"But do you know he is?"

"I didn't know Stanford was until he told me. I don't need that bullshit again, so I sent Durban a text that said thanks for everything, our arrangement's done," I say glumly.

She gawks at me. "You really can be your own worst enemy sometimes. Durban is not Stanford. That giant douche of an ex broke your trust, and it's ruining what might be a good thing."

I fail at holding the tears back. She throws an arm around my shoulders. "I'm making this worse," I wail.

She releases me and slaps her hands on her knees. Tavis throws his hands in the air, eyes still closed, and goes back to sleep. I smile and she chuckles.

"How about this?" she says. "We quit talking about it, we get you through this wedding, and we see how Durban acts at the reception. Then we'll plan our attack."

I don't want to wait and see. I don't want to monitor Durban's behavior like I'm trying to read tea leaves. I don't want to manage January and Stanford's nonsense just to get them down the aisle. I don't want to be responsible for booting my uncle off our family's land and out of our business. I just want to lie in bed and cry. I want to be taken care of. I want this wedding to crash and burn and for it not to be my fault.

But today is about what everyone else wants. What they need. And I'm going to go and do my job and get through it all so I can lie in bed and be miserable for the next week.

Durban

I dump the wire stretcher into Haven's truck bed. We dragged the steer out of the ravine. The damn thing fought us until it saw the chance for freedom instead of more rocks and brush. It was easy after that, and then we repaired the portion of the fence that sagged and got trampled over by the cattle.

"Damn." Haven takes his cowboy hat off and wipes his hand across the back of his forehead. We both smell like horse sweat and our own perspiration. "Natalie have you that messed up you gotta take it out on the tools?"

I tilt the brim of my cowboy hat down to hide my scowl. I told him about Natalie's missed call and the text, and then I forgot about her. It's Campbell's message streaming through my head on repeat. I didn't tell him about that. I'm too raw.

Did she mean it? She's done with me? Without even stopping to ask me about what she saw? She might be on a strict schedule today, but I want to mean more to her than that. I should be more than a quick note to end things when she's stressed.

I know she read the message. The timing was either lucky or the crappiest in the world. I got to see how little Campbell's invested in me. Again, I was building up what I had with a woman until she walked away after the first inconvenience.

Is tonight going to be the first taste of what living in the same town with her when I can't have her will be like?

I slam the tailgate shut and stalk around the pickup to get into the passenger seat.

Haven climbs in. "So you ran Natalie off and you're regretting it?"

"Jesus, can you quit with Natalie?" I snap. "It's over. We're done. I'm not interested in her."

I'm being a moody bastard. He doesn't know the whole story, and every time he opens his mouth, I'm tearing him a new asshole.

"I think Campbell saw the texts from Natalie, the ones where she said she had a job offer in Bozeman."

He whistles. "That would look fishy to a woman."

"I got a 'thanks for everything, see you around' text from her after she left." I sink into my seat and glower out the window as he pulls away from the fence and bumps across the pasture. "So I guess we're done."

When we hit the road, he doesn't take the turn to his place.

I sit up. "I need to get my pickup."

"Yup." He continues going straight.

"It's parked at your house."

"Yup."

He's being obtuse on purpose. "I have to be at the reception in three hours."

"You sure do."

The wedding starts soon, and I sure as hell won't go to that. I won't witness two people who hurt Campbell get a happy ending, and I can't watch Campbell and not be able to hold her. I take my hat off and stuff a hand through my sweaty hair. "Is this payback for being an asshole?"

"You can't pay back an amount that high," he says dryly and turns down the road that'll take us to Iverson's.

"Dammit, Haven. Are you and Ivy going to crawl up my ass?"

He slides his dark gaze toward me. "You deserve it."

Why? Because I'm easy for women to walk away from?

Iverson's garage door is open and the sawhorses are lined up on the concrete with some boards across the top. He's brushing them with stain, the brim of his ball cap shading his face. Kacey has a giant pack of sidewalk chalk and there are stick figures all over the concrete pad in front of the garage.

Lane and Cruz are watching the distillery so we can be free for the wedding, since we're all tied to the bride through the Hawthornes. Haven's going to help me serve the reception tonight, and Iverson's staying with his family.

My niece sprints toward us after Haven parks, arms out, and her sandals slapping against the ground. Her ponytail swings behind her. It lifts my destroyed heart out of the gutter. Not far, but enough to get me out of the pickup to swoop her into a big hug. Iverson clicks off the music playing, some Dolly Parton song.

"She just saw me this morning," Haven says as he climbs out, "or she would've hugged me first."

"Daddy said it's almost quiet time," Kacey says solemnly. She studies my face with her doe-brown gaze. "You need quiet time."

I must look as bad as I feel. "I could use some, but I think Haven has other plans." I set her down, and she runs to Haven for a hug.

After he places her on her feet, he cocks his head toward me but keeps his gaze on Iverson. "This guy needs some girl talk."

"I like girl talk," Kacey says.

Iverson holds his hand out. "Time to go in. I'll read you the first book."

She looks to us, like she's hoping we'll insist she stays for girl talk. Her lips turn to a pout, and she takes her dad's hand.

Coal runs around us while we're waiting for Iverson. I lean against the pickup and tip my head back.

After several minutes, Haven says, "Beautiful day for a wedding."

I glare at him.

"So it's really Campbell, then." He nods. "What a relief. I thought you were gonna go running after Natalie."

I hold my hard stare until Iverson pushes out the door. "What's going on? Is the wedding imploding?"

"Natalie was trying to get a hold of Durban about moving to Bozeman, and Campbell saw," Haven answers. "Durban told Natalie to take a hike."

"Good," Iverson says, coming to a stop in front of us. "She's not good for you."

"I know," I say woodenly. Knowing isn't doing me any good right now.

He folds his arms. "So what about Campbell?"

I tell him about this morning and how it ended, and how I had been planning to wait until after the wedding to ask Campbell if she wants something more serious. Felt pretty goddamn serious to me. "But she walked away without looking back or letting me explain. I know she's stressed, but I thought what we had was worth more than a 'see you around.' "

Iverson whistles and folds his arms over his chest. His eyes are shaded by his ball cap when he pins me with his gaze. "I think both you and Campbell are spinning your wheels going in the same direction."

He's the oldest, but that doesn't make him always right. "I'm done spinning my wheels and getting nowhere. My time with Natalie at least showed me that I deserve more than that."

Haven shakes his head. "And Campbell's time with her ex, and this whole goddamn wedding hubbub, showed her that she can't trust a guy."

His words are a frigid splash in the face. "She can trust me."

"Or . . ." Iverson says, "she panicked, thought history would repeat itself, and left before she could get hurt more."

Ah, hell. I didn't factor in her history. Mine was too busy clouding my view. She might've looked at those messages, and fuck. Her mind could've gone anywhere about me and Natalie, even that I'd lied about her in the first place.

"Campbell is crazy about you," Haven says. "I only had one meal with the two of you, and it was like you'd been together forever."

"Pretty sure she's devastated," Iverson adds.

My heart wrenches at that. "Why would you think that?"

His expression turns thunderous. "Because Jamison's been gone since Campbell called. I heard the sobs from the phone, and now I know it wasn't because today's the wedding day."

"She was crying?" Shit. I push off the pickup. If she's distraught and it's my fault? I have to get to her. I have to reassure her and tell her how I really feel. A few minutes ago, I was so righteously upset about how she could leave without talking to me, but I was doing the same thing. Natalie's texts made us both revert to our old hurt selves when we got together in order to move on from all that. "Give me your keys."

Haven doesn't move. "I've never seen you think less, Durban."

"I need to find her." I advance on him, but he starts backing up.

I can take him in a fight and wrestle the keys from him. If Iverson jumps in, I'm in trouble, but the adrenaline pumping through my blood will make me a formidable opponent.

"And then what?" Iverson asks.

I stop and gravel skitters around my boots. What will I do? She'll be at the lodge, helping the bride and all the guests, overseeing the staff. Do I just march in, pick her up, and carry her off?

That's exactly what I want to do. "I don't care about the goddamn wedding. It never should've happened."

"William agrees with you. Jamison said her parents have been bickering about how they should've just told Rayburn to pound sand and deal with the consequences, but once the planning started, Campbell was too embroiled. They don't want her to look bad."

They're too afraid to start the drama. "She wouldn't look bad if the truth came out about everything. If people were fucking honest about how they're screwing her over, she wouldn't have to absorb the blame."

"So you're going to what?" Haven asks. "Ride in and sweep her off her feet and to hell with everything else?"

All of the work she's been doing runs through my head. Coordinating, planning, even goddamn riding lessons.

"Yeah," I say. "That's a great idea."

CHAPTER TWENTY-TWO

Campbell

I linger outside of the room January and her bridesmaids are getting ready in. My flats are usually comfortable, but I've been on my feet for hours running from the kitchens to pepper Chef with questions, out to the pavilion to ensure setup is following the timeline, and here, to check on my cousin, who's turning into a last-minute bridezilla.

The door next to me opens.

"—why would she wear that?" January's stricken voice comes through. "Only brides wear white at the wedding!"

"Yep." My cousin Sydney ducks out. She closes the door behind her, leans her head back, and blows out a big exhale. She's wearing the dusty-rose, off-the-shoulder dress that's the color and style I had my heart set on since I was five. The shade and style have been updated over the years, but Sydney is exactly how I thought she'd look on my wedding day, from the fun white cowboy boots to her simple chignon. Though the beige cardigan she's holding in her hand wasn't part of my plan.

My cousin cracks an eye open and slowly turns her head toward me. She puts her hand on her chest and sags against the wall, relief scrawled across her face. "Oh, good. It's you. I thought Hannah came back and caught me wishing I was anywhere but here."

Hannah's a coworker of January's. She's taking my place in January's lineup of bridesmaids.

"That bad?" I ask.

She rolls her gray eyes. "I'm tasked with giving this sweater to Aunt Margaret to put on for the rest of the night. She's wearing a white dress," Sydney finishes in a scandalous tone. She smirks and looks around. "Taking a breather?"

"Sticking close for when she beckons. She doesn't want me in the room, and she made it clear when I arrived that there'll be no checking on Stanford."

She groans. "Fucking Stanford. I wish I could pick my brother-in-law."

"I wish she hadn't picked my boyfriend, but I'm so glad she opened my eyes."

"They had to be closed real tight."

I bark out a laugh. "One hundred percent." I let out a long exhale. "I didn't know how good it could be, but when you're stuck with something that's not terrible, you start to confuse that with good. Then you find out what amazing is really like and realize how low your standards were."

I swallow past the lump in my throat.

Sydney squeezes my arm, sympathy in her eyes. "She

thinks you're sleeping with one of the distillery brothers. I guess it's more than sex."

"I thought so."

Her compassion deepens when she hears the past tense. My vision gets blurry again. I cannot cry. I came to work with a splotchy face and bloodshot eyes, and I'm finally some semblance of normal. I only look anemic now.

"Yeah. That's all it was." I check my phone. Twenty minutes to showtime. "I should go out to the pavilion. Can you make sure January's ready to walk in fifteen minutes?"

"Mom's got the countdown going." She gives me a sad smile. "For what it's worth, my parents aren't happy about this. My mom doesn't like the rift it's caused between her and your mom. Dad is so damn grumpy and I think he really wants to talk to Avery and Thea about Thea's job."

Thea's the manager of a baseball stadium. My uncle mines her for information each time he sees her. Except at this event.

Sydney shrugs. "They're avoiding him."

Well, he's basically extorting us so . . . "It's messed up."

"It is. And I'm sorry. I'm really, really sorry you've been put in this situation."

"Thank you." Her apology is the first I've gotten from that side of the family. It hits me hard. Without this wedding, I'd be spinning my wheels and wondering where I messed up. I'd be looking for where to go next, where I wouldn't be haunted by another selfish prick who'd screwed me over.

Instead, I've coordinated events with three different

businesses in town, and I have a city street fair to help plan. I don't care if it's this year, next year, or in five years. It's going to happen. When I checked my email a moment ago, I already had a query from a woman asking if Hawthorne Guest Ranch had openings for a wedding next summer.

I kept thinking that if I could get through today, I could establish myself. I could grow the job I wanted. The reality is that I'm already doing it, and the wedding hasn't even happened.

If January implodes right now, will I still be able to pull off a career in Huckleberry Springs? I'd still have three events to show off at. More chances to build my reputation.

And there's my love life. When I moved home, I didn't know what was wrong with me. Why couldn't I hold a job? Why couldn't I keep an underwhelming guy like Stanford happy? Why did I need my family's name to get ahead?

Thanks to Durban, I know the answers to all those questions now. And I know what I'll never settle for again.

My heart's just a little lighter as I head toward the pavilion to take my post in the back.

When I reach the venue, Mom crosses to me, the skirt of her pale blue dress swirling around her legs, and gives me a quick hug. Avery and Thea are on her heels. Avery's a bolt of sunshine in her yellow dress, while Thea's wearing a light gray pantsuit with a deep *V* down the front.

"Jamison said she was over to the house," Mom says quietly.

I nod as my throat thickens again. "Nerves, I guess."

She rubs my back, gives me the look that says she knows I'm not telling her the whole story, but she doesn't press.

Avery speaks out of the side of her mouth. "Get a load of that lady in white. Jan's going to lose her shit."

At the end of one of the aisles of chairs is January's aunt Margaret. Sydney's talking to her and holding up the cardigan. The aunt's gesturing with her hands, and Sydney's shrugging.

"She already has," I say, scanning the guests. It's a small, intimate wedding, more out of necessity than choice. It was like January could never create her own network. She had to siphon from mine. Mine would've been bigger. "Daddy at the barn?"

Mom nods. "Ready to bring the horses up right before the vows are said."

"That's going to be the highlight," Avery says, pushing a strand of dirty-blond hair off her face. "Hailstorm looks so purdy with white bows in his mane."

"I think Clyde likes his bling too," Thea says.

I laugh, wishing it wouldn't be so bittersweet to see the horses ride up. Wishing I wouldn't get so wistful. "They're the chillest creatures around today."

"Want me to stand back here with you?" Thea asks. "It'll look more Team Campbell versus Team January."

I shake my head. "Have a seat and enjoy the uncomfortable show. I might have to rush off any second."

Out of the corner of my eye, I see Stanford escorting his parents over the lily-lined trail to the pavilion. He's in a tux, looking like the businessman he is. After he leads them to his seat, he wanders back down the aisle, nodding at all his friends and relatives.

Shit, he's heading in my direction. I clutch my clipboard and look as impassive as possible.

"Is January ready?" He adjusts his bowtie. It's crooked, but I keep that information to myself.

"She'll be ready." My emotions are raw, and I've had a rough morning. I'm also sick of men at the moment. I run my finger around my necklace to make sure it's showing. "I'm good at what I do." Before he can open his mouth, I make a point of looking at the time on my phone. "Take your place and wait for your lovely bride before you put me behind schedule."

Annoyance crosses his face, along with something that resembles regret, but the countdown is on for when Stanford is not my problem. He spins sharply on a heel and stomps to the front.

I lean against the corner beam of the structure. It's begun.

My melancholy returns, but there's a relief chaser right behind it. This day is almost done. I can cry into my pillow tonight, and tomorrow will be Baldwin-free.

Stanford takes his place under the flower arch and glares at me. I hold his gaze, my unimpressed expression unwavering. He's the first to blink, sliding his attention away to the flurry of activity at the end of the path where the attendants are gathering and crowding around January for the big reveal—right on time. A muscle in his jaw jumps, and he lifts his chin.

What's the matter, Stanford? Second-guessing today?

I turn my attention to where he's looking. Sydney took charge for me, and she's ordering everyone to line up. Stanford's douchey best friend is first to walk with her, then two of January's cousins with Stanford's cousins, and finally the coworker and an old frat buddy of my ex's that I never liked.

One of Daddy's staff kicks off *Pachelbel's Canon in D.* A lovely version with piano and violin drifts through the air. My favorite. But instead of being nauseous like I thought I'd be, I'm bored.

This isn't the wedding of my dreams.

This? It lacks heart. There's no vision, just echoes of mine. It's a forgery when the real thing still exists in my head.

Today is just a launchpad for me to jump off and meet someone who'll treat me right. Someone who won't lie or cheat. Someone who knows what I really need and will rearrange heaven and earth to provide it.

January didn't take anything from me. She gave it all back.

I fold my hands quietly and wait for the procession.

Sydney takes a step, but she swings her head to the side and stops. The man on her arm almost tugs her off her feet, but he glances in the same direction, doing a double take. A murmur goes through the crowd, and heads swivel in the same direction that captivates Sydney.

What's going on?

I peer over the heads of all the guests. Someone chortles, and I swear it sounds like my mother.

Then I see it. A rider on horseback, cowboy hat tipped down low, charging over the lawn.

What the . . .

The ground drops out from under me, and I feel weightless, like I'm floating. A handsome cowboy in— ohmigosh—a white dress shirt and black jeans charges toward the pavilion on horseback.

The murmurs grow louder as he approaches.

"What the fuck?" Stanford hollers.

Hailstorm thunders closer, and I push away from the corner post. I stand on the very edge of the slab the pavilion sits on and hope lurches high in my chest.

Why is he here? Why on horseback?

Is he really . . .

When Hailstorm's twenty feet away, Durban switches the reins to his left hand, leans over, and holds his right arm out.

Without thinking, I reach for him.

Durban doesn't have to steer Hailstorm close to me. The big horse knows the drill, and this time he knows he's got a competent rider.

My adrenaline surges seconds before I grab Durban's arm and jump. He swings me in front of him so my legs spill over the side. I tuck them close to me, to him, and to Hailstorm and hug Durban. He's got me snugged to him so tight that the saddle horn isn't even prodding my ass.

Whoops rise up behind us—Avery and Thea.

"What are you doing?" I ask with my face tucked into his chest. I really don't care what's going on. I'm in his arms again, but Natalie's pretty face flashes in my head. This can't be real.

"I'm sweeping you off your feet." His deep voice rumbles through my cheek. "So you know there's no one else for me but you."

His seat is solid, and he's slowed Hailstorm to make the ride smoother for all of us.

What about the wedding?

I really don't care. Because this day finally got exciting.

Durban

She's in my arms. I rode in like a madman, sure to ruin the event, and she reached for me like it was a reflex, like there was nothing else she could have done.

She knows—she has to—that I'm all hers. I'll show her soon enough, and every other day she'll let me.

Hailstorm heads for the barn. Clyde whinnies, and William pumps his fist in the air. He's surrounded by Haven, Iverson, and Jamison. Kacey's on Iverson's shoulders, and Jamison is swaying side to side with Tavis. All of them are grinning.

I stop Hailstorm by William and hand the reins off, but I don't set my damsel in distress down. She clutches me, and I vault off. She yelps and buries her face in my chest. My feet hit the ground, and I'm holding her like a groom looking for a threshold to cross. We've definitely crossed something.

She lifts her face, her expression filled with wonder and confusion. She's so goddamn beautiful in her prudish pink shirt and a gray skirt that gives me all sorts of ideas, and a lot of them start with me putting her panties in my pocket again.

"Why?" she asks softly.

Hailstorm is between us and our family, but I don't care who hears. My why was obvious to everyone around us. I had to get my ass kicked into gear.

"Seems I've fallen in love with you, Belle. I found everything I've wanted in you, and if you don't feel that way, it's fine. I won't pressure you." Though I'll experience a real broken heart. "But the least I could do was take the blame for tanking the wedding, so you don't have to waste one more minute on that couple."

Her eyes shimmer. "You love me?"

"So damn much. I don't care if Natalie moves to Bozeman or Huckleberry Springs, I'm not interested." My gaze dances over her face. "She's kind of a dick." I lift her silver chain out of her top and rub the horseshoe charm with my thumb. "I was stupid enough to let your text stop me."

"It was all a lie," she whispers. "I was so certain you finally had your chance with your dream woman, and I tried to save face."

"Campbell Joanna Hawthorne, I'm holding my dream woman in my arms. I don't want to put you down until you're in my house, where you belong." I swallow, hoping this is a slam dunk. "If you want to."

"I'm a messy person."

"I like seeing signs that you're in my house, that it's not a big, empty tomb I'm going to grow old alone in."

"I have a lot of timers."

"I ordered a pack to keep around the house."

Her red lips part. "You did?"

I nod.

"I'm a nepotism baby." She says it mostly without shame.

"No reason not to use the connections you have."

"I like to drink whiskey straight from the guy who makes it." She licks her bottom lip. "Because I love him."

My mouth stretches wide. "You love a guy who wrangles cattle and turns grain into alcohol?"

"I also love a guy who rides off with me into the sunset."

"You're it for me, Belle. Look at my face. Have I ever looked like this when I've talked about anyone else?"

Her eyes are liquid when she shakes her head.

"I'm setting you down only so I can kiss you."

As soon as her feet hit the ground, I lift her into a kiss. Her mouth lands on mine, and there's cheering around us. Hailstorm's hooves stamp, and he huffs.

She smiles against my lips, her arms twined around my neck. "I think we have an audience."

I set her back down, but keep her tucked close to me. "Haven said he'll do the reception tonight. Your dad's going to deal with your uncle, and I'm going to make sure no one bothers you about any of it."

"Durban," she whispers and rises to her toes to kiss me.

"Don't worry about a thing, kiddo," William says. "I'm going to tell my brother what I should've said in the beginning—shit or get off the pot. I'm not playing around."

"Hey, Daddy," Kacey says, tapping Iverson on the head, "Grandpa said—"

"I heard." Iverson smirks. "Grandpa's allowed to say it. Not you."

A "woohoo" rings up from the pavilion. Avery and Thea are sprinting toward us. Avery's holding her shoes in one hand.

"I'm going to take that as a good sign," Jamison says.

William leads Hailstorm to the holding pen that Clyde is in, and returns just as Avery and Thea skid to a stop.

"It's pandemonium up there." Avery doubles over, laughing so hard.

Thea grins, a short lock of her dark hair falling on her forehead. "Stanford demanded someone stop you and bring you back, and the bride lost her ever-loving mind."

"*Lost it!*" Avery wheezes while frantically nodding.

"Mama Hawthorne and Sydney are coordinating the chaos," Thea continues, grinning like she's won the lottery, "but last I heard, Stanford was screaming that he deserves better than a hillbilly bride, and Rayburn was shouting that Stanford's a two-timing cocksucker who should be castrated."

Avery recovers enough to get out, "You missed January telling him that she deserves someone who can find the clit and doesn't obsess about his ex."

I rub my thumb up and down Campbell's shoulder. "Couldn't have happened to a better couple."

She puts her hand on my abdomen.

"Oh my God!" Avery pushes both hands through her hair. "Jamison, I recorded it. You have to watch Campbell get swooped up by her man."

Jamison grins. "Can't Stanford practiced for hours, and he couldn't nail it."

"Durban didn't need a second to master it," Campbell says and pats my chest.

Damn, I'm going to blush, and my brothers will never let me hear the end of it. "A good horse helps."

"A good cowboy," she murmurs.

I tip her face up to capture another kiss. My brothers groan.

"Get a room," Haven calls.

"I happen to have a place." I pick Campbell up again.

She giggles and throws her arms around me. I'm parked by the barn, where I sped to in order to take Hailstorm from William.

I didn't do it just to be flashy. I did it to steal something back that had been taken from her. I'll give every piece of her dream back to her, even if it's bit by bit.

Carefully, I deposit her in the passenger seat. I brace my hands on the frame as she buckles in. "I'm going to take you home, and we're not getting out of bed until every guest for this wedding is gone. You're mine. And long after they're gone—you're mine." I lean in, the muscles in my arms stretching. "You're who I want."

A playful glint enters her eye. "I feel like you need to prove it."

"I will, Belle. Every damn day."

CHAPTER TWENTY-THREE

Campbell

I'm naked and stretched out on Durban's bed, and I'm up one orgasm. He laps his tongue over my belly button, where he poured some Chapel House whiskey. The party favors were still in his truck, and he brought in a few with him when he carried me into the house.

When I left this morning, I thought it was for forever. But Durban makes me feel like forever started as soon as he brought me home from Bootleg Tavern that night.

"The best infusion is you." His hot breath gusts over my fevered skin. I arch into him as he prowls up my body and nudges my legs open.

He pushes inside, slow and sensual like he's savoring it, like he was afraid we wouldn't have this chance again.

I hook my ankles around his hips and run my hands over his shoulders and into his hair. "I need you so bad."

"You have me," he says, pumping in and out in a

steady rhythm. "You know why I'm not mad about those years I wasted waiting for the wrong person?" He thrusts hard, and a moan leaves me. "I was really waiting for you."

My heart swells so big I'm going to burst before I shatter for the second time. "I can't be upset that something awful made me move back home." He pulls out and plunges inside, and my brain fractures. The man scrambles me from the inside out. "It was when a moody cowboy could take me home."

"I'm not going to quit taking you home." Pump. "I'm not going to quit making you smile." Pump. "I'm not going to quit making you laugh and showing you that we're fucking perfect for each other. You were made for me. This pussy is mine."

"All yours," I groan as pleasure soars through me. It's the second time today I could float away, but he anchors me.

"One day, I'm going to propose." He hooks his arms behind my thighs and spreads me wide. "You're going to plan your dream wedding." He rises to his knees and pistons his hips back and forth, hitting a spot only he's ever been able to find. "And I'm going to make it happen. Whatever you fucking want."

I fist my hands into the blankets so I don't scoot across the bed. Waves of pleasure undulate through me, cranking me closer and closer to my peak. "What do you want?" I barely have the air to ask.

"I want you. That's all I need." He licks the pad of his thumb. When it lands on my already stimulated clit, my back arches, and I come so damn hard I can't feel anything but him moving inside me. The rest of me is electrified.

"Durban!" I ride the storm, shaking and clawing at the bedding.

"Give it all to me, Belle." He grunts and thrusts hard, burying himself to the hilt, and he comes with me.

I mourned losing this only hours ago, but here I am, connected to Durban, and he not only wants me forever, but he also wants to make my dreams come true.

He collapses over me and gently slips out while rolling us to the side. I curl into his hard, bare chest and inhale the faint scent of horse sweat, vodka, and his caramel-and-oak smell.

"Is it bad to admit I'm curious about what happened?"

He reaches for his nightstand and checks his phone. A chuckle vibrates in his chest, and he shows me his screen.

Iverson: Having the party anyway. Just Hennessys and Hawthornes. Invited the Fosters.

Haven: If you ever get off your girl, you should come out.

Haven: Bet you're coming enough.

I laugh and stretch over Durban for my phone.

Waiting for me is a selfie of Jamison, Kacey, Avery, and Thea. Mama and Sydney are in the background.

Jamison: Bridal party all packed up and left. Except Sydney. She always was the fun cousin. Uncle Rayburn signed over the land.

Jamison: Sydney got 80 acres. And when January asked about hers, Uncle Ray screamed at her that the damn wedding is her land.

Avery: You should've heard Daddy read Rayburn the riot act. In front of everyone! Epic.

Thea: We'll save you some cake. Two pieces from each tier.

I toss my phone to the edge of the bed. "This blew up so loud that I don't think my name will be mentioned at all unless it's to talk about how a hot cowboy rode off with me."

He puts his phone by mine. "They're going to hear that you plan some memorable events."

I settle myself back into him. "I'll certainly remember this forever."

"Good. If you ever forget, I can talk to Hailstorm."

I laugh, and we lie in comfortable silence. This is really happening. I'm Durban's girlfriend. All of our family knows.

"I want to take you out," he says. "A real date."

I pretend to think. "Hmm. I might be busy."

He growls and rolls me over, pinning me on my back. I laugh and link my legs around him again. I'm wet and messy, and he doesn't mind at all.

"Where do you want to go?" he asks.

"Um . . ." I think about all the places in town we could go. There's Dee's Sweets. We could do a tasting or go out for Chinese. "I want to try the Mexican place that opens next month. I have to talk to them about a future street fair."

"I'll take you there, but we're going out earlier. I want to show my woman off."

He really says all the right things. "Bootleg."

The corner of his mouth tips up. "Where it all started."

"Seems fitting."

He rolls out of bed and takes my hand, bringing me

with him. "I said I was keeping you in bed until everyone's gone, and it sounds like they've left. Let's go out."

"Now?"

He grabs my skirt off the floor and tosses it to me. "Now." He picks his jeans up and steps into them. "We snuck around for weeks. I'm ready to lay my claim on you."

The horse-and-sunset part probably did that already. I step into my skirt. "What if I don't wear underwear?"

He drops his hands from the button of his jeans. "I'm going to be hard the whole time."

"Good."

I've never looked forward to a date more. I'm freshly fucked and wearing wrinkled clothes that smell faintly of horse sweat. It's the most impromptu night out I've had, and it's going to be the best.

Durban will make sure of it.

EPILOGUE

Campbell

One year later . . .

I'm holding a bouquet of white lilacs, facing a groom so handsome I couldn't have imagined it. The temperature is perfect, and fluffy white clouds dot the blue sky. I stand at the front of the pavilion. Instead of a flower arch, the whole space is decorated with white and blush-colored roses. Same with the chairs. When those are moved to make space for the tables for the reception, each tabletop will have a fragrant bouquet of white lilacs, picked fresh an hour ago.

"You may now kiss the bride." The pastor who baptized me, confirmed me, and caught me drinking with his daughter in high school and made us mow the church lawn for a month, finishes the ceremony.

Durban lifts the bouquet from my hands and gives it

to Jamison. She's wearing a dress in the blush color that's perfect for a late spring day. I told them the color and asked them each to pick out their own style. My oldest sister is my maid of honor. Then Avery, Thea, and Sydney. I've gotten closer with my cousin over the last year as she distanced herself from her family.

Maybe she'll reconcile. I don't care if I see January again. The trust is gone, and she's somewhere in Costa Rica, eating, praying, and loving. My aunt and uncle aren't in the crowd either. My new husband said if they made me uncomfortable, they weren't coming.

He dips me for the kiss, and our guests cheer.

When he sets me right, he whispers in my ear, "You're blushing."

I grin and turn so my mouth brushes the shell of his ear. "Don't dip me too far. I'm also not wearing underwear."

He groans. "As soon as we reach the barn, I'm taking you to the tack room."

Hailstorm's led to the pavilion. Riding off was a part of my dream wedding, so Durban's making it happen again. Along with the honeymoon in Tahiti. Iverson and Haven will feed the chickens and horses, the barn cats that are no longer kittens, and Wolf, our border collie, that the rescue swore was a blue heeler.

My groom, dressed much like the day we rode off together last year, swings onto Hailstorm and pats his withers. "Ready, wife?"

"Ready, husband."

He rides Hailstorm in a wide circle, and just like a year ago, he swoops me into his arms. My shoes stay on, and my dress drapes over the side with my legs.

"Hang on, Belle. I've got you."

"I know," I say, and I cling to my husband as we ride off into the sunset.

———

Thank you so much for reading Durban and Campbell's story!

There are still some Foster House bachelors left, but that's going to change when Cruz catches a quiet baker busting a move in the early morning hours. He knows she's a cupcake worth unwrapping and he's determined to prove that the heat between them won't burn them both in Whiskey Flirt.

Join Durban and Campbell on their first real date after he rescues her from her ex's wedding in a bonus epilogue you can receive after signing up for my newsletter at walkerrosebooks.com/newsletter/.

ABOUT THE AUTHOR

I live the dream in my own slice of paradise where I get to enjoy colorful sunsets from my rocking chair while I'm working. I have my very own romance hero with Mr. Rose and there's more than a few little rose buds running around. A couple aren't so little anymore! We keep things interesting with cats and a dog and the critters that roam though the yard (fingers crossed the mountain lions stay away).

walkerrosebooks.com

ALSO BY WALKER ROSE

Foster House Series

Whiskey Cowboy

Whiskey Bargain

Whiskey Flirt

Bourbon Canyon Series

Bourbon Bachelor

Bourbon Lullaby

Bourbon Runaway

Bourbon Promises

Bourbon Harmony

Bourbon Summer

Bourbon Sunset

* 9 7 8 1 9 5 1 0 6 7 8 2 3 *